A KILLER HOLD

A KILLER HOLD

A Larkspur Library Mystery

Leah Dobrinska

LEVEL
BEST BOOKS

For anyone who wanted to be Nancy Drew when they grew up

Praise for A Killer Hold

A *Killer Hold* delivers a killer mystery in the Larkspur Library Mystery series.

"Greta Plank is juggling a *lot* right now: a Wisconsin library conference, a friend's engagement party, a new romance, and the return of her ex. But everything is put on hold when a dead body is found in the heart of Larkspur. What unfolds is a tantalizing mystery that blends history, treasure, and treachery together in the most page-turning of ways. Greta goes *National Treasure*-meets-Miss Marple as she begins digging into Larkspur's past for clues. With a cast of quirky new suspects and lovable returning characters, *A Killer Hold* is the perfect addition to this charming, cozy mystery series."—Sarah E. Burr, author of the Trending Topics Mystery series

"*A Killer Hold* is an excellent addition to Leah Dobrinska's Larkspur Library Mysteries. With a present-day mystery woven intricately around a legend from the early twentieth century when gangsters roamed the Wisconsin woods, you couldn't ask for more twists and turns, false leads, and gasp-worthy reveals. Full of cozy warmth, friendships, bookish puns, and the intrigue of a bygone era, this fast-paced mystery is everything cozy mystery fans could ask for. I devoured every page!"—Janna Rollins, author of the Zen Goat Mystery series

"It's spring in the beautiful Wisconsin Northwoods, and spunky librarian, Greta Plank, is faced with another murder to solve. Expertly intertwining the modern-day mystery with gangster legend, Leah Dobrinska takes the reader on a page-turning ride that will leave them guessing to the end. Intrigue with a touch of romance, *A Killer Hold* is a delightfully enthralling cozy mystery readers won't want to miss!"—Kara Lacey, author of the Vermont Camera Mystery series

Author's Note

With its quaint small towns and tree-dense setting, the Wisconsin North-woods served as a hideaway for early twentieth-century gangsters, including Al Capone, John Dillinger, and Baby Face Nelson.

In April 1934, the fledgling FBI, then called the Bureau of Investigation, or BOI, was given a tip that members of John Dillinger's gang were staying at Little Bohemia Lodge in Manitowish Waters, a lakeside town in northern Wisconsin.

Throwing together a bare-bones plan to capture the gangsters, BOI agents approached the lodge on foot, under the cover of darkness. When three men exited the lodge and got into a car to leave, the federal agents called out and ordered them to stop. Because the car's radio was turned up, the men in the vehicle did not hear or heed the order. These men were innocent civilians, but the BOI agents opened fire on the car, killing one passenger and injuring the other two.

The noise of the shooting tipped off the gangsters, who were still inside the lodge playing cards. John Dillinger and two of his compatriots grabbed their cash and weapons and escaped out the back door of the lodge. They fled through the woods and commandeered a car from an unsuspecting elderly couple and their neighbor, escaping the federal agents.

Baby Face Nelson was in a cabin near the lodge when the first shots were fired. He engaged the federal agents in a gunfight before disappearing into the woods. He, too, escaped capture.

The agents' bungled job was a national embarrassment for FBI director J. Edgar Hoover.

To this day, Little Bohemia Lodge bears the bullet holes from the shootout. It is one of many stops on the Wisconsin gangster trail. For more information, visit littlebohemialodge.com.

The actual events of the Little Bohemia Lodge Raid served as the jumping-off point for the historical aspects of *A Killer Hold*. Any inaccuracies and liberties taken are my own.

Chapter One

"What do you call a group of librarians?"

Greta Plank looked up from her notes. She peered across the table in the small meeting room at Larkspur Community Library and scrunched up her nose at her friend and fellow librarian, Fitz Atwood. "Is that a serious question?"

"Humor me." There was a glint in Fitz's eye that seemed to bounce off his dark-rimmed, square glasses and further illuminate the already sun-streaked meeting room.

It was spring in Larkspur. The small town nestled in the Wisconsin Northwoods was beautiful at all times of the year, but especially so now. Vibrant pink and yellow tulips were beginning to pop up along the perimeter of the cardinal red brick library building, making it seem straight out of a storybook. The crisp, dew-scented air and sun's rays were a welcome relief after the frigid, gray winter.

Fitz, Greta, and Iris, one of Greta's Larkspur co-librarians, were meeting to put the finishing touches on the schedule for the Wisconsin Library Organization's annual spring conference. In a few days, librarians from all over the state were set to arrive to take part in a week of programming.

As library director in Larkspur, Greta carried the weighty responsibility of pulling off this conference, and she would take all of the sunshine and spring breezes Larkspur wanted to throw at her. Better that than rain storms or tornadoes. Good weather would set the stage perfectly.

"How about a collection?" Greta flattened the collar on her daisy-printed dress and considered Fitz's question. "A collection of librarians seems

1

fitting."

"I like it." Fitz rocked back in his chair. "I was thinking a chapter. Sounds very official."

"That reminds me of a fraternity," Greta said after a second's thought. "Is that the vibe you want? We're a little less drunken debauchery and a little more skillful and scholarly, don't you think?"

Fitz frowned. "Good point."

"An index of librarians. A volume of librarians. A folio of librarians." Iris collected her brunette hair into a tail and secured it with a claw clip. "Oh! That one's my favorite."

"Very Shakespearean." Greta grinned. "What about a shush? A *shush* of librarians. Has quite the ring to it, doesn't it?"

"A shush." Fitz clapped his hands. "Perfect. Let's implement it next week when everyone arrives. Maybe it'll catch on. We'll be trendsetters."

Greta had grown used to Fitz's bursts of enthusiasm. He always kept things entertaining—from his bookish-themed dress socks to his off-the-wall, out-of-left-field commentary.

She'd met Fitz about six months before. Cindi Fields, the Larkspur Library Board president, had volunteered—or more like volun-*told*—Greta and her team as hosts for the WLO conference.

Cindi, who was like a pesky fly constantly buzzing around Greta at a picnic, contaminating everything, didn't seem to understand—or care—how much effort it would take to pull off a major industry conference with less than six months' notice. Greta could count on Iris as well as the third prong of their Larkspur librarian trio, Josie, who was currently manning the desk in the library while they held this Saturday morning meeting, but she'd also known she'd need reinforcements. Enter Fitz. He was a veteran librarian in the neighboring town of Karrington, and they'd become fast friends.

"Next up on our agenda,"—Greta checked her notes—"we need to go over the breakout sessions."

"We should be all set in Karrington," Fitz assured her. "I've got staff scheduled all week to direct folks to the proper meeting rooms as well as to answer questions about the conference and the commute between there and here."

The three librarians went over a few other bits of minutiae before wrapping up their meeting.

Fitz slung his messenger bag over his shoulder and stood to leave. He was in his early fifties, but he still dressed like a preppy twenty-something. Today, he was wearing well-fitting khakis and a denim button-up that peeked out beneath a navy-blue cardigan. "Any big plans for the weekend before the chaos of next week?"

Greta beamed. "Actually, yes. Josie doesn't know it yet, but this is about to be the best day of her life."

"I'm so excited!" Iris did a little jig, and Greta joined in.

Since moving to Larkspur the previous summer, she had made two close friends among her coworkers. Their similar ages and interests allowed the three librarians to bond quickly, and their friendship had seen them through the highs and lows of the past year.

Fitz paused with his hand on the doorknob and shot Greta and Iris a questioning look.

"Ed's proposing," Greta whispered.

Josie had been dating fellow Larkspur resident and owner of the local log cabin resort, Ed Kennedy, for almost eight months. The engagement might seem quick to some, but their relationship was forged in fire. Greta had no qualms about the timeline, not that it was any of her business anyway. "He's got a whole afternoon of surprises planned, and it's going to be so happy and romantic."

Fitz *aww-ed*. "How exciting! Ed's been so great opening up his cabins for the librarians to stay at."

"He's the best." Iris nodded, but held her finger to her lips. "Mums the word, though. Act natural when we go out there."

Fitz mimed zipping his lips, and opened the door, letting Iris go ahead of him.

Greta hurried to collect her notes and to-do lists and file them in the appropriate manila folders. She hoisted the stack into her arms and flitted through the door Fitz was still holding, her floral frock swishing around her

3

knees.

They walked together toward the circulation desk. "What about you?" she asked. "Any weekend pl—"

A meeting room door banged open directly in front of Greta, cutting her off midsentence. She lost her grip on her paperwork, and it spilled to the ground. She and Fitz bent to retrieve it as two people stormed out in front of them.

"We are not finished here! How *dare* you?" Cindi Fields was hot on the heels of a woman, whom Greta vaguely recognized. The woman had on a figure-hugging black dress that hit mid-thigh, with a cropped denim jacket that rested above her hips. The relatively basic ensemble was elevated with a whole lot of bling. Her ears glittered with sparkly earrings that dangled down to her chin; a gold necklace disappeared into her décolletage, and she was wearing a whole assortment of rings affixed with different colored gemstones.

The rubies and diamonds glinted as the woman waved her hand back and forth. "Give it a rest, Cindi. I don't owe you a thing. You're jealous you won't have something groundbreaking to share at our event."

"That's not it at all! We're a club. You shouldn't be withholding information. Especially if you're telling the truth and there is a major development."

Club? Greta culled her memory, and it quickly dawned on her that the True Treasure Seekers were scheduled for their monthly meeting this morning. The True Treasure Seekers, or The Seekers for short, met at the library to discuss and debate historically significant lost treasures. Think Ted Binion's silver stash, hidden somewhere in Nevada. Or Blackbeard's treasure, rumored to be in any number of places along the Atlantic coast. Greta had never attended a meeting, but she'd overheard enough of the excited conversations of the club's members as they'd left their monthly gatherings to understand that they took their studies seriously.

The rest of The Seekers skirted around the two arguing women, shooting side-eyed glances at the spectacle and apologetic looks in Greta's direction before making themselves scarce.

"Oh, it's major, alright." The woman shot Cindi a cloying smile. "Like I said, it's going to change everything and make headline news. This will put Larkspur on the map. Wait and see."

"I don't want to wait and see!" Cindi's voice was shrill. "I am the president of the True Treasure Seekers. I should have a say. Tell me now!"

"No can do." The woman looked like she was taking pleasure in antagonizing Cindi.

Greta felt a strange sensation in her stomach. Was she actually feeling defensive on Cindi's behalf? The woman may be a fly at a picnic, but she was *her* fly, dang it. Had there been an opening in the argument, Greta might have been compelled enough to step in. But the angry pair kept at each other, giving her no chance.

"Then I don't believe you." Cindi crossed her arms.

The woman snorted and leaned in. "I'll have proof before you know it. When I present it at the anniversary event of the Little Bohemia Lodge raid, it's going to bring the house down."

At this, the jewelry-clad woman turned on her heel and stalked toward the front of the library.

Cindi followed closely.

Greta stood and shoved her thick, curly, strawberry-gold hair behind her ears. Fitz handed her the papers he had collected, and the two exchanged wide-eyed glances before hurrying forward.

"You think you're so smart, Blythe, but you won't get far without a partnership. We're supposed to be a team." Cindi was almost pleading now, switching tactics from angry demands to more subtle begging.

The woman in question—Blythe, apparently—spun around, sculpted eyebrows narrowed. A few strands of her white blonde hair had fallen out of the tight bun she wore on top of her head. She flicked her gaze toward Greta and Fitz before turning her attention back to Cindi. She held herself up to her full height and pointed at the library board president. "My discovery. My glory. I shouldn't have even mentioned it to you. Forget about it for now because no one, and I mean no one, is going to steal this from me. In a few short weeks, everyone will know my name."

With that, she whipped around and strode out of the library, pausing only to shove a stack of books in the return drop-off slot before making her grand exit.

Nobody moved for a second or two. Behind the circulation desk, Josie and Iris stood with identical *did that just happen?* slack-jawed expressions on their faces. Next to Greta, Fitz shifted the weight between his khaki-clad legs.

Cindi, with her hands balled into fists at her sides, was the first to break the silence. "That woman is infuriating! Why...why...I could MURDER her!"

Chapter Two

Greta flinched at Cindi's outburst. She was so shocked she couldn't even enjoy not being the one on the receiving end of the library board president's wrath...for once.

Fitz cleared his throat. "*O-kay.* On that note, I'm going to go and let you handle whatever this is. Call me if you think of anything else you need before the conference."

He left the library, giving Cindi a wide berth.

Greta took a step forward, not sure exactly what to do. "Is everything okay?"

"No, Greta," Cindi huffed, her eyes blazing. "In case you couldn't tell from that exchange, everything is *not* okay."

"Do you want to talk about it?" Iris offered.

"Clearly, there's not much to say, is there? Since Blythe won't tell me anything."

"Back up. Who's Blythe?" Greta asked.

"Blythe Prescott. A know-it-all, overly dramatic member of the True Treasure Seekers. Honestly, she's a scourge to our club's good name." Cindi worked her jaw. "I don't even know why she comes. All she does is gloat about her own findings and big ideas, but she never considers the rest of us worthy enough to be let in on all the secrets she's uncovered. Supposedly uncovered," Cindi added with a scoff.

"What sort of secrets?" Josie asked. Greta found herself nodding. If there was one thing the trio of librarians shared, it was their innate curiosity. It came with the territory in their line of work.

"We're doing a big event to celebrate the anniversary of the Little Bohemia Lodge raid at the end of April. You should know that." Cindi shot a pointed look between the three of them.

Greta refused to take the bait. "Of course. Nico Eddison is coming to speak about the raid and the gangster history in the area. We're looking forward to attending."

The True Treasure Seekers Club had been planning this event for several months, and they were bringing in Nico—who authored one of the most comprehensive histories of the comings and goings of early twentieth century gangsters in the Midwest—to drum up extra interest and hopefully attract a wider audience of book lovers, treasure seekers, history buffs, or all of the above. He was set to arrive as the librarian conference was winding down.

"Well," Cindi sniffed. "Blythe *claims* to have made some massive discovery that pertains to Larkspur and the gangster trail. But that remains to be seen." She smoothed the front of her denim vest. "You know what? I'm being ridiculous."

Acknowledgement is the first step to recovery.

Greta couldn't help the snarky thought.

"I doubt Blythe's findings are anything ground-breaking," Cindi continued. "This is hardly the first time she's gone off about some such thing. When we were studying the millions of dollars' worth of treasure supposedly lost in the Great Lakes, she swore she was going to go deep diving in Lake Michigan to find some cache of hidden gold. She's all smoke and no fire." Cindi stuck up her nose. "Now, I trust everything is in order for the conference on Monday?"

Greta was so busy picturing Blythe Prescott scuba diving—with all the jewelry the woman had been wearing, she would have been lucky not to sink to the bottom of the lake herself and become the next piece of lost treasure—she almost missed Cindi's conversational lane-change.

"Uh, yep," she recovered. "We're all set. Librarians will arrive between ten and noon, and we'll have our welcome mixer at Bobber's Bar beginning at three thirty."

Cindi gave a decisive nod. "I'll be on hand to make sure everything runs smoothly, though I do have my monthly book club and my weekly genealogy club meetings to run. So, I won't be able to oversee all the events. This is a big deal. A big stage for Larkspur. I don't want us to be embarrassed by any miscues."

"It's going to be great." Iris laced her voice with extra sweetness, but Greta didn't miss the glance she stole at the clock. It was ticking past noon. The library was officially closed, and they had a friend to hustle off to her surprise engagement. Iris moved toward the exit. "I'm going to lock the doors behind you."

Cindi took the hint and sauntered out of the library. Iris swung the doors closed, sagging into them as she turned back to Greta and Josie. "Is it me or was there more drama in our library just now than at a family reunion?"

"Do either of you know Blythe Prescott?" Greta cut behind the circulation desk, joining Josie.

"She looked semi-familiar, but I think that's because I've seen her at The Seekers's meetings before." Josie lifted a shoulder in a shrug.

"That's what I thought, too," Greta agreed. When Josie went to grab the books from the return slot, she stepped in front of her. "You know what? It's a beautiful day. That job can wait until Monday."

"Sounds good to me." Iris grabbed Josie's bag and shoved it into her arms. "Let's go, Jos."

Josie's eyebrows hitched up. "You sure?"

Greta was usually a stickler for not leaving for tomorrow what they could get done today, and she liked a tidy library, but if ever there was a good excuse to shirk some of their bookish responsibilities, it was the fact that Ed was waiting for Josie in the parking lot, ready to sweep her off her feet.

"Definitely." She'd check the books in on Monday. It would give her something to do while she was nervously anticipating the arrival of the majority of the librarians in the state. She waved Josie and Iris out the door, and after switching off the lights and locking up, Greta tugged on her long cardigan and trailed them into the hallway and through the exterior doors of the municipal complex. Larkspur Library was housed in the same building as the town hall and police station. Since it was Saturday, the parking lot was empty except for their cars and Ed Kennedy, leaning up against a Kennedy's Cozy Cottages pick-up truck.

The grin on Josie's boyfriend's face doubled in size when his eyes landed on her.

"What are you doing here?" Josie stepped toward Ed. "I thought you had an investment meeting?"

Ed wrapped Josie in a hug, and Iris grabbed for Greta's hand. They looked at each other and silently screamed before composing themselves.

"Nah. I've got something more important in mind. Something I've been thinking of doing for a long time."

Swoon.

Greta sighed happily. The front-row seat she'd had to Josie and Ed's relationship was like getting to live inside the pages of one of her favorite romance novels.

Greta's thoughts flitted to Detective Mark McHenry, her boyfriend of six months. The two of them weren't anywhere close to marriage or engagement. But as Greta neared her thirtieth birthday, she would be lying if she said she wasn't taking their relationship seriously.

McHenry was currently in Chicago visiting his brother. He'd been gone less than forty-eight hours but already Greta missed him. A lot. She couldn't deny she was falling hard for the detective.

Ed tucked a strand of Josie's chin-length black hair behind her ear. "You ready to go?"

"Sure." Josie stared at him for a second before facing them. "See you guys later?"

"Yup." Greta bobbed her head up and down, trying to act natural, and Iris waved. "Have fun, you two."

After Ed pulled out of the parking lot with Josie sitting shotgun in his truck, Greta let loose her pent-up shriek. She and Iris jumped up and down for a minute before scurrying across the street to Mugs & Hugs, Larkspur's go-to coffee shop and community meeting grounds. They had an engagement party to pull together.

***

Later that evening, the glass door to Mugs & Hugs swung open, and Josie stepped inside. Her eyes widened as she took in the space. The cheery yellow walls were festooned with white crepe paper streamers. Greta and Iris had decorated all the tables with glass mason jars overflowing with baby's breath and greenery. Rose gold balloons spelling out *She Said Yes* floated along the side of the dining room, creating the perfect photo-op backdrop. A crowd of friends stood beaming at Josie. Ed had texted ahead, confirming that she had, in fact, said yes.

"Surprise!" Greta chorused with the rest of those in attendance.

Josie spun around to where Ed had held the door to Mugs & Hugs open for her. "You planned this, too?"

"All for you." He placed a kiss behind her ear. "My amazing bride-to-be."

A renewed round of cheers went up in the café.

Josie's mom and dad hurried forward to embrace her, and Greta swallowed back happy tears.

Ed had coordinated getting Josie's family to town, which meant her parents came in from the Twin Cities in Minnesota to be here for the celebration. And—

"Jake!?" Josie squealed her brother's name before throwing her arms around his neck.

Josie's older brother Jake had flown in with his wife, Caroline, from the East Coast in order to surprise her.

"Congrats, Jos." Jake stepped back, giving Caroline a chance to hug her sister-in-law. After her, Greta and Iris rushed forward.

"Did you know about this?" Josie asked into Greta's neck.

"Sure did. Were you surprised?"

"Shocked," Josie admitted. "In the best possible way." She reached for Ed's hand, dragging him into their circle before showing off her engagement ring, a sparkly, square-cut diamond on a simple gold band. It was so perfectly Josie—sleek, classic, and stunning.

Greta gushed over the ring before hugging Ed, and as Iris was offering

11

the pair her congratulations, she took a beat to study Josie. Her friend was glowing. She was always a stunner, all angular features and willowy lines, but today, the heightened blush in her cheeks and the twinkling in her eyes made her look even more gorgeous.

"We should make the rounds." Josie peered around the crammed café. "My gosh, it looks like the whole town showed up."

"As they should." Iris laughed. "We're thrilled for you both. Now go, mingle."

As the couple of the hour moved on, Iris occupied Josie's parents with chit-chat, and Greta offered to get everyone a drink. Allison, the owner of Mugs & Hugs, and one of Greta's favorite people, wasn't known for her nighttime beverages, but she'd made an exception for Josie and Ed's celebration. She'd created a custom menu for the engagement festivities filled with coffee-flavored drinks. The list of available options was stenciled on the chalkboard menu above the counter. Greta took orders, and when she got to Caroline, Josie's sister-in-law asked for an espresso martini as her phone buzzed. She glanced at the screen. "Shoot. This is my mom. She's watching our kids. I should make sure everything is okay."

Caroline stepped out of the noisy café.

"I'll help you grab drinks," Jake offered to Greta.

She gladly accepted his help. Six glasses were a lot for any one person to carry, and she was more known for her clumsiness than her grace, so she'd rather not chance it.

They made their way to the counter, where the pastry case was stocked with delectable offerings like melt-in-your-mouth chocolate chip cookies, light and fluffy sponge cakes, and an assortment of colorful macaroons.

"Hey, G!" Allison stood at the register. The bandana she always wore to keep back her dark, natural hair was a pale green color today and was complimented in a way only Allison could pull off with neon orange tulip earrings. "What can I get for you?" Her umber eyes bounced up to Jake's face. "You must be Josie's brother!"

It was easy to see the resemblance between siblings. Like Josie, Jake had angular facial features and was tall and lean. He also shared her dark black hair, though he wore his in a messier mop and looked every bit the stereotypical academic.

After Jake introduced himself, Greta rattled off their collective drink order and asked for a couple of cookies for good measure.

"This place is pretty awesome." Jake glanced around.

Greta took a deep breath, savoring the bold smell of coffee as it mixed with the sweet aroma of baked goods. Even without all the decorations they'd brought in for the engagement party, Mugs & Hugs was adorable. The sunshine yellow walls and white beadboard that hugged the room made it feel both clean and welcoming. Allison was a total plant lady, and the bright green leaves and vines of her collection were on proud display, hanging over the large picture windows at the front of the café.

"It's the best," Greta agreed.

"There's nothing like the vibes of a local coffee shop. I get some of my best work done at the one near the university."

Greta was interested in hearing more about his work. Josie had told her some about her brother's efforts as a history professor at Chesterton University in Maryland. Before she could ask him about it, a familiar voice rose up from a table tucked into a nearby alcove.

"Relax, Tuck. You know I'll take care of you." Blythe Prescott was sitting with a man Greta had never seen before. "Leave it to me."

The man—Tuck, apparently—leaned forward, but his nasally voice carried. "You can trust me, you know that, right? Heath, on the other hand…"

"Leave Heath to me." Blythe patted her white blonde hair, which, since her outburst at the library earlier in the day, she'd re-secured in the tight bun on the top of her head. There wasn't a strand out of place. "When I break the news about the Dillinger gang, he'll be putty in my hands. And I do trust you, but—"

"Here you go!" Allison's chipper voice made Greta jump. She spun around to find the six beverages and a plate of cookies sitting on the tall counter.

"Thanks, Allison." Greta reached for the drinks, and Jake stepped forward to grab several. Blythe and Tuck lowered their voices, and Greta wasn't able to catch any more of their conversation, though, from the way their heads were pushed together, she would guess it was serious.

"Was that woman talking about John Dillinger?" Jake asked as they wove back toward his family and Iris.

"That's what I heard, too. She was actually in the library today." Greta explained the True Treasure Seekers group. "They're planning an event for the end of the month."

Jake nodded. "Makes sense. It's amazing the history that's tied up in these small, northern Wisconsin towns. I had half a mind to extend our trip and do some hands-on research around here myself. I always loved the legend of Little Bo."

"What are you guys talking about?" Iris took her drink from Jake.

"We overheard a woman talking about John Dillinger." His eyes were lit with excitement.

"The gangster?" Iris grimaced. "What about him?"

"Not sure. I actually don't know a ton about the Little Bohemia Lodge raid." Though Greta hated to admit it, the history of gangsters was not an area of expertise for her.

Jake swallowed a sip of his drink. "The raid at Little Bo, as it's called, is actually one of the biggest guffaws of the fledgling FBI. They'd been tipped off that John Dillinger and his gang were at the Little Bohemia Lodge in Manitowish Waters, Wisconsin, relaxing and recuperating. Dillinger was one of the most notorious gangsters and bank robbers of the early twentieth century. He was wanted after he escaped prison in Indiana. The feds drove up this way and tried to apprehend him and his gang. But when they breached the Little Bohemia Lodge supper club, they fired on a retreating car of supper club diners. One of them died from gunshot wounds. These were innocent civilians, and they were only guilty of not hearing the agents' calls to stop their vehicle, because their radio was turned up too loud. When the FBI opened fire, the ruckus alerted the actual gangsters, who were still inside, of the law's presence. They fled out the back. The FBI gave chase, but they escaped, and the whole raid was sort of a bust."

Caroline appeared at Jake's side. "Is he boring you with historical commentary?" She gave him a playful nudge and took her drink from him.

"Actually, it's fascinating. I wonder what Blythe knows about it. Or thinks she knows about it," Greta said. "She's the one who mentioned John Dillinger," she added for Iris's benefit.

"You said she's part of a treasure-hunting group?" Jake asked.

Iris and Greta nodded.

"Maybe she's looking for a suitcase of money that the gang supposedly left buried in the woods of Northern Wisconsin."

"Wait. For real?" Iris's eyes went wide.

"That's what legend says, though there have been reports that dispute it." Jake shrugged. "It's still fun to think about. These sleepy little Midwest lake-side towns were host to some of the most notorious criminals of recent history."

* * *

An hour and a half later, after seeing Ed and Josie happily ensconced among friends, Greta quietly left Mugs & Hugs. She was exhausted by the events of the day. Happy, but exhausted. She'd parked her car down the block, where they'd all stashed their vehicles so as not to draw any attention to the surprise party. The Larkspur streets were quiet as Greta's high heels clicked on the sidewalk. She tugged her cardigan closer around her neck as a chill rippled through the air. Spring was here, but winter wasn't fully gone.

Greta rounded the corner to where she had parked her car, but pulled up short when angry voices met her ear.

"I want you off my property now."

Greta pressed her lips together. A man was speaking. She froze in place, staying in the shadows even as she peered forward and tried to get a better look.

Blythe stood underneath the spotlight outside the backdoor to Bobber's Bar, one hand on a hip, and the other holding onto what appeared to be a dowel that had been removed from the handicap accessible ramp into the restaurant.

"Oh, come on, Ace. Aren't you at least a little bit curious?"

"No. I most certainly am not. I have bigger things to worry about than you and your ridiculous ideas. I'll say it again. Get away from here. And stay away." Ace spat the final words with such force, Greta could see spit fly in the glow of the overhead light.

Blythe sneered back at him. "Play nice, Ace. If you're not careful, this could all be mine, and then I'd be the one telling you to get off my property."

"In your dreams."

Blythe stuck her nose in the air. "I intend to make those dreams my reality."

With that, she tossed the dowel onto the ramp. It rattled and rolled to the base of the structure as she sauntered away.

Greta tucked herself further into the shadows as Blythe walked past, headed for a vehicle that was parked a few paces ahead. She stayed still until Blythe drove off. Only then did Greta return her gaze to Ace Hawler, the owner of Bobber's Bar. He was pacing along the back of the building, muttering to himself. Greta was too far away to make out what he said. Whatever it was, he didn't seem happy.

Blythe Prescott seemed to be at the root of a lot of displeasure around town. What was her story?

Chapter Three

Monday morning dawned with sunshine and the scent of copy paper in the air. Greta was at the library early, putting the finishing touches on the handouts for the conference and trying to calm her nerves. She wished she could say she was excited about the upcoming conference, but she was more anxious than anything. Hosting the members of the WLO was a big deal.

That, and the event would bring her ex-boyfriend and fellow librarian, Nathan, into town.

He'd registered for the conference, and Greta wasn't surprised. He was the library director at a large branch in Green Bay, and he liked to network. Mostly, he liked to hear himself talk. Greta sighed. Nathan was the type of person who thought he knew everything and was all too happy to tell everyone else what he thought he knew. When the two of them dated, they liked listening to cold case and true crime podcasts together. Well, Greta had enjoyed it at first. Until Nathan would drone on and on about how he had everything figured out. If Greta so much as brought up a contrary point, he would shut her down. Looking back, there were lots of red flags in their relationship, culminating in the largest horror of all: finding out that Nathan was married.

Greta tapped the printed copies of the week's itinerary more firmly than necessary against one of the worn tables in the library's research area. She looped around the circulation desk. Thoughts of Nathan and Cindi Fields and Blythe Prescott and John Dillinger vied for her attention, making her brain feel like it was about to explode, but she was determined to stay calm and focused. She opened up the software program they used for book returns and scooped out the titles she'd left in the return slot on Saturday morning.

Not much soothed Greta more than methodically scanning books back into circulation. She back-dated the return date in the system so that no one would be penalized for late books and then scanned each title twice, for good measure. That greatly reduced the off chance that a book would get shelved without being checked-in, thus inducing panic when a patron received notification that there was an issue with their account.

Greta was so much in the zone that, at first, she didn't register the feel of the worn cover of a paperback copy of *Pride and Prejudice* by Jane Austen. It was lacking the familiar library binding and protective coating they applied to many of their soft-covered titles. Flipping open the cover and turning the book over in her hands confirmed her suspicions. This book wasn't part of the Larkspur collection. It didn't seem to belong to any library at all. Greta set it aside and finished scanning the remaining titles before gathering and checking in the books that had been returned through the outside drop box over the course of the weekend.

That accomplished, she turned her attention back to the errant copy of *Pride and Prejudice*. It was a truth universally acknowledged that anyone who misplaced such an outstanding piece of literature would want it returned to them post haste. Greta inspected the title page, inside cover, and back cover once more, searching for a name or a defining feature and trying to determine who this book belonged to.

No dice.

She paged through the weathered crème pages, familiar words jumping out at her. *Dancing, even if one's partner is barely tolerable... A pair of fine eyes... You are too generous to trifle with me... They walked on...*

But as much as Greta would have loved to sink into her favorite love story, she was pulled out of her perusal by the constant notations scribbled all over the pages.

Greta herself was a proponent of writing in books. Maybe not in library copies, but those in her personal collection she annotated to her heart's content. In this case, though, the pages of *Pride and Prejudice* were less highlighted for specific lines and more marked up. As far as Greta could tell, there was no rhyme or reason to it. There were individual letters underlined and page numbers circled. Dashes were made aside individual lines. In a couple cases, there were exclamation points in the margins, but in Greta's humble opinion, the punctuation marks weren't written near particularly gripping or pivotal scenes. This sort of marginalia made no sense.

"You look perplexed."

Greta's gaze bounced up from the book, and she met the onyx eyes of Detective Mark McHenry, or simply McHenry to his friends. Her heart leapt even as her shoulders rolled forward and her spine softened. Greta thought of the detective as *her* McHenry now that they'd been dating for six months, and while she called him Mark on occasion—usually when she was feeling extra affectionate or when she had a major point to get across—she still mostly referred to him by his last name. There was a comfortable familiarity that came with it.

"I thought you weren't getting back until later." She dropped the paperback and came out from behind the desk, meeting McHenry in the still dimly lit library atrium.

He opened his arms, and she stepped into a hug. Resting her head on his chest, she inhaled his trademark scent—worn leather and sandalwood. She sighed, already feeling better about the day.

"Change of plans." He leaned back, scanning her face like he was reading lines of a book—left to right—no inch left unstudied. He never failed to make Greta feel seen and cherished.

She studied him right back. He had dark stubble lining his jaw, like he hadn't bothered to shave before he left Chicago. There were slight bags under his eyes, and though he looked entirely attentive—and entirely handsome— he also looked tired.

She twisted her mouth to the side. "That's it?"

"What?" McHenry shrugged. "Aren't you happy to see me?"

"Obviously. I just thought you had"—Greta searched for the word—"*things* to take care of with your brother." McHenry had been tight-lipped about his brother, and Greta hadn't pressed, so she wasn't entirely sure what had sent him to Chicago. One thing she'd learned about her boyfriend over the past half-year was that McHenry would open up to her when he was ready. She didn't want to nag him. Still, she was an over-communicator. She always appreciated some context and conversation.

"I did," he said. "And they're done. For now," he added under his breath.

A twinge of concern pinched at Greta's sternum. What wasn't McHenry telling her about his brother? Was he in danger? Was he in trouble?

"Okay," she said carefully. "You know you can talk to me about it if you want to, right?"

"I know." McHenry sighed, gazing at her with his slate-colored eyes. They looked like smooth stones beneath lake water. "I wanted to be here for you today."

Greta felt as if someone had pushed her backwards onto the most comfortable mattress in the world: shocked but equally delighted. "You did?"

"Of course I did. I know you have to face Nathan."

Greta wrapped her arms around McHenry's waist. "Thank you," she whispered.

She'd been embarrassed to tell McHenry about her history with Nathan. Greta hadn't known her ex had a wife. But the whole experience left her jaded and uncertain where dating was concerned. To his credit, McHenry never judged her. He listened. And he showed up for her. He might not have been the most outspoken of men, but she didn't doubt him or his intentions.

She released him from her hug. "Check this out." Greta reached for the copy of *Pride and Prejudice* and handed it to him.

McHenry paged through the book. "Who scribbled all over it?"

"No clue. It's not the library's copy. I'll have to hunt down the owner."

"That's a mystery I can get behind you solving. Low stakes."

Greta made a face. She had found herself in the middle of not one but two of McHenry's cases in the past year. While her quest for justice ran deep, so did her survival instincts.

"I have no plans to do any more actual detective work, thank you very much. I'll be leaving that to you."

"Can I get that in writing?"

"Look who went to Chicago and came back with a sense of humor," Greta teased. "Got any more jokes hiding in there?" Greta went to pat his pockets.

McHenry wrapped her up in a swift hug, burying his nose in her neck. "You can search me anytime, Miss Plank."

Greta blushed.

She had to hand it to McHenry. Every other thought in her over-crowded brain had dissolved since he showed up.

She kissed his jaw. "I'll remember that."

The pair separated when Iris and Josie arrived.

Greta showed them the copy of *Pride and Prejudice*. "Do either of you recognize this?"

Iris shook her head.

Josie's gaze bounced to the stack of checked-in titles Greta had set in piles on the circulation desk to be shelved or shipped back to other branches. She pointed at the books on the bottom of the stack. "If it was with those, they were the titles Blythe Prescott dropped off before she left on Saturday. Maybe one of her own copies got caught in her returns."

"I'll give her a call." Greta took the book back from Iris and turned to McHenry. "You're working today?"

He nodded. "I'm planning to swing by your mixer this afternoon, though."

"Good." Greta longed to hug him again, but the two kept their PDA to a minimum while at work. "See you then," she said with a smile she hoped conveyed how grateful she was that he was here.

"Have a good day." McHenry held her gaze, eyes warm and intense, before glancing at Josie and Iris. "All of you. Good luck with the start of the convention."

"Thanks, McHenry," Iris said in a sing-song voice as the detective walked into the hallway and made his way to the back entrance of the police station.

Greta watched him through the floor-to-ceiling windows on the south side of the library, a happy flutter in her chest. When she pivoted to face her friends, they were smirking at her.

"What?"

"You two are cute, that's all," Iris wagged her eyebrows. "I wonder if I'll have not one but *two* friends engaged in the not-so-distant future."

A rush of heat spread up Greta's neck. She and McHenry hadn't talked about marriage. They hadn't even said they loved each other yet. She was taking it slow in the aftermath of the Nathan debacle, and he...well, he had underlying issues with his brother and his past in Chicago that he was slowly opening up to her about.

For now, she was enjoying every minute she got to spend with him. Still, the idea of marriage to a man like McHenry made her pulse kick up for all the right reasons.

"Maybe someday," she said with a smile. "I'm going to try to get in touch with Blythe, quick."

Josie and Iris dispersed to tend to their daily tasks, and Greta pulled up the patron contact page for Blythe Prescott. She grabbed the library phone and dialed the number on Blythe's account. After four rings, Blythe's recorded voice came on the line.

Greta hung up without leaving a message. It was the millennial in her. She'd try again later or get in touch with Blythe some other way.

She turned her attention to her work, and when she unlocked the doors to the library a little while later to open for the day, she was met by a familiar-looking man waiting in the vestibule.

"Oh! Hello." Greta squinted at him to make sure he was who she thought he was. "Nico Eddison, right?"

The man smiled self-consciously, straightening the baseball cap he wore over his pale blond hair. "Guilty."

"You're—"

"Early. I know." He gave a good-natured shrug. "My schedule opened up and I decided to come to town ahead of the program next weekend."

Greta's mind turned over, and she mentally calculated what this meant. On top of hosting the librarians, she was now on the hook to show a visiting author a good time. Here went nothing.

"Come on in. We're opening up for the day." Greta ushered Nico inside and introduced him to Iris and Josie.

"I don't imagine my cabin is ready this far in advance?" Nico had the wherewithal to look chagrined.

"I'll make some calls, and we'll get you all set," Greta assured him.

While Nico set off to wander the stacks, Greta convened with Josie and Iris.

"I'll call Ed and see about a cabin for Nico," Josie offered. "But—"

"He's booked with librarians through Friday. I know." Greta frowned.

"My parents still have a small house here in town. It's probably a little dusty, but nothing some elbow grease wouldn't fix. In a pinch, it could work." Iris got out her phone. "I'll text them now and see if it's okay to use."

Greta punched out a breath, scanning the library, her gaze connecting with Nico's. Greta smiled and waved before turning her back to him. It was odd he showed up a whole week early. Unannounced. But what could she do about it? He was here. "I'll reach out to Cindi. She can be Nico's tour guide for the week." With a shake of her head, she added, "Whoever said being a librarian was all old books and shushing people never spent any time in Larkspur."

* * *

A couple hours later, after seeing the first wave of librarians settled at Kennedy's Cozy Cottages in Larkspur, Greta drove to Karrington. The conference would begin at the library there, and she needed to touch base with Fitz before the first speaker took the stage to discuss this year's theme: *Libraries: Curators, Creators, and Collaborators.*

Glancing at the clock on her dash, Greta stepped on the gas. If she hurried, she would have enough time to stop by B'Jeweled on her way into town. The tattered copy of *Pride and Prejudice* was sticking out of the canvas tote she had set on the passenger seat, and she wanted to try to return it to Blythe in person so she could check one item off her to-do list.

Greta navigated her car off the county highway and slowed as the speed-limit dropped as she approached the Karrington town limits. Karrington was bigger than Larkspur, but it had many of the same quaint, small-town vibes. B'Jeweled was located on the outskirts of town, in the corner unit of a strip mall that was attached to the satellite location for the local technical college.

Greta parked in the lot, taking in the façade of the jewelry store. Much like Blythe herself, the place shimmered. The awnings over the front windows were pink and silver striped, with iridescent fringes hanging down. Large, three-dimensional light-up letters spelled out *B'Jeweled* above the doorway.

After double-checking that she had the book in her bag, Greta locked her car and hustled toward the entrance. She stepped inside onto the padded indoor-outdoor carpet and took in the room.

There was one other customer inside. His back was to her, so she couldn't make out much besides his well-fitting blue jeans and a worn flannel shirt. He was leaning over the display case, his face only a few inches from the man behind the counter, who hadn't looked up upon her entrance. A younger man stood off to the side, polishing a watch face. Greta recognized him as Tuck, the guy whom Blythe was with at Mugs & Hugs the night of Josie's engagement. He was scowling at the scene in front of him. Blythe herself was nowhere in sight.

Greta jumped and tore her gaze from Tuck when the customer slammed his hand onto the glass counter, making the jewelry inside rattle.

"Hey!" The salesman growled. "Don't do that unless you want me to sue you for damages."

The man in flannel snorted. "I should be the one suing you. This place is such a sham."

"You have your copy of the authenticity documents, don't you?" the salesman pressed.

"Yes. But I don't believe one word on them."

"That's your own problem."

"I want to talk to the owner. This needs to be made right."

The man behind the counter stood to his full height. His gaze pinged to Greta and then to Tuck, who scrubbed the watch with more force and didn't return the eye contact.

The salesman turned back to the angry customer, his eyes narrowed menacingly. "She's not here at the moment. If there's nothing else I can help you with, I'd kindly ask that you leave. I have someone else I need to assist."

The customer snatched a jewelry box off the counter and clutched it in his fist. "Don't think this is the last of me. You'll be hearing from my attorney!" As he stormed past Greta, he muttered, "Learn from my mistakes and shop elsewhere. This place is as crooked as they come."

The door rattled on its hinges as he made his departure.

"You'll have to excuse him." The salesman behind the counter drew Greta's attention from the angry customer. She turned to see him smiling at her. His teeth were dazzling white and perfectly straight. He wore crisp black pants and a white button-up shirt with a pale gray suitcoat over the top. Greta would place him at around forty-five or fifty years old. His dark brown hair was lighter at the temples, but aside from the heightened color in his cheeks, he looked every bit the successful seller Greta would expect to find at a high-end jeweler. "I'm afraid he's in here every other week claiming we've done something wrong with jewelry he's purchased from us over the years." The salesman gave a good-natured shrug and flicked his wrist at Tuck, in the universal signal to get lost. Without a word, Tuck disappeared down the hallway that led away from the showroom. "Anyway, what can I help you with this fine morning?"

Greta stepped forward. "I'm looking for Blythe Prescott." She pulled the book from her bag. "I believe this is hers."

The guy eyed the book. "Blythe isn't here. I'm her husband, Heath." He reached out his hand. Greta toggled the book to her left hand and shook it, fighting a cringe when he held onto her fingers a couple of seconds longer than necessary.

"Greta Plank." When he finally dropped her hand, she tucked it behind her back, flexing.

Heath pointed at the book. "I don't recognize that."

Greta frowned. "I'll hang onto it then. Maybe I'm mistaken." She slipped the copy of *Pride and Prejudice* back into her bag.

"While you're here, you should check out these diamond necklaces. One of a kind, truly. They'd look simply lovely on you."

"Thank you, but I have to go. Busy day!" She was already retreating. Something about Heath was smarmy, and the words she overheard between Tuck and Blythe at the café on Saturday night came back to her in a flash: *Heath can't be trusted.*

Tuck would know, if he worked alongside him every day.

"Stop in to see us sometime soon, then," Heath called.

With a noncommittal wave over her shoulder, Greta escaped outside, lamenting the wasted trip. Heath gave her the heebie-jeebies. She was thinking about him as she eased her car out of the cramped spot. She was about to turn onto the main road, but she had to slam on her brakes when a pick-up truck came barreling into the B'Jeweled parking lot and shot across the pavement in front of her.

Greta gasped as the driver gave her an apologetic *toot-toot* of the horn. A bumper sticker on his tailgate read *I Brake for Bigfoot.*

Greta let out a shaky breath and drove to the library across town, where Fitz was waiting for her with a Styrofoam cup of coffee in hand. "You look frazzled."

Greta huffed out a laugh. "Don't sugarcoat it, now."

"Sorry." Fitz winced. "I'm nothing if not honest."

"It's fine. It's true." Greta took a sip of her coffee, letting the warmth of the drink and the zip of caffeine rejuvenate her. "How's everything here? We about ready?"

"Librarians are trickling in as we speak." Fitz glanced over Greta's shoulder and waved. "Hello, everyone."

Greta spun around with a fixed smile, ready to greet their guests. Her expression slipped when she saw Nathan.

She had braced herself for this moment. According to the event's registration list, Nathan would be in attendance with the group of librarians from Green Bay. They were her former co-workers. And as library director there, Nathan was her former boss.

All of the shame and humiliation that went along with her past relationship rushed to the surface, making her skin painfully hot. Greta pressed her lips together, trying not to let her discomfort show.

If she expected Nathan to be bashful, repentant, or seem in any way affected by their history, she was sorely mistaken. The only indication that he felt any guilt for his behavior where she was concerned was the way his eyes popped ever-so-slightly wider before he schooled his features.

"Greta! Great to see you again!" He stepped forward, arms outstretched as if he expected her to hug him.

No way in Dewey Decimal's System.

Greta thrust out her hand, arm fully extended. She didn't waver when Nathan's chest knocked into it. He adjusted and shook her hand.

She offered him a shaky, close-lipped smile before clearing her throat and turning to greet those who had arrived alongside him.

"Welcome, everyone. So glad you could make it. This is Fitz Atwood, one of the head librarians here in Karrington. He'll help get you settled after you check in."

Fitz waved the group toward the registration table, but before he left her side, he grabbed her wrist. "I'll take *Awkward Encounters* for two thousand, Alex," he whispered.

"You don't know the half of it," she whispered back.

He eyed her meaningfully. "I can handle this group, then."

Before Greta could express her appreciation, he spun on his heel and went into full-on host mode.

She took a deep breath, turning her back and taking a moment to collect herself.

She'd done it. The Band-Aid had been ripped off. For the past year, she'd dreaded the thought of seeing Nathan again. Now, it was over.

The day could only go up from here, right?

Chapter Four

Later that afternoon, Greta made the rounds, chatting with the librarians attending the Welcome Mixer at Bobber's Bar. Appetizer platters were piled high with loaded French fries dripping with melted cheese and topped with lettuce, green onions, and vine-ripe tomatoes; bottomless baskets of chips waiting to be dunked in creamy artichoke dip; and deep-fried cheese curds still steaming.

Bobber's was authentically *Wisconsin*. The rustic bar and grille was a Larkspur staple. Located off Main Street and about a block from Mugs & Hugs, it had wood-paneled ceilings and scuffed, parquet floors. The lighting from the single strand bulbs over each table was dim, but the windows on all sides of the large eatery let in natural daylight for the librarians' afternoon mixer.

The owners of Bobber's Bar, Ace and Suz Hawler, had graciously agreed to host the outing in between their lunch rush and the busy dinner hour.

Greta wound around to the bar to touch base with their hosts. "Thanks again for everything, Suz."

"It's no problem, sweetie. Seems like everyone is having a good time."

"I'd say so." Greta glanced around as laughter broke out from a table of Milwaukee Public librarians who were a couple drinks in. One of them was doing an impersonation of Oprah. *You get a book. You get a book. You get a book. Everyone gets a book!*

"I can help you get things back in order when we're done here," Greta offered.

Suz waved her off. "Nonsense. Mondays are usually slow. And Rob will be coming in for his shift anyway, so we'll have all hands on deck."

"A family affair," Greta said with a smile. Rob was Ace and Suz's twenty-year-old son. "That's so nice."

A crash sounded from the kitchen, and Suz's smile slipped. "I better go see if I can help out in there. Your crew is keeping us busy."

As if to prove her point, a server swung out from behind the bar with a tray full of ice-cold drinks.

"Thanks again, Suz. And please thank Ace for me. I haven't seen him."

"I'm guessing he's back in the middle of the madness." She hooked her thumb toward the kitchen. "I'll give him your best. Holler if you need us!" With a finger wave, she scuttled off.

Greta turned, and her eye caught on a familiar figure outside. Blythe Prescott was picking her way across the grounds alongside Bobber's Bar. She disappeared from Greta's view, but Greta had no doubt it was her. She'd recognize that top-knot of white-blonde hair anywhere.

Greta wondered whether or not she could sneak out and grab the copy of *Pride and Prejudice* she'd left in her car and return it to the woman. She could hardly leave her own party, but she didn't relish another encounter with Heath at B'Jeweled.

She turned toward the door, and, because she had the worst luck, the table of Green Bay librarians happened to be directly in front of it. Nathan was staring back at her, almost as if he was waiting for her to look in his direction. He stood up from his seat and scooted out from behind the table.

Josie appeared at Greta's side. "Is that who I think it is?"

"Unfortunately, yes. I was about to leave." She told Josie about seeing Blythe. "Now I'm boxed in."

Nathan crossed in front of the doorway and wove through the tables toward them.

"Why does he feel like he has any right to talk to you?" Josie's brusque tone told Greta exactly how her friend felt about the situation. "If you want, I'll create a diversion so you can escape."

Before Greta could take Josie up on her offer, the door to the bar opened behind Nathan, and McHenry stepped inside. Greta immediately relaxed.

"Greta." Nathan came to a stop right in front of her. His blond hair was slicked into his trademark coif. He had on grey, tight-fitting dress pants and a navy polo shirt with a tiny animal embroidered on the upper left side. The buttons were opened to reveal a white t-shirt and a braided leather necklace. Greta used to think his prep-school-like attire was endearing, but now, he seemed like he was trying too hard. All he needed was a popped collar to complete his boy-band look. But instead of seeming trendy, he came across as desperate.

Nathan had an easy smile on his face as he gave her a once-over. How could he be so shameless to have led her into an unwilling affair and now act like they could be buddy-buddy? "This is quite the party."

Greta met his eye. She wouldn't cower. "Thank you."

"Josie Sinclair." Josie held out her hand. "I don't think we've met."

"I'm sure Greta has told you about me." Nathan shot Greta a grin, which slipped when McHenry came up alongside her.

Josie, bless her heart, had her focus solely on Nathan. She frowned back at him and shrugged. "Actually, no. She hasn't really mentioned you."

"Hey, you." McHenry's low voice spread over Greta's skin and instantly soothed her tattered nerves. She smiled up at him after he placed a firm, lingering kiss against her temple.

Nathan stuttered, his gaze darting between Josie and Greta and then bouncing up to McHenry. Greta almost laughed when she looked at the detective. He had on his interrogation scowl and was aiming the full force of it at Nathan.

"I...uh...see someone I should talk to." Nathan swallowed so hard his Adam's apple bounced. He tugged on the leather necklace. "Greta, maybe we can catch up later?"

Without waiting for a response, he scurried away.

"Good riddance," Greta mumbled. She fell into conversation with Josie and McHenry and caught sight of Fitz coming out of the men's restroom. He signaled to the bar and mimed tossing one back. Greta nodded and shot him a thumbs-up. She needed a drink.

"Hello, everyone!" Iris cut into their circle with a cheery smile. "Nico was outside, so I invited him to join us." She pulled the author forward.

Greta introduced McHenry to Nico before asking him, "Did you get everything sorted out with your short-term rental?"

"It's perfect." Nico offered Iris a grateful glance. "Thanks again for hooking me up. The cabin is going to give me just the privacy I need to get to work on my next project."

"Are you drafting another book?" Josie asked.

"Trying to." Nico winced. "I need to make sure my idea is solid. I want this book to be a success. I need some redemption."

Before Greta could ask Nico a follow-up question, Nathan reappeared like an ill-timed boomerang. "Nico Eddison? It's a pleasure. I'm Nathan Balker. Love your work."

Greta was more than happy to let the two men slip into their own conversation. Nathan was an extrovert. It was one of the things that had drawn her to him. He had no problem talking to strangers.

She made a mental note to look into Nico's previous publications. Why did he need redemption?

McHenry placed a hand on Greta's lower back. "You okay?"

"I am now." She leaned into him. "Need anything to drink? Fitz is at the bar."

"I'm good. I've got to go back to work after this."

Greta nodded. She'd grown accustomed to McHenry's fifty-hour-a-week schedule. "Want to wander outside for a second? I was going to see if I could catch Blythe."

The woman was probably no longer around, but Greta could use some fresh air.

McHenry nodded and guided her out of the crowded bar.

The spring sun had dipped lower in the sky, and a cool breeze tossed Greta's curls into her face. She tugged them aside and leaned into McHenry's warmth. She angled them toward the parking lot where she'd left the book in the front seat of her car, but they both jumped when a woman's scream pierced the air.

Chapter Five

McHenry, whom Greta had long ago realized always ran toward screams and not away from them, took off in a sprint around the side of the bar. Greta followed him, because while she didn't love screams or the situations that usually caused them, she always felt safer when she was near McHenry.

When she came around the corner of Bobber's Bar, she spotted Suz Hawler standing with her hands over her mouth. McHenry was crouched down in front of her, hovering over—

Greta gasped and pulled up short next to Suz.

Blythe Prescott lay flat on her back in the dirt. She looked dazed, with color in her cheeks, and her eyes opened and glassy, as if she'd fallen down or fainted. But the large gash at her temple and the trickle of blood pooling beneath her head told another story.

McHenry removed his finger from where he was checking for Blythe's pulse and leaned back on his heels. "She's gone."

Greta matched Suz's pose, hands flying up to cover her mouth, as the woman next to her let out a guttural sob. While it could have been an accident, Greta doubted it. She didn't see any way Blythe could have fallen in the middle of the bar's backyard, managed to hit her head in such a way, and then landed on her back.

McHenry stood and retrieved his cell phone, shooting Greta a concerned glance. "I've got to call this in."

"Right," she whispered. Unfortunately, Greta knew the drill. She massaged her temples as miserable memories resurfaced. Larkspur had seen two other murders in the past year, and that was two too many, as far as she was concerned.

McHenry said a quick word to Suz, asking her to hang tight for a minute, before he stepped toward the body.

Suz turned away, crying into her hands. The back door to the bar opened and Ace came barreling outside. "What is it? What happened?"

Suz's sobs increased as Ace wrapped her in his arms. He glanced over at Greta, who winced.

She motioned to where McHenry was blocking most of the gruesome scene. "I'm afraid she stumbled upon Blythe Prescott. She's dead," she added in a hushed tone.

Ace stiffened, and a look passed over his face that Greta didn't want to admit looked a lot like relief. Sometimes, she hated that her brain was constantly reading people, assessing them, and drawing conclusions. Sometimes, those conclusions were premature and inaccurate, but often, she was spot on.

Before she could study Ace any further, he turned his wife away from the dead body. "This is a shock. I'm going to get you something to drink."

Suz nodded numbly and allowed herself to be led to a wooden bench that sat against the back wall of the bar, likely there for the staff to use when they stepped outside on their breaks. A slew of yard equipment was leaning up against the bar's log exterior—a rake, a hoe, and even a pair of outdoor working gloves were tossed on the ground. The shovel was missing. Greta glanced over to where it lay near Blythe's body. She could see a fresh trickle of red blood on the end of it. To Greta's untrained eye, it looked like someone blasted Blythe over the head with the shovel's metal edge. But who?

She spun around in a slow circle, taking deep breaths in an attempt to quiet the buzzing in her ears and cataloging her surroundings in hopes of making sense of the scene. It was a gorgeous early evening in Larkspur. The late-day sun glinted through the pine trees scattered throughout the Bobber's Bar property. Wood violets had sprung up at uneven intervals around the yard, so the ground was a carpet of dirt brown, grassy green, and floral purple. A tattered-looking cabin sat a stone's throw away from the rear of the property. It was tucked behind the bar proper, nearly hidden from the road but in line with where the murder had taken place. If someone was inside, they may have seen or heard something.

McHenry was still talking into his cell phone, crouched next to Blythe. Greta had seen Blythe less than an hour ago. She'd been marching around the outside of the bar with purpose. It was impossible to believe she was lying here, lifeless, now. It was terrible to think that a killer was close at hand.

The thought had Greta opening her eyes and peering around again. The soft, spring ground was damp, and footprints would certainly be found in the mud, but there appeared to be a whole swarm of them, crisscrossing in every direction surrounding the spot where Blythe was killed.

Sirens carried on a gust of wind, and noise from the front of the bar drew her attention. Nico appeared with Nathan, the two still knee-deep in conversation from the looks of things. Behind them, a squad car sped into the parking lot, lights flashing. Officer Clarkson, a junior member of the Larkspur police force, hopped out in full uniform. He jogged forward, passing Nico and Nathan and jostling them from their conversation. As Officer Clarkson joined McHenry on the scene, Greta begrudgingly headed for the two other men.

"What's going on?" Nathan peered beyond Greta.

"I'm afraid there's been an accident. Or, well, not an accident. A woman is dead," Greta stuttered.

Nico's eyes flared, and he stood upright. "Here? Now?"

Greta nodded.

A crowd gathered behind them as Officer Clarkson hurried to affix crime-scene tape around the backyard of the bar. "Stay here, folks. This is an active scene."

"Wait a minute. What's going on?" A young man wearing a baseball cap and a thick flannel over the top of a white t-shirt pushed up against the barrier. "Are those my parents? Let me through."

Rob Hawler. He must've shown up for his shift. Poor kid.

"Sir, I'm afraid you'll have to hang tight." Officer Clarkson hooked his thumb over his shoulder. "We can't have anyone else contaminating the scene."

"What scene? What happened?"

"I'm not at liberty to discuss details at the moment."

"Screw that." Rob lifted the tape and took off toward where his mom still sat on the bench behind the bar.

Officer Clarkson was on him in an instant, catching him by the elbow and pulling him to a stop. "This is for your own good."

McHenry appeared and said a few hushed words to the junior officer. Greta overheard him mumble, "Keep an eye on them."

"Alright, then. Let's head in through the back. We'll grab your parents, too." Officer Clarkson led Rob to where Ace and Suz were, and together, the four of them disappeared into the back of the bar.

"Greta!"

Greta turned to see Josie and Iris flagging her down. Fitz was standing with them, too, worrying his lip. She cut under the police tape and joined them.

"What happened?" Josie asked.

"It's Blythe Prescott." Greta swallowed around a knot in her throat. "She's dead."

She turned to assess the scene again, only to find Nathan right behind her. Nico stood beside him. Greta took a step toward Josie, putting plenty of distance between her and her ex.

Her friends circled her, asking questions and making sure she was okay.

"Don't you live for this, Greta?" Nathan asked the second there was a lull in the conversation. His eyes held an excited gleam.

"What are you talking about?"

"You know. You sort of do this...for fun, right? You're like a mystery-solving librarian."

Greta silently cursed the local newspaper that had coined that nickname for her following the events of the previous fall. That was the only way Nathan could have discovered that she'd become enmeshed in the past two murder investigations to happen in Larkspur. She did not see history repeating itself, though. She had no intention of inserting herself in this case. The police were the professionals, and she'd seen enough crime in the past year to last her a lifetime. The knowledge that Blythe's lifeless body was directly behind her made Greta feel sick to her stomach.

"It is *not* fun." Iris looked horrified.

"Come on." Nathan scoffed. "Think about it. All of us librarians here. What are we, if not little investigators, every day? Sniffing out books that people ask us about using the most benign of clues. We could be real assets."

"You're a real *ass*et of some sort, alright," Josie said under her breath.

Fitz let loose a snicker, but he covered it with a cough.

"I don't think it's our place," he said when he recovered. "The best thing to do is to stick to the game plan for the week. This is a tragedy, but there's nothing we can do about it now."

"Absolutely." Greta agreed, forcing herself not to picture the expression on Blythe's face. "McHenry will take care of it."

Nathan eyed her appraisingly. "How long have you two been together?"

"Long enough to know he's good at his job." Greta worked to keep her voice even, but under the surface of her skin, she could practically feel her blood boiling. Where did Nathan get off?

"Well, you may not want to get involved, but I sure do. This is like a mystery novel come to life before my eyes. How can I not do a little off the books investigating of my own?"

The rest of them looked at Nathan like he had grown five extra eyeballs. He shrugged and sauntered off.

Greta shouldn't be surprised by Nathan's comments, cavalier though they may sound. Hadn't she determined he was a narcissist? He thought he knew best—and could do everything the best—all the time. Put his narcissistic tendencies together with his fascination with solving crime, add in the present circumstances, and here they were. This could spell disaster.

Greta started to count to ten to lower her blood pressure, but she was interrupted before she got to five by another unwelcome voice.

"What is going on here? What are you all doing outside?"

The circle turned and watched as Cindi dodged through the crowd. Her eyes zoned-in on Greta and she made a bee-line for her.

"Greta, what's the matter? I thought you were hosting the librarians at the mixer. What are you doing out here?"

From Greta's perspective, most of the librarians had disappeared. It was almost time for the mixer to be over anyway. A few lingered. Some of the Green Bay crew chatted with Nathan on the far side of the yard.

Greta steeled herself and addressed Cindi. "There's been a situation. Blythe Prescott was found dead."

Cindi stumbled, and Fitz caught her by the elbow. "Blythe? Dead? No. That can't be."

"I'm afraid so."

Cindi craned her neck toward the scene before she snapped her gaze back to Greta. "Why does this sort of thing always happen around you?"

"Hey, now. That isn't fair." Josie stepped forward.

Cindi stuck out her chin defiantly. "Where's the lie?"

"Maybe we should be considering the loss of life here," Iris said pointedly.

"Right. Of course." Cindi sniffed, put in her place for the time being. "It's a tragedy to be sure. Blythe's husband will be distraught, no doubt."

"Heath." The name tumbled out of Greta's mouth.

Five pairs of eyes gazed at her curiously.

"I met him at B'Jeweled, the jewelry shop Blythe owned, when I tried to return her book," Greta explained. "He introduced himself as Blythe's husband."

"I don't believe they had kids, though I'm not quite sure. She didn't talk much about her personal life," Cindi said. "I wonder what will happen with her research. Oh dear, this will throw a wrench into the programming for the gangster trail presentation next weekend."

Greta couldn't help but recall Cindi's forceful outburst at the library on Saturday morning. Something about wanting to murder Blythe. Word choice that was not aging well. Greta guessed it was a coincidence, but it was only years of good manners and toeing the party line that had her refraining from asking Cindi where she'd been that afternoon.

Nico cleared his throat and pointed across the backyard of the bar to the decrepit cabin. "Is there another way to get back to my place?"

Greta faced Iris. "Wait. That's your parents' rental unit?"

"Sure is." Iris turned to Nico with an apologetic grimace. "I can show you the alley entrance around back. It's more out of the way, but it looks like that'll be your best option until they get this taken care of."

"They look like they're going to be a while." Fitz motioned to where McHenry had his phone to his ear again.

Greta knew from experience that the state forensic team would be called along with the medical examiner's office. It would be a long night for McHenry.

She caught his eye as their group dissipated: Fitz back to Karrington, Josie to connect with Ed, and Iris and Cindi to ensure Nico was looked after.

McHenry jogged over.

"You okay?" she asked.

He nodded once. "I'll try to text you later."

"Do what you need to do. I understand. But I'm here if you need me."

Greta swallowed a lump of unease, knowing that McHenry's high-stress job wore him down. She reached out and gave his hand a squeeze. She said a silent prayer that this would be an open and shut case for him.

He squeezed her hand three times, and she took a moment to savor the way his near-black eyes flickered with warmth when he looked at her—like they contained fireflies in the night sky.

"We'll talk soon." With one last glance, he turned and strode to where Officer Clarkson knelt over the body, a frown on his youthful face.

Greta walked slowly back to the front of the bar. She thought about going inside to check on the Hawler family, but she didn't want to intrude or insert herself. Instead, she wandered to her car. She pulled up short when the bar door swung open, and Rob Hawler exited. His phone was pressed to his ear as he strode over to a pick-up truck.

He looked left and right and when he spotted her, she waved and dug into her purse, looking for her keys.

Rob spun so his back was to her, but she still overheard him say, "Just cover for me, alright? All day."

Greta didn't hear anything else except the door to the bar opening, and when she looked up, Rob was gone.

She unlocked her car and plunked down in the driver's seat, exhaling heavily.

She put the key in the ignition, but the worn copy of *Pride and Prejudice* taunted her from the passenger seat. She tugged it out of her tote bag and flipped it open, running her fingers over the ink-stained pages. If this was Blythe's book, and that was a big if, Greta wouldn't ever have the chance to return it.

Would she ever know what all these funky notations meant?

She'd been so tied up with the WLO conference kickoff, she hadn't had a chance to try to decipher the scribbles herself.

No time like the present.

She flipped to the opening page and read the all too familiar first line of Austen's Magnum Opus. Greta paused at where the letter A was circled in the word "acknowledged." She turned several more pages, recording the circled letters in her phone's notes app.

She wasn't sure how long she sat there, but by the time Greta looked up, the sky had turned grey, and the dinner crowd had arrived at Bobber's Bar. Someone had tacked a handwritten *Closed for the Night* sign to the front door. Dinner-goer after dinner-goer walked up to the entrance, read it, and retreated.

Greta glanced down at the letters she'd accumulated in her notes app. She wasn't even halfway through the book, and what stared back at her was a whole lot of gobbledygook. She wasn't sure what she had been expecting to discover, but this effort seemed like a waste of her time. She gently closed the book and set it in her passenger seat. She put her car in drive and checked her surroundings. She did a double take when she saw the *I Brake for Bigfoot* bumper sticker on the truck Rob had been leaning against. Had he been the one to cut her off in the parking lot outside B'Jeweled this morning? If so, was it merely a coincidence that the owner of the jewelry store ended up dead behind his parents' bar?

Greta's head spun as she made the quick drive down Larkspur Lane, circling around on Lakeside Drive toward her cabin. Tucked in amidst the trees on the west side of the Larkspur Lake basin, Greta's cabin was her oasis.

When she walked inside, she dropped to the floor to greet her adopted Siberian cat, Biff. He meowed his welcome, weaving between her legs before flitting off. Greta stood and stretched. Her stomach felt out of sorts.

Nathan's suggestion that she'd dive headlong into this case rattled her. She wasn't reckless, and she didn't like to meddle, especially since she got an up close and personal look at the time and work McHenry put in to serve the community and keep everyone safe. She didn't want to do anything to jeopardize it.

And yet…

Greta winced. Wasn't she already meddling? Trying to figure out the story behind the marked-up book? Wondering about Rob and his connection to the jewelry store. Heck, even her checked desire to question Cindi.

Putting a teapot on the stove to warm, Greta resolved to turn the book over to McHenry the following day and leave this case to the professionals. She had a group of librarians who demanded her focus, anyway. Better to be bookish than brash.

Chapter Six

The jovial-sounding bell above the door at Mugs & Hugs announced Greta's entrance the following morning. It was only ten o'clock, but she was exhausted. True to his word, McHenry had texted after midnight, and the chime on her phone had startled Greta out of her restless sleep. She hadn't managed to sleep soundly for the remainder of the night.

She'd seen the librarians off to a good start at the conference, helping to lead the large group program and guiding folks to the proper break-out sessions. Now, she was taking a minute to regroup.

She walked up to the counter and placed an order with one of Allison's employees for an iced hazelnut latte as well as a raspberry and white chocolate scone. When Greta turned, she spotted Suz Hawler hunched over a mug at a two-person table near the register. Suz's face was smeared with day-old makeup. Her hair was a rat's nest on top of her head. Greta's heart squeezed.

When the server set her drink and pastry on the counter, she thanked him and walked toward Suz. The woman didn't look up until Greta's shadow fell over her.

"Oh, Greta. Hi." Suz glanced down into her coffee mug.

"How're you holding up?" Greta asked kindly.

Suz opened her mouth but clamped it shut again when only a strangled moan escaped.

"Can I sit?" Greta motioned to the empty chair.

Suz nodded and took a sip of her drink.

Greta was content to sit in silence with the shaken woman. Sometimes, being present was all a person could do. Honestly, words failed in the wake of a tragedy like Blythe's death.

"How did you recover from it?" Suz whispered after a minute.

"Pardon me?"

"You found Franklin dead last fall, right? How does life ever go back to normal after something like that?"

Greta broke off a corner of her scone, popped it into her mouth, and sat back in her chair. She could viscerally remember the moment when she'd stumbled upon her neighbor's lifeless body at the base of his deck. She wouldn't wish the sort of premature death Franklin and Blythe suffered on anyone. She wouldn't wish the role of being the one to see someone like that on anyone, either. Her heart went out to Suz, whose hands trembled where she clutched her mug. Greta reached forward and covered one of them with her own hand.

"It doesn't go back to the way it was, but you adjust to a new normal. It will get easier. I promise you that." There had been a time when Greta thought she'd be haunted by her neighbor's death forever. It had been just over six months, and while the loss was still fresh, Greta had learned to cope. She'd been fortunate to be able to adopt Franklin's cat. Biff was a daily reminder of everything she did to find justice for her neighbor and friend. The good-natured tabby also provided some levity and companionship during some of the dark moments.

"Every time I close my eyes—even when I'm blinking—I see that poor woman lying there on the ground." Suz shuddered. "She looked stunned, didn't she? Like she hadn't expected to die in that moment."

Greta pressed her hand against Suz's once more before letting go and taking another drink. Suz was right. Blythe hadn't seemed like a woman who was terrified for her life when Greta had spotted her through the window of the bar. She'd looked determined, as if she'd been going about her business the same as any other day.

Since Blythe was lying on her back, that would indicate that whoever had murdered Blythe had done it head-on. Did that mean that she knew her killer? Were they in the middle of a conversation? Blunt force trauma with a weapon that was found on the premises seemed uncalculated. Like a crime of passion.

"Did you or your husband know Blythe Prescott?" Greta asked.

Suz's gaze bounced up to meet Greta's, and there was a slightly panicked look in her eye before she blinked it away. "Not really," she said slowly. "I mean, I've seen her in the bar over the years, but I hadn't spoken to her. My husband told the police the same."

Ace lied.

Greta had seen him and Blythe fighting. Was Suz aware, or had Ace kept her in the dark?

Either way, something about the measured delivery of Suz's response struck Greta as significant, but she told herself not to borrow trouble.

"She was a member of some library clubs," Greta said. "I saw her after the True Treasure Seekers meeting last weekend."

Suz paled. "Oh?"

"Yeah. But I never talked to her myself. From what I gathered, she seemed like an"—Greta searched for the right word—"animated sort of woman."

Suz made some sort of humming sound in response and shifted uncomfortably.

Greta switched courses. "Surrounding myself with people who care helped me after I found Franklin. I'm glad your husband and your son could be there with you yesterday."

Suz's eyes brightened. "They're both rock solid in a crisis, that's for sure. I don't know what I would have done if they hadn't been there. Might have had a full-blown panic attack. Rob was great. He took over sending staff home and cleaning the dining room and kitchen for us so Ace could tend to me."

"Sounds like you've raised a good kid." Greta offered Suz a smile. "I saw Rob in Karrington yesterday morning, actually, but I don't know that we've been formally introduced."

"That can't be right." Suz frowned.

"It's okay. I'm still relatively new to town. I'm sure our paths just haven't crossed."

"No, no. Not that." Suz shook her head. "Rob wasn't in Karrington yesterday. He spends Mondays with his girlfriend, Sadie, before he works the dinner shift."

"Oh." Greta sat back in her seat. "My mistake, I guess."

"No biggie." Suz straightened her mug. "I will introduce you to him sometime. We're so proud of him. We weren't able to have kids for years, and when we'd all but given up, we found out I was pregnant with Rob. He's our pride and joy. All set to take over the bar for us, too."

"How wonderful." Greta scooted her chair away from the table. "I've got to get back to the library, but it was good seeing you. I'm here if you need someone to talk to."

"I might take you up on that." Suz's eyes clouded over again. "I hope the police get this sorted out quick. I don't like the thought of a killer roaming around the Larkspur streets."

"They will," Greta assured her.

But as she left the café, Greta was on edge. She swore she saw Rob in Karrington yesterday morning. So, the question was: was he pulling one over on his own mom, sneaking off to Karrington, and doing who knows what when she thought he was with his girlfriend? Or was she covering for her only son? And why did Ace lie to the police about not interacting with Blythe? What was the connection between her and the Hawler family?

Greta huffed as she walked into the library.

"What's wrong?" Iris asked from behind the circulation desk.

Greta joined her, peering around before lowering her voice. "Sometimes, it's a big fat bummer to have a curious mind. I spent the past fifteen minutes talking to Suz Hawler." Greta relayed what the woman had said for Iris. "I don't know what to make of it."

"Seems suspicious, if you ask me."

"Right? But I don't want to be suspicious. I don't want to prove Nathan right."

Iris waved her off. "Don't beat yourself up over it. Anyone would have drawn the same conclusions you did based on what you told me. Why don't you go talk to McHenry? Give him the book. Get it off your chest."

McHenry always had a way of calming her down.

That, and he would tell her in no uncertain terms to stay out of his investigation. She could use a firm reminder.

"Good idea. You good here?"

"Everything's running like clockwork." Iris shooed her out the door. "Go. You'll feel better."

Greta made the quick walk down the hall to the rear entrance to the police office. Lori Lamponee, the department's secretary and a good friend of Greta's mom, was at her usual spot behind the desk. She waved when Greta entered, but then her eyes bounced to the other side of the room.

Greta followed her gaze to find Chief Sorenson and McHenry with their heads together, talking in low tones.

Lori held up one finger, encouraging Greta to wait a moment.

"When do you leave?" Chief said.

Greta stilled.

"I should head out today. They need me in court tomorrow to testify." McHenry dragged a hand through his hair. "I was hoping it wouldn't come to this."

Chief Sorenson pressed his lips together and nodded. "You obviously have to go. But this puts us in a bit of a bind with the investigation."

"I know." McHenry winced, and his gaze pinged to Greta.

She held up a hand in a weak wave.

"Greta. Hey. We were—"

"I didn't mean to interrupt." Embarrassment prickled in Greta's cheeks. "I only wanted to drop this off in case it was helpful to your investigation. I think it belonged to Blythe."

Greta held up the book, and Chief Sorenson and McHenry joined her in front of Lori's desk. The chief took the copy of *Pride and Prejudice* from her after she explained why she had it.

"Her husband, Heath, said he didn't recognize it," Greta said with a shrug.

McHenry's gaze, which hadn't left her, seemed to burrow into her face with more intensity. "You've met Heath?"

"I brought the book over to B'Jeweled yesterday morning on my way to the library in Karrington…before Blythe's death. She wasn't around, and he brushed me off."

McHenry's mouth flattened into a straight line.

Greta got the sense McHenry didn't get good vibes from Blythe's husband. She longed to ask why, but she really, truly was trying not to press into the investigation.

"You're not sure what these notations mean?" Chief Sorenson flicked through a couple pages.

"I'm afraid not. They seem random."

"Could they have something to do with Blythe's death?" Chief Sorenson turned his attention to McHenry with this question.

"Anything's possible," McHenry conceded.

The chief looked to the ceiling. If he had a beard, Greta could imagine him stroking it, lost in thought. After a couple seconds, he dropped his gaze to her. "Do you think you could look into it for us, Greta?"

"Pardon me?" Greta frowned.

"Chief," McHenry said, his tone laced with apprehension.

Greta glanced between the two law enforcement officers. Chief Sorenson held up his hand to stop McHenry's protests. "Hear me out. We're short-staffed as it is. You're going to be out for at least a day or two. Greta, here, could prove to be a valuable help to the case."

"She's a civilian," McHenry ground out.

"I'm not asking her to arrest anyone," Chief Sorenson said. He turned to Greta. "Would you be willing to look into these scribbles for us? See if you could figure out a pattern or a hidden meaning?"

"You…you actually *want* my help?"

"Yep." Chief Sorenson said.

"With an active investigation?"

The chief nodded. "With the book. The actual book will need to be logged and kept as evidence. But we'll make photocopies for you."

"I think I've entered an alternate dimension," Greta mumbled, causing Lori, who had been watching this exchange like a tennis match at Wimbledon, to snort into her coffee mug.

Greta's lips quirked. "I'd be happy to do anything I could to help, Chief."

"I don't think it's a good idea," McHenry said.

"Nonsense." Chief Sorenson waved McHenry off with a flick of his wrinkled hand. "Greta has proven that she's quite capable of handling herself. And the lady's whip-smart."

"Not arguing with you there, but—"

"We'll hire her on as a contracted consultant. A book expert. Exactly what we need for this sort of thing. How does that sound, Greta?" the chief asked, ignoring McHenry completely.

"Sign me up." A familiar tingle of excitement, nerves, and anticipation thrummed through her veins.

"That's settled then. I'll bring the photocopies down to the library for you later today. Then you can touch base if and when you learn anything."

"You got it, Chief."

Chief Sorenson disappeared into his office, and Greta said goodbye to Lori before she turned to McHenry. "Walk with me?"

Without a word, he opened the police office's rear door and held it for her so she could exit first into the hallway. She felt him step out behind her.

When the door to the police station swished shut, she spun around.

"Don't be mad," she said at the same time McHenry blurted, "I'm sorry."

Greta crossed her arms. "For what?"

McHenry sighed. "Come on."

He strode halfway down the hall and pulled open the door to the storage closet. Greta's lips twitched when she walked inside. She never thought a supply closet that smelled distinctly of lemon and floor cleaner would be romantic, but here she was.

McHenry shut the door after he stepped into the space, and Greta flipped on the light. They stood chest-to-chest, as the wall shelving and leaning tower of mops, brooms, and buckets didn't allow for much floor space. McHenry's eyes were like lasers on her. "I'm guessing you overheard me talking to the chief?"

He posed it as a question, but from his tone, it was obvious he knew the answer.

"You're going back to Chicago?"

A muscle in McHenry's jaw pulsed. "I am. I'm sorry for not telling you. I was planning to yesterday night, and then everything happened outside the bar, and I wrapped up late, and I didn't want to share it over text. So, I'm sorry."

That was fair. Greta didn't love finding out McHenry's schedule after Chief Sorenson, but she understood. She reached out and grabbed his hand, squeezing it. "It's not a big deal. Don't worry about it."

"But it is a big deal for me." McHenry's gaze bore into her. "I want to be honest and upfront with you. Given your"—he paused—"past," he said with kindness, "I want to show you that I'm not like that."

Greta's heart tugged in her chest, like it was trying to hop from her body to his. "I *know* you're not like that, Mark." She reached up and cradled his cheek. "Thank you for recognizing why it might be hard for me if I feel like you're withholding information."

McHenry covered her hand with his. "I have to go down to testify on behalf of my brother. He was mixed up with some bad guys, and one of them is standing trial for drug trafficking. My brother testified and his lawyers initially thought that would be enough, but they wanted the credibility of having a cop on the stand. So, I got called up."

Greta's head spun. This was more than McHenry had ever told her about his brother. She worried her bottom lip. "These bad guys will see you and know you're testifying against them? Doesn't that put you in danger?"

"I don't think so. It'll be a quick trip, and then I'll head out of town and be back here, hopefully for good. Those guys have bigger fish to fry than me."

Greta let out a slow breath. "If you say so."

She had to put it out of her mind. She knew that. She trusted McHenry to do his job. He wouldn't be the man she was falling in love with if he didn't work on the side of justice and the good guys.

"About this little arrangement you and the chief cooked up." McHenry's eyebrows formed a V as he stared her down. "I'm not thrilled."

"You don't say," Greta said dryly, poking him in the side.

He grabbed her finger. "Promise me you'll be careful. Stay in your lane.

Don't do anything rash or draw any unnecessary attention to yourself."

"I'm hard to miss," Greta teased.

"I know." McHenry's dark eyes flickered with an undercurrent of heat.

Greta's stomach fluttered. "I'll be careful and stick to the book. Promise."

McHenry studied her with his intense gaze before giving a single nod. "I'll be back the day after tomorrow."

Greta stood up on her tiptoes and pressed a light kiss to his cheek, savoring the grit of his stubble against her lips. "Can't wait."

McHenry turned and caught her mouth with his. "Me either," he said, leaning out of the kiss.

He opened the door to the hallway and motioned for her to go out first.

Greta stepped out under the harsh fluorescent lights and smoothed down her sun dress. Giggles erupted from near the library as McHenry appeared behind her. Greta followed the sound to a pair of meddlesome sexagenarians.

Dolores Jenkins and Celeste Janowick were two of her favorite library patrons. They were also Larkspur royalty. They knew all the comings and goings around town, and, as such, were expert sources of information. The only downside to their busy-body ways was the interest they'd taken in Greta and McHenry's relationship. Even before there was an actual relationship to have an interest in, these two ladies were scheming.

"Well, well, well." Celeste rubbed her hands together, causing her trademark bracelet stack to jangle on her arm. "Aren't you two cute?"

"A clandestine meeting in a closet," Dolores cooed. "Very romantic. Good work, Detective."

"Hey." Greta pretended to be offended. "How do you know I wasn't the one who lured him inside?" She wiggled her eyebrows, and the older ladies tittered.

"I'll leave you to it," McHenry said with a chuckle. "You seem to have this under control."

"Text me?" Greta said as he turned to head back to work.

"I will." He strode away, and Greta joined Dolores and Celeste, checking her watch. She had about ten minutes before she needed to be at the next WLO event. "What brings you two by today?"

"What else?" Dolores widened her eyes. "Can you believe there's another murder in town?"

Celeste glanced around to ensure they were alone. "What do you know?"

Greta opened her mouth to respond, but slammed it shut when the outside door to the municipal center whooshed open and Heath Prescott ambled inside.

Chapter Seven

"Hold that thought." Greta waited a minute, letting Heath make it into the library, before she followed behind. Dolores and Celeste were hot on her heels.

Josie was attending the morning conference session, so Iris was staffing the circulation desk alone. She glanced up from her computer, her eyes landing on Heath, who shoved a cardboard box onto the counter. It was long and narrow, like the type of container that could slide underneath a piece of furniture. There was orange script writing on all the sides of the box. It read, *Bigger Is Better* with an image of a diamond on either side of it.

Greta scrunched up her nose at its crassness.

"Can I help you?" Iris asked Heath.

He appraised Iris and flicked his gaze to Greta, who rounded the corner of the desk to stand near her friend. Heath's brows narrowed before his eyes bugged, recognition dawning. "You," he said. "The one with the book."

"Hello, Mr. Prescott." Greta greeted him with a practiced smile. Iris stilled next to her, and she imagined their thought processes were synced. What was Blythe's husband doing in their library? And what had he brought with him?

"Can we help you with something?" she reiterated Iris's question.

Heath shoved the box toward them. "I'm here to drop off this rubbish. Wanted to donate it."

Greta tentatively opened one flap of the cardboard, revealing a portion of the box's contents. It appeared to be mostly paperwork, some handwritten, some typed.

51

"What, exactly, is it?" Iris peered into the box from over Greta's shoulder.

"My late wife's research." Heath made air quotes as he said the last word. "A bunch of hogwash if you ask me. I know there are others around here who like to waste their time like she did, searching for lost treasure that doesn't exist. I figured instead of tossing this junk, I'd spread the love."

Greta reached for the box, even as she internally recoiled at Heath's callous and dismissive treatment of his wife's belongings. The woman had only been dead a day. Still, Greta had a feeling Cindi Fields would love nothing more than to page through these documents and unearth the gangster trail discovery Blythe was bragging about ahead of the Little Bohemia Lodge anniversary.

"We'll take care of it," she said to Heath. "That's very thoughtful of you."

Heath rocked back on his heels, sticking his hands into his pockets and shooting Greta and Iris an oily smile. "What can I say? I'm a thoughtful guy. You give any more thought to some bling? I could hook you up."

Behind Heath, Greta caught the eyes of Dolores and Celeste, who were frowning and looking like they'd enjoy giving Heath a piece of their minds. Greta gave them a subtle shake of her head.

"Not in the market at the moment, but I'll keep B'Jeweled in mind when I am. Speaking of, I'm sorry about your wife." Greta softened her tone. "I should have led with that."

"Appreciate that." Heath hummed. "But what can you do, ya know? We're all gonna die someday." He shifted his gaze, taking in the library. "Nice setup you got in here."

"Thank you," Iris responded, shooting Greta a look.

Greta shrugged back.

"Well, better be going. Lots of business to take care of."

"Speaking of business, are you taking over now that Blythe is gone?" Greta asked. According to the angry customer she'd overheard at B'Jeweled, Blythe was the CEO, not Heath.

Heath stopped in his tracks and lasered a scrutinizing look at Greta. It was the first time he looked anything other than slimy. "Who's asking?"

A bolt of unease tightened into Greta's spine. "I wanted to make sure you'll still be around when I decide to come in and look at that bling." Greta batted her eyelashes and fought back a gag.

Fitz appeared in the library doorway, but pulled up short next to Dolores and Celeste, waiting for Greta to conclude her conversation.

Heath fell back into his salesman good humor. "Definitely. I'm doing some housekeeping. It'll be a one-man show from now on."

"You're firing your staff?"

"It was just Blythe, me, and Tuck before." Heath leaned in. "You saw him when you came in, didn't you? Between you and me, I don't trust Tuck as far as I can throw him. Actually, I wouldn't be surprised if he had something to do with her death."

Greta sucked in a breath. "That's a serious accusation."

Heath shrugged. "He's got some skeletons in his closet, that's all I'm saying. Had I known his history, I wouldn't have let Blythe hire him in the first place. But then he leeched onto her, and what could I do?" Heath reached over and patted her hand. Greta had to fight not to snatch it away. "Anyway, you come see me whenever you're ready, and I'll get you taken care of. Don't be a stranger."

With a wink, he left the library.

Greta wanted to take a shower, but Fitz approached the desk, and she knew she was needed at the conference.

"Ready?" he asked.

"Or not," Greta replied. She surveyed the library, which wasn't super crowded. A few people were browsing the stacks, and some kids squealed from the train table area in the children's section. Nico must've arrived when she was talking to McHenry. He sat with his nose buried in a book at one of the tables lining the wall of exterior windows. She had to smile at that. Book people were drawn to book places. It was science.

Or literature, she supposed.

"Sorry, I can't chat longer, ladies." She offered Dolores and Celeste an apologetic smile. "Duty calls."

"We know you're busy, dear." Dolores stepped forward. "You keep us posted if there's anything you need."

53

"We're happy to help. Even if you need someone to fend off guys like that." Celeste flicked her wrist to the exit where Heath had disappeared. Her bracelets clanked.

"I will." Greta chuckled. "Thank you." The two older women left, and Greta turned to Iris, motioning to the box of Blythe's belongings. "Can you put this somewhere?"

Iris nodded and lugged it off the desk. "Nothing like Heath leaving Blythe's garbage for us to take care of," she said with a huff.

Greta wasn't so sure it was garbage. In fact, she was dying to go through it and see what, if anything, she could learn about Blythe's research. Now that she had the official go-ahead from Chief Sorenson to investigate, she couldn't wait to get started.

But first, there was a room full of librarians waiting on her.

"All good?" Fitz asked.

"I think so." They walked together toward the large conference room at the back of the stacks. This was the space Greta had hoped to convert into a rare books room. She'd love to make it a destination for book collectors and local book lovers alike, but as it turned out, Larkspur's late mayor's request to put that project on hold had worked out for the best. The large space was the only one with enough capacity to seat the full group of conference attendees.

The first thing Greta noticed when she and Fitz entered the room was Nathan. He was sitting up on the table with one leg propped on a chair.

"He's super eager to collaborate with me," Nathan was saying. "He said he'd been in contact with the deceased, so I'm sure we'll have a lot to go on as we look into this mess."

A murmur of *ohhs* and a buzz of intrigue zipped around the room. Greta and Fitz exchanged wary glances.

"What are you talking about?" Fitz asked, approaching the group.

"The murder, what else?" Nathan said easily. His eyes found hers. "I tell you what, you're not the only one who caught the amateur sleuth bug, Greta. I'm starting to think I missed my calling."

"Why would you say that?" Fitz was the picture of skepticism.

"I've been talking to Nico, and he and I have formed a bit of a partnership. I like our chances of sorting this all out. Can you imagine the news?" Nathan dragged his hand across the air in front of him. *"One for the books! Librarian and author crack case.* The headlines will write themselves."

"You're getting way ahead of yourself, Nathan." Greta hadn't wanted to get drawn into this discussion, but...desperate times.

"I disagree. As soon as we're done here for the day, Nico and I are meeting up. I'm sure we'll start questioning folks ASAP."

"You can't go around accusing people. No one in Larkspur will appreciate that."

"I didn't come here to make friends."

Greta squinted at him. "You came here for a librarian conference, but that's neither here nor there at this point. All I'm saying is I hope you're not planning to start pointing fingers to satisfy your amateur sleuth craving."

"I have more tact than that. You, of all people, should know."

Greta's cheeks flamed. "In any case, let's leave the investigating to the professionals. We've got library work to do."

Greta strode to the front of the room to announce the speaker for the session, effectively ending Nathan's pontificating.

But even as the discussion about how libraries could collaborate with local school districts began, Greta's mind wandered to the box Iris stowed for her. What had Blythe been working on? Had it gotten her killed? What did Tuck think about getting fired? Why did Heath say he was bad news? And where did the copy of *Pride and Prejudice* fit into the mix?

Before she knew it, Fitz was nudging her, and the room was clearing out. "Lunch time."

Greta pressed her lips together. She hadn't heard a word of the presentation.

Josie joined them from across the room. "You two want to grab a bite?"

"I'm heading over to Bobber's," Nathan announced to a nearby table before Greta could answer.

She exchanged a pointed look with Josie and Fitz. "We better follow and make sure he doesn't ruffle too many feathers."

* * *

After a quick walk, Greta, Josie, and Fitz found a table in the center of the bar's dining room. Nathan took a seat at the bar. Suz appeared and took their drink orders, promising to be back with them shortly.

As Greta was pulling a menu from the slot behind the napkin dispenser, the door to the bar opened, and Nico walked in. He took a seat next to Nathan.

"What do you make of those two?" Josie asked.

Fitz eyed the two men. "Not sure when there was time for that bromance to develop, but it's obvious they're thick as thieves.

Greta sighed. "I hope they don't make any trouble."

Suz buzzed back with their drinks, and they placed their order with her. The bar door swung open behind Greta, and Suz left their table and walked over to greet the newcomer.

When Greta turned to see the new arrival, she stiffened. It was Tuck. He kept popping up.

"Suz seems in good spirits, despite the circumstances." Josie took a sip of her iced tea.

"Much better than when I ran into her this morning." Greta stirred her straw around her ice-cold Diet Coke and kept her eye on Suz as she slipped behind the bar.

Ace was drying a highball glass with a bar towel. Suz whispered something in his ear, and his jaw tensed, though he didn't look up from his task. Suz flitted into the kitchen.

Nathan waved to the bar owner, beckoning him to the end of the counter where he and Nico sat.

Ace walked over. His deep, booming voice carried throughout the relatively empty eatery. "What can I get for you, gentlemen?"

"Hoping for some information," Nico said.

"Regarding?"

"Bobber's Bar and its connection to John Dillinger's compatriot, Julian 'JuJu' Vance."

Behind her, Greta heard a growl emanate from Tuck's table. She covertly glanced back at him, and his gaze was focused on the bar. She swiveled her head around and eyed Ace, who had cocked his head to the side and was staring between the two men seated at his bar.

"Come again?" Ace's eyes were narrowed.

"Who's Julian 'JuJu' Vance?" Fitz asked in hushed tones.

"No idea," Greta muttered. "Never heard of him."

Josie shushed them, and they all held their breath.

"We have reason to believe that after fleeing from the FBI during the raid at Little Bohemia Lodge in 1934, Dillinger and his gang, including JuJu Vance, escaped and made their way south en route to Chicago. JuJu stopped here, in Larkspur, and more specifically here, at Bobber's Bar. You know anything about that?" Nico pressed.

Ace's lips curled into a sardonic frown. "You realize that was about ninety years ago, right? How old do you think I am?"

Nico gave a good-natured chuckle. "We're not suggesting you were literally around at the time, but according to your website, this bar has been in your family since about that time. Are you sure there hasn't been any family lore passed down about the infamous gangsters passing through?"

"If there was, I must've missed it," Ace said coolly.

Greta couldn't help but notice that Ace didn't meet Nathan or Nico's eye as he said it. Instead, he looked beyond them and in Tuck's direction before cutting his gaze out the window.

"So, you're saying you don't know anything about JuJu Vance's connection to this place?"

"Why would I?" Ace snapped, his tone suddenly hostile and his focus tuned into the men directly in front of him.

Suz bustled out of the swinging kitchen door with plates of food. "Honey, can you take these for me?" She tipped her chin to where Greta and her friends were sitting. "They go to that table over there."

"Excuse me, gentlemen," he said to Nathan and Nico as Suz handed over the meal.

Ace approached them, expertly balancing three plates on his arm. He set them down in front of Greta, Josie, and Fitz.

"This looks delicious," Fitz said. If he was at all startled by Ace's outburst at the bar, he hid it well.

"Anything else we can get you?"

"I think we're good." Greta smiled at Ace. "I hope you're all doing okay here after everything that went down yesterday."

"I certainly never expected to find that woman dead here." Ace paused and added, "Or anyone dead here, for that matter."

"Did you know her?" Josie asked. "Blythe, I mean."

"No. I didn't." Ace tugged on his collar. "Such a shame, though."

Greta offered him a kind smile. "I'm most sorry for Suz. I ran into her this morning, and she still seemed unsettled by it all. How's she holding up?"

"She's a tough nut, that one. She'll be alright." Ace puffed up his chest. "We all will be. We get through it as family does. Together."

As if on cue, Rob appeared from the kitchen. Nathan waved him over to where he and Nico sat. The three struck up a conversation, though Greta couldn't make out what was said. Ace trained his eyes on the bar and clenched his jaw.

"Were those guys giving you a hard time?" Fitz wiped his mouth after taking a giant bite of his crispy chicken sandwich.

Ace pulled his gaze from the bar. "No, no. A slight misunderstanding. If you'll excuse me, I've got to get back to it. Holler if you need anything else. Suz will be by with drink refills."

Ace strode away, and stopped next to Rob, effectively ending whatever conversation his son was having with Nico and Nathan. Rob looked to his dad with a quick side-eyed glance before returning to the kitchen.

Greta itched to talk with the younger Hawler. To ask him about his Monday morning trip to B'Jeweled. She wasn't sure how to approach him, though. Not when the two hadn't been formally introduced. She was also keen to figure out what was going on with Tuck. Why did he keep popping up? What was with his strong reaction to the name JuJu Vance? Did he know anything about Blythe's research? If so, he might be able to help her sift through the documents Heath had left, or at least help her figure out what she was looking for.

Then again, Greta had promised McHenry she would stick to the book research. She had marginalia to decipher, and that should be her first priority. She checked her watch, and if he hadn't hit traffic, McHenry was probably almost to Chicago. She said a quick prayer for his safety and that everything went smoothly for him down there.

* * *

The three librarians managed to enjoy the rest of their lunch without paying too much attention to Nathan and Nico. The two men left the bar while Greta's table was splitting the check, and they were nowhere to be found when Greta, Josie, and Fitz stepped out into the sunshine.

"I should get back to Karrington and make sure everything is set up for this afternoon." Fitz stretched his arms over his head as they walked down the quiet backroad.

"I'll be right behind you." Greta gestured to the library. "I have to swing back in and grab my bag."

The librarians separated, and Greta trailed Josie and Iris behind the circulation desk.

"Tweedle Dee and Tweedle Dum beat us here," Josie said under her breath. She bobbed her chin toward the research area.

Nico was seated at his laptop with Nathan hovering over his shoulder. They were speaking in hushed tones, but Nathan's low voice carried.

"This is huge, man. Don't you think? I can't even believe it. I've always had a thing for true crime, and this is like living it."

Nico nodded, not taking his eyes off his computer. "Let me just pull this up quick."

A few patrons approached the desk and blocked Greta's view of the two men. Iris set to work checking out their books.

"Nathan's going to be late for the afternoon session if he's not careful," Greta said to Josie. "I should get going, too."

Cindi bustled into the library but barely glanced in their direction. Her focus was solely on Nico.

"Oh good, we can get rid of that box." Josie reached under the circulation desk and wedged a corner of it out.

"Hold on a sec." Greta nudged it back with her toe. "I want to go through it first."

"You think you'll find something in there?"

"Won't know until I look." *And I'm not even sure what I'm looking for.* "I figure I'll start by keeping my eyes peeled for the name JuJu Vance."

Chapter Eight

J osie gave her a knowing nod.

"Who's that?" Iris asked.

"Tell you later," Greta promised before turning to Josie. "Actually, would you mind asking your brother if he's come across that name?"

Jake and Caroline had flown back to the East Coast first thing Monday morning.

"I can do that. Jake loves a good mystery as much as the next guy, and with his resources at the university, he could explore this further. I'll text him now."

Josie stepped into the office, and Nathan sauntered over to the desk.

"You heading out?" Greta asked him.

"Sure am. Want a ride to Karrington? I have to come back this way since I'm staying at Kennedy's Cozy Cottages."

"I'll drive myself. I may need to stay later and finish up some prep work for tomorrow," Greta lied. There was nothing to prep. But spending time in the car with Nathan was high on her list of things that made her want to puke…right up there with book bans and book burning.

"At least let me walk you to the parking lot, then."

Seeing as they were literally headed in the same direction, there was no way to avoid this. Greta said goodbye to Iris and grabbed her bag.

"So." Nathan pushed open the exterior door and held it for her. "I finally get you alone. It's been too long."

"Please don't, Nathan." She stopped and faced him. "I'm not interested in whatever it is you think you're doing. Stop flirting with me. You have a wife at home. I'm trying to be civil here, but you're not making it easy."

"What do you mean? I haven't done anything."

Greta sighed and turned to walk away. There was no reasoning with Nathan. He was a classic narcissist who thought he was above everyone else. She didn't know how she'd been blind to his true character when they'd dated.

Nathan jogged up to her. "Come on. I don't want any trouble. I miss talking to you and hearing what's rattling around in that brain of yours."

Nathan's sweet-talking and compliments about her mind used to charm her. Now, she saw right through them. He would say anything to try to get his way—or to get the information he wanted. She wasn't about to give it to him.

"Not much besides the library conference at the moment," she said lightly.

"Doubtful." Nathan stepped in front of her and cut her off before she reached her car. "What have you learned about Blythe Prescott's death?"

Greta managed to pull up short before she collided with him. "I'm staying out of the way on this one."

"I don't buy that for a second." Nathan's eyes glittered in the midday sun. "Local woman smacked over the head with a garden tool basically in the library's backyard. Tell me you're not intrigued."

He had her there, but Greta wasn't about to admit it. She also wasn't about to tell him the police had brought her on as a consultant. He'd be insufferable. "I don't have time for this."

"Come on. We could pool our resources. I've found out some mighty interesting things about Blythe."

Greta refused to take the bait. She walked around him.

"Don't you want to know what I know?"

"Not really."

Besides, Greta had a feeling she could figure it out, based on what she'd overheard at the bar and what Blythe herself had said to Cindi.

The woman's death seemed to be connected to the research she was doing about some type of hidden treasure buried by the gangsters of the 1920s and 1930s—as out there as that sounded.

"Nico has been very interested in my help," Nathan put his hand on the lip of her door as Greta pulled it open, stalling her progress.

"We're going to be late," she grumbled.

"Want to know what I think?"

"No, but you're going to tell me anyway," Greta muttered.

"I think you're jealous that I'm working this case. I think you're dying to know what I know."

Greta rolled her eyes. "Nathan, this may shock you but I actually don't spend much of my time thinking about you, and I haven't spent that much time thinking about Blythe's death."

Not yet, at least. She planned to have a date with the photocopies of *Pride and Prejudice* later that evening, though.

"Let me let you in a little secret—one that'll whet your appetite for the case, then." Nathan leaned in. "Did you know Blythe had been in touch with Nico? She's the reason why he's in town early."

"Of course, she was in touch with him. She was helping to coordinate the event that he's speaking at."

Nathan looked smug. "But she was communicating with him on the side about this huge bit of news she unearthed. She wanted to collaborate with him, using that information to pen another book."

Greta threw up her arms. "What information?"

Nathan rocked back on his heels, looking delighted that he'd gotten a rise out of her. "She never said. He's only puzzling things together based on what she did say."

"Which was?" Greta prodded. She was in the conversation this far; she may as well see it through.

"Something went down at Bobber's Bar back in 1934, on the heels of the Little Bohemia Lodge raid. We're not sure what yet, but Nico and I will figure it out."

Greta elbowed Nathan aside. "What you should do is share all this with the police. Chief Sorenson has a tip line set up."

"What about your boyfriend?" Nathan leaned over the edge of the door and stared her down.

"What about him?"

"Shouldn't I speak to him directly?"

Greta wasn't sure how she ever had feelings for this man. Between him and McHenry...there was no comparison. She'd actually relish the opportunity to watch a confrontation between the two. McHenry would eat Nathan for breakfast. The thought made her lips twitch.

"You can if you want," she said breezily. "But he's out of town until at least tomorrow night."

Her heart squeezed, even as she kept her face blank. She missed McHenry. A lot. She was still figuring out how to be in a relationship with a guy whose job demanded so much of him. All Greta knew was she wanted to support him, like he showed up and supported her. They were building a solid partnership. That was something she'd never had with Nathan.

Nathan clicked his tongue. "Shame. Guess I'll wait and see what else I can find out in the meantime and then show him that I can basically do his job."

Greta gripped the steering wheel. She wouldn't let Nathan see her sweat, even if he was completely disrespecting the efforts of law enforcement, McHenry included. She felt a twinge of guilt for any instance in the past when she thought she could do it better. She'd learned that she didn't know it all. But that didn't mean she couldn't be helpful. On the contrary, Nathan's arrogant attitude and cavalier approach was all wrong. He was going to make an even bigger mess of things if he wasn't careful.

"You should leave the investigative work to the professionals. You don't want to get mixed up in something. You could get hurt."

Nathan put his hand to his chest. "If I didn't know better, I'd say you cared about me."

She drew in a breath to compose herself before responding. "I'd just hate to see anyone else end up injured or worse because they overstepped. This isn't a game."

"Maybe not," Nathan said with a smirk. "But I intend to win."

Chapter Nine

Greta spent the ride to Karrington trying to catalog her thoughts into some semblance of order and to shake off Nathan's arrogance and the general ick she felt being around him. She coasted through the afternoon breakout sessions and lingered after the final session of the day, waiting in Fitz's periphery as he spoke to one of his fellow librarians.

When he spotted her, Fitz turned and beckoned her forward. "Greta, this is Wren, one of our library assistants. She's been helping keep the library afloat while I'm at the conference."

Greta shook the young woman's hand. "Pleasure to meet you. Thanks for your work."

"Of course. Happy to take some things off this old man's plate." Wren grinned.

Greta's gaze snagged on a couple old books on the desk nearby. They appeared too vintage to be in circulation. "What do you have going there?"

Wren held up an old diary. "Family heirlooms my dad found. I was showing Fitz."

"You know how much I love a good book artifact," Fitz quipped. "Speaking of that, I've got to run. Online orientation tonight."

Greta gasped and grabbed Fitz's arm. "Oh my gosh, that's right. I can't believe I forgot! Are you excited?"

"Not sure if I'd call signing up for five to ten more years of schooling exciting," Fitz chuckled. "But it'll be good to touch base with some folks in my program."

Fitz was starting a PhD program in the fall. He was hoping to become an archivist.

"I can't wait to hear all about it. I'll see you tomorrow." Greta waved to Wren and left the library. She drove toward Larkspur and slowed as she approached the strip mall that housed B'Jeweled. The letters spelling out the jewelry store's name were illuminated and flashed at even intervals.

Greta slammed on her brakes and veered to the side of the road when the door to B'Jeweled opened and Tuck walked out. He was carrying a box, and he didn't turn around when Heath exited the building after him.

Greta rolled down her window, but from her position, there wasn't much of a chance that she'd be able to hear what they were saying to each other. From the looks of things, Heath was kicking Tuck out. He was gesticulating wildly and pointing at the younger man.

Tuck, for his part, walked calmly to his car, deposited the box and turned to face Heath.

Greta strained her ear, but it was no use.

After a minute, Tuck got into his car. Heath stepped back, his arms crossed over his chest. He looked on as Tuck navigated out of his parking stall.

"Shoot." Greta rolled up her window and shielded her face with her hand. She heard more than saw Tuck's car rumble past her. She gave it an extra minute before pulling back out onto the road. She glanced in her rearview mirror, and Heath had disappeared.

"Thank goodness." Greta exhaled.

She tapped her brakes when she'd driven about a half mile and spotted Tuck's car on the side of the road. He'd blown a tire.

Greta turned on her flashers and pulled up behind him.

He was standing on the shoulder side of the road, hands on his hips, glaring at the flat tire as if it would change itself.

Greta stepped out of her car and waved. "Hey, there. What luck, huh?"

"You can say that again," Tuck snorted. His sour mood was evident in the scowl on his lips and the ruddy undertone of his cheeks.

"Need a hand?"

Tuck sized her up. "From you?"

"Looks like I'm your best option," she said easily. "Happy to help."

Tuck shifted on his legs. "I don't know the first thing about changing a tire," he gritted out after a moment.

"Lucky for you. I do." Greta would never forget the day her dad took her and her older sister, Kelly, into the garage. It was below freezing outside and not much warmer in the unheated garage, but he wouldn't let them go back inside until they both successfully changed a tire on his car. He insisted it was a life skill and he wanted his girls equipped. He put the ABBA Gold CD in his old boom box and set to work teaching them. It took Kelly and Greta several tries to get the hang of it, and their fingers were numb before all was said and done. But the quality time together—singing, teasing, and laughing—had been worth it. Looking back, it was one of Greta's last significant memories with Kelly before she passed. She was grateful her dad had made them learn and that they'd done it together. *This is for you, Kell.*

With Tuck looking on, she proceeded to jack the car up, get the old tire off, and put the spare tire on in record time.

Tuck was mostly quiet while she worked, although he did offer her a sweatshirt from his backseat so she didn't have to kneel in the dirt. He earned some brownie points for that. She'd hate to ruin a perfectly good sun dress.

"All set." She stood and dusted her hands after lowering the car with the jack and fastening the lug nuts in a star-shaped pattern.

"Where did you...? How did you...? Thank you." Tuck dropped his chin, defeated. "I'm sorry. I'm not usually such a jerk."

"It's alright. Like I said, I was happy to help." Greta decided to press her advantage. She did save the man's behind, after all. "You moving out?" She gestured to the box in his backseat.

Tuck laughed, but there wasn't any humor in it. "I wish. I was fired. Can you believe that? Tossed out of a job and, as I'm driving away, I bust a tire. What's next?"

"They do say bad things come in threes." Greta offered him a wry smile. "I'm sorry about the job. I'm sure something else will present itself. You worked at B'Jeweled, didn't you?"

Tuck gazed at her, narrowing his eyes. "How'd you know that?"

"I stopped by earlier this week. I was looking for the owner. I saw you before Heath sent you to the back."

Tuck looked at her more closely, but he didn't seem to recognize her.

"It's alright. My face is pretty forgettable," Greta joked.

"It's not that." Tuck stared her down. "You had the book that belonged to Blythe, right?"

A flush of unease burned at the base of Greta's jaw. Something told her that the book was significant, and at the very least, she didn't want too many people to know about it.

"I *thought* it belonged to Blythe." She tried to emphasize the point. "But I never was able to track her down before..." Greta trailed off. "I'm sorry. Were you two close?"

"We were." Tuck swallowed. "She was like a big sister to me. She took me in and mentored me. I liked working for her. Heath, on the other hand..."

It was Tuck's turn to leave a thought unfinished.

"He's Blythe's husband? Was her husband, I should say," Greta amended. "Right? What's his deal? He stopped by my library today with a bunch of Blythe's research."

Tuck's sour expression returned. "He isn't a good dude. I probably sound like a disgruntled employee, which I guess I am, but if Blythe had believed what he was capable of, we might not be in this mess."

Greta had so many questions, but she asked the first one that came to mind. "You don't think he had a hand in her death, do you?"

The spouse or partner was always looked at closely when foul play was involved in a death. The thought made Greta shudder. To think that the person you're closest with is the most likely to off you is wrong on so many levels. She considered McHenry, and her chest warmed. She didn't have to worry about him. He was one of the good ones.

Tuck stuck his hands in his pockets. "I'm not trying to point fingers. But, like I said, Heath is not a good dude. He's involved in some shady business, and yeah, it might have come back to hurt Blythe. She was the head of the store, after all. The buck stopped with her, even if he was behind it all."

"What is he up to?" Greta couldn't mask her curiosity.

"Why do you care?" Tuck's voice held a bit of censure.

"He's been on my case to come in and buy from him. I'd like to know if I should avoid B'Jeweled." That was a half-truth, at least.

"I would avoid that place like the plague."

"Because...?" Greta prodded. "Heath offered me a great deal."

"I don't trust the jewelry he's selling."

"Why not?"

"I don't know. There's something off about it. He always works with this one, particular supplier. No one else. And I wasn't allowed to interact with the guy. I got my level one jeweler's certification and everything. It should have been part of my job. I mean, I talked to Blythe's other suppliers for her all the time—but Heath insisted on micro-managing. And I don't know. The quality of those pieces seemed second rate."

"Have you told the police this?"

Tuck scoffed. "I don't have any proof. Not anything solid, anyway."

"Still, they'd probably appreciate your perspective and your experience."

"They don't want to hear from me." Tuck didn't meet her eye.

She opened her mouth to tell him he should share what he knew—or at least what he thought—with law enforcement, but a truck rumbled past, heading toward Karrington.

Greta couldn't mistake the *I Brake for Bigfoot* bumper sticker. It was Rob Hawler.

Tuck growled. "What's he doing here?"

Chapter Ten

Greta swung her head to Tuck. "How do you know—"

"Gotta go. Thanks for your help with all this. Sorry to have unloaded on you." Tuck rushed around to the driver's side of his car. "You know what? I was probably reading into things with Heath. Forget about it." He waved over his shoulder, revved up his engine, pulled a U-turn, and headed back in the direction of Karrington, tailing Rob.

Greta was left on the side of the road in a cloud of dust.

Which, admittedly, sounded a lot like a lyric from a country music song, but wasn't nearly as glamorous.

She wrestled with the angel and devil on her shoulders. The angel looked a lot like McHenry and was patiently reminding her that following the two men would not end well. She'd already been told that one had a dangerous history. The other was a wildcard.

The devil on her opposite shoulder, which strangely resembled Chief Sorenson, was whispering a reminder that she was an official police liaison and consultant on the case. Shouldn't she do what she could to help gather evidence?

In the end, Greta's cooler head prevailed. That or maybe the image of McHenry as an angel did it for her. Either way, Greta pulled off the side of the road and headed toward Larkspur.

It was a quick drive, and when she pulled back into the sleepy downtown, it was only seven o'clock. Plenty of night ahead to work on the notations in Blythe's copy of *Pride and Prejudice*.

Greta had the photocopies stashed at the library, so she swung into the

70

desolate parking lot and went inside the municipal center. Josie had closed for the day an hour before, so Greta unlocked the door and headed for the office behind the circulation desk.

Tucking the pages safely in her tote, her eye caught on the box Heath had dropped off that morning. She made the split-second decision to take it home with her. She had a feeling the book and the contents of the box may be connected. If they weren't, she was still curious about what Blythe had been working on.

Greta hoisted the box up onto her hip, tucked her tote bag tightly against her side, and palmed her keys. She used her back to push open the exit and twirled around before the door could smash the box.

"Smooth move," a male voice said.

Greta jumped and looked up and into the smiling face of Nico Eddison and the scowling face of Cindi Fields.

She gripped the box a little tighter. She glanced from Cindi to Nico and back again. What were these two up to? "I didn't know anyone else was here."

"Nico needed a quiet work space. I told him he could use one of the library study rooms," Cindi said.

"We're closed for the day." Greta straightened.

"I know that." Cindi shrugged. "But we can make an exception for our author in residence." She beamed in Nico's direction. "Especially since he's hard at work on his next book."

"I don't think—"

"Nonsense, Greta. Move aside. Under our former library director, I used the facilities after hours all the time." Cindi brushed by her and grabbed the door, holding it open for Nico. She motioned Greta away. "I have my own key, so I'll lock up when he's done. Don't you worry."

Greta opened her mouth to argue. She didn't like the thought of leaving her library unsupervised. Then again, Cindi was there. The woman was basically staff. "I'll be at home. If you need me for anything, call."

"You're not that important, Greta." Cindi patted her on the shoulder.

Nico offered her an apologetic smile as he walked by her. "Need any help with your box?"

"No, no. I've got it." Greta turned to leave. She didn't want to answer any more questions about Blythe's possessions, and that was incentive enough to get out of there. Even if what she wanted to do was give Cindi a piece of her mind. Greta may not be important in Cindi's eyes, but the library was important, and she was looking out for its best interests. Why couldn't the library board president cut her some slack?

Greta deposited the box in her car, tucked her tote on the floor of the passenger seat, and made the quick drive down Larkspur Lane toward the lake. She circled around to her cabin.

Once inside, she bypassed the kitchen and plunked the box down on the corner cushion of her couch.

"Hey, buddy." Greta bent to scratch the dark markings between her cat's eyes while he meowed a greeting. He allowed her petting, but only for a second. Then he was off. He leapt up onto the couch and sniffed the box of Blythe's papers. Finding nothing of note, he abandoned that effort and pranced into the kitchen.

Greta followed him, stopping to fill his food and water bowls before palming her cell phone. Her home screen was lit up with notification badges.

She winced. It had been such a busy day; she'd failed to check any of her messages.

There were a couple from McHenry. An hour ago, he had messaged that he would have to stay the night in Chicago but he planned to head back to Larkspur late the following day. She responded and said she couldn't wait to see him. She asked if he had time to chat later that night, and then clicked over to her group text with Iris and Josie while she waited for a response from him.

Greta: Are either of you free? I've got a bit of a situation.

Greta set her phone on the counter and grabbed a glass container of leftover broccoli cheddar soup from the fridge. She deposited it into a pan and reheated it for a late dinner. Her neighbor, Richard, was trying his hand at bread making, and he had dropped off a loaf of sourdough late yesterday. Greta had slathered a slice with avocado and enjoyed it for breakfast, and now she couldn't wait for more.

Her phone vibrated with a new message, and Greta gave the soup a stir before checking it.

Josie: Ed and I are just sitting down to a late dinner at his cabin. What's up?

Iris: I'm around. What do you need?

Greta quickly detailed her plans to go through the book pages and the box. She ended her message by saying she'd take all the help she could get.

Because she had the very best of friends, she wasn't surprised by their responses.

Iris: Be over in fifteen minutes. I'll bring my Sherlock Holmes cap. <detective emoji> <magnifying glass emoji>

Josie: Can I bring Ed? We could be to your place in an hour or so.

Greta: Yes! Come whenever. See you soon!

Greta pocketed her phone, took the soup pan off the burner, and poured it into a bowl. She sliced a piece of bread from the loaf and buttered it before taking her dinner into the living room and setting it on the tray she kept on her coffee table. As she ate, Greta couldn't help but feel her heart squeeze as she thought of McHenry. She wished he was here. She wished she wasn't eating dinner alone. She'd never been a clingy partner, but something about seeing Nathan around town in the past two days was raising all sorts of insecurities in her. That, and she really liked spending time with McHenry. Dueling sensations of admiration for him and unease surrounding the circumstances in Chicago rose up in her chest, but she swallowed them down with a giant bite of bread. She trusted McHenry.

Greta ate a final spoonful of soup and brought her dishes to the sink before returning to the living room. It was her favorite spot in the whole cabin. Wide glass sliding doors took up the entire wall on the backside, giving her a perfect view of the navy-blue lake waters below her deck. Greta opened the slider, letting the cool springtime breeze in through the screen. She looked out over the lake and took a deep breath. Spring smelled differently in Larkspur. Whereas fall was tinged with the scent of crunchy tree leaves and summer always held the lingering scent of campfire smoke, this time of year had a freshness about it—a smidge of floral and a splash of rain made for an exhilarating aroma that reminded Greta of new beginnings and hope.

With hope on her mind, Greta retrieved the pages from her bag and started at the beginning. She pulled up her phone where she'd already made a note of what letters were circled in the early pages. She did a quick search on her laptop for any type of coding as it related to, first, *Pride and Prejudice*, and second, books in general.

She was reading through an article on book ciphers when a light knock sounded on her front door.

"It's open," Greta called.

A moment later Iris walked into the living room, trailed closely by Biff.

"Alright, tell me where you're at with everything. Any book breakthroughs?" Iris asked after seating herself opposite of Greta.

Greta stretched her arms over her head. "Actually, yeah. I think so. Check this out."

She handed over the laptop and waited quietly while Iris skimmed the article she was reading.

"An Ottendorf Cipher? Like in *National Treasure?*"

Greta agreed. "It's the easiest answer to the question of the marked-up copy of *Pride and Prejudice*. Sometimes, the most straightforward solution is the correct one. We have the book, which is basically the key to the code. But we don't have the ciphertext, or the message that we're trying to decode."

"You think Blythe was leaving coded messages within these pages to share some type of details about buried treasure?"

"Either Blythe was leaving messages, or someone was leaving messages for her. Or maybe she was using this book to generate the number sequence for her ciphertext that she'd then give to someone else so they could decode it into plaintext."

"My head hurts already," Iris grumbled.

Greta chuckled. "In either case, we're missing a key element of the equation—the sequence of numbers that'll tell us the order we need to put these markings in to make them make sense."

"Maybe it's here." Iris scooched forward in her chair and tipped the box of

Blythe's papers toward her. "Have you gone through any of this?"

"Not yet." Greta scooped out half the stack of papers and handed it to Iris. She took the rest. "Let's look for any sort of sequence of numbers first. We need to find that in order to decipher what secret message someone was sharing through this book."

The two worked in silence for the next twenty minutes.

When Iris gasped, Greta looked up from what she was reading. "What? What is it?"

Iris held up a pile of old letters. "Love letters to JuJu Vance from a woman by the name of Viola Douglass." Iris held one out and Greta took it, scanning the contents.

"Wow. The woman sounds smitten."

"The woman is definitely smitten," a third voice echoed.

Greta jumped, and Iris yelped, even though the familiar voice was Josie's. She walked into the living room, smirking, followed by a red-cheeked Ed. "Honestly, Jos." He shot Greta an apologetic glance. "Sorry for barging in."

"Nonsense." Greta waved him off. "Come on. Look at this."

Josie and Ed circled the couch and sat down. They all took turns reading the letters.

> JuJu,
>
> I'm scared. I want you here, and I'm afraid you're risking everything getting messed up with those awful men. That's not like you. Come home. Marry me. We can make a life together here. I don't care about money. I don't care what Mother and Father think of you. All I care about is you and this child of ours. I don't know how much longer I can keep the baby a secret, and I'm worried what my family will do when they find out. I need you. Please tell me you'll come back to me. I feel like I'll die if you're not holding me in your arms soon. Write me as soon as you can, my love.
>
> Viola

Ed was the last to read the final letter. "So, Viola was in love with JuJu and having his baby. Did he return the sentiments?"

"I think so. Check this out." Greta held up a jeweler's receipt. "He spent a pretty penny on a three-carat engagement ring. It looks like it was purchased in the Minneapolis area in early 1934."

"That would have been before the Little Bohemia Raid," Josie said, taking up the story. "By the way, I talked to Jake, and he's going to do some digging on JuJu for me. He wasn't familiar with the name, but he has access to a lot of resources. I'm waiting to hear back from him."

"Thanks for doing that." Greta leaned forward on the couch and pointed into the box. "Based on what I've read, Blythe seemed to be under the impression that JuJu Vance was still in possession of the diamond ring during and immediately following the Little Bo Raid. He got separated from Dillinger and fled south, hiding out somewhere here in Larkspur, and—"

Biff chose that moment to catapult himself into the center of the living room, knocking the empty box from the coffee table.

"Biff! Careful." Greta grabbed the box and turned it upright. "Wait, what's this?" A paper was wedged between the panels on the side of the box. She'd missed it until now.

She unfolded the paper and found a crude drawing of a map. Greta squinted at it. "Is this what I think it is?"

She held it out, and Iris took it from her, studying the sketch. "It's a map. If I'm not mistaken, the X is right over—"

Ed let out a low whistle. "The place where Blythe was killed."

Josie frowned. "So, Blythe foretold her own place of death? That doesn't make any sense."

"I'm wondering if it's a coincidence and that X is actually the location of some buried treasure." Greta waved the receipt in the air. "Namely, a diamond ring."

The four took a collective breath.

Biff hopped up onto the coffee table. Greta grabbed him and nuzzled his fur. "Good work, buddy!"

"Add him to our detective team," Iris said. "Do you think Blythe was hunting for the ring when she was killed?"

"Or was she killed because someone else wanted to get to it first?" Ed proposed.

"But who? Who would kill over something like this?" Josie asked.

"I have an idea." Greta stood from the couch, setting Biff on the ground. He let out a proud *meow* and scampered out of the room and toward the kitchen. Greta followed him as far as the hall closet. She dug behind her winter coat and snow pants, which she had only recently stowed away until next season, and retrieved a medium-sized whiteboard.

"What's that?" Iris asked when she returned to the living room.

"I used it to study in college, but for now, it's going to serve as our crime board."

Ed shifted his gaze from Josie to Iris and finally to Greta. "Have you ever made a crime board before?"

"This'll be a first. But I've never been an official police consultant, so I'd say it's merited. Besides, it'll be a good way to list out and organize our thoughts." Greta grabbed a marker from the junk drawer in her kitchen and wrote *Suspects* in the top left corner of the board. On the opposite side, she wrote *Motive? Means? Opportunity?*

"Alright. Who do you got?" Josie sat forward, rubbing her hands together.

Greta wrote Heath's name first. "A logical starting point is Blythe's husband."

"The spouse is always a suspect," Iris agreed.

"Right. And in this case, there's something shady going on at B'Jeweled, according to Tuck, a former employee, and I think it all stems from Heath. Maybe Blythe found out and was going to turn him in, and he killed her to keep a lid on it?" Greta jotted down all these ideas on the board.

"Did anyone see him at or around Bobber's Bar on Monday?" Iris asked.

"I didn't, but that doesn't mean anything," Greta mused. "He may have been trying to keep a low profile. He was pretty crass when he dropped off this box. Didn't seem heartbroken at his loss at all."

"Maybe he doesn't consider it a loss," Josie speculated.

Greta nodded sadly. "Which brings us to another suspect. Someone Heath was quick to throw shade at. Tuck White. Former B'Jeweled employee. Jake and I saw him talking with Blythe the night of your engagement. She mentioned Dillinger to him, so perhaps he knew about her treasure findings and the two had a falling out and he killed her to keep the findings for himself."

Iris hummed. "Tuck knew his way around Larkspur, if he was at Mugs & Hugs. He could have slipped in and out of the Bobber's Bar area undetected."

"He and a lot of other people," Ed argued.

"Including the owners of the establishment." Greta winced as she said it, writing Ace Hawler, Suz Hawler, and Rob Hawler's names on the board.

"You think they could have had something to do with Blythe's death?" Iris asked on a gasp.

"You missed lunch today," Josie told her. "But there was some obvious tension when Nico and Nathan questioned Ace about the bar's association with JuJu Vance."

"Right." Greta nodded. "It's too much of a coincidence to ignore. I also overheard him and Blythe fighting behind the bar the weekend before she was killed. People are allowed to argue, but..." she trailed off, knowing her friends would follow her train of thought.

"I'll give you that," Ed said after a beat. "But what does Rob have to do with anything?"

"I'm not sure. But I've seen him in Karrington near B'Jeweled a couple times now. Once, when his mother insisted that he wasn't there. It was obvious today that Tuck wanted to follow Rob. For what, I don't know." Greta paused. "Also, he was on the phone with someone, asking that person to cover for him right after the murder. Who knows what that was about, but I'm curious."

"I'll tell you what I'm curious about." Iris crossed her legs underneath her. "Our author in residence."

Greta scribbled *Nico Eddison* up on the now cramped whiteboard. "Do tell."

"First of all, the guy shows up unannounced. Early. So, he's here before the murder happens. His house"—Iris paused—"my *parents'* rental," she added, "literally butts up against the crime scene. He could have used that to his advantage. Cleaned up, cooled off, slipped out from scrutiny after, well, you know."

Greta nibbled her lip. "Nathan said that Nico told him that Blythe contacted him personally, outside the scope of planning the Little Bo Anniversary event. Maybe she wanted his opinion about what she'd discovered about JuJu Vance and Viola Douglass?"

"Maybe she told him what she'd found, and he wanted to keep it for himself, so he killed her and was planning to take credit for the findings. Write a whole book about it." Josie's voice rose with excitement. "I could see that."

"He's a question mark," Greta agreed. She stood back and studied the board. It was so full now that her writing had grown cramped. "There's one more name that we might want to consider. Cindi Fields."

"You've been waiting for this day, haven't you?" Josie said with a wry grin. "Pinning a murder on your work nemesis would be sweet revenge."

Greta chuckled. "I don't think Cindi had anything to do with it. But the three of us had a front-row seat to the argument she and Blythe had on Saturday morning."

"Cindi did use the exact words, 'I could murder her,' in reference to Blythe," Iris put in.

"And she was around the bar at the time of Blythe's death," Josie finished.

Greta nodded. "I don't think she would go so far as to kill Blythe, if for no other reason than it throws a snag in the program she's been planning for the Little Bo Anniversary. But let's leave her on the board, so our bases are covered. She's at the library with Nico right now."

"What?" Josie exclaimed at the same time Iris said, "Why?"

Greta explained the situation. Her friends didn't look happy about it.

"I should have stood up to her more firmly. Put my foot down," Greta sighed. "She makes me feel so small."

As if sensing her guilt, Iris held up a hand. "Not your fault."

"We'll keep an eye on her—and take a good look around the library tomorrow, too, to make sure nothing's up with Nico or Cindi."

Greta was grateful for her friends' support.

"What do we do now?" Iris asked. "I have access to Nico Eddison because of my parents' rental. I could drop in on him and try to scrounge up some more information."

"What would your excuse be, though?" Josie countered. "You shouldn't go sniffing around suspects all willy-nilly. We've learned that in the past."

Greta recalled one particularly harrowing visit she and Josie made to a man who turned out to be innocent, but things could have gone sideways really quickly.

"Josie's right. And you shouldn't do anything alone. If you want to talk to Nico, I'll come with you. We can even loop Cindi in. Maybe frame it as a conversation about how the event will look going forward. Would it work to set something up for tomorrow?"

"I'll coordinate it." Iris agreed.

"I have a thought." Ed raised his hand. "We happen to be in the market for a particular kind of jewelry at the moment." He pointed to Josie's engagement ring and his bare ring finger. "We need wedding bands. We could shop at B'Jeweled."

Greta sucked in a breath. "I don't think you want to buy anything from there, not based on what Tuck said and what I overheard from an angry customer."

"'Course not," Ed said easily. "But we can act like we're going to shop. Ask some questions. I could even bring along my friend. He's the jeweler I bought Josie's diamond from. He could help us figure out if there's something shady happening at B'Jeweled."

"I like it." Josie rubbed her hands together again. "I'm all about the covert ops."

"I won't stop you." Greta grinned before turning serious. "I'm planning to talk to Chief Sorenson tomorrow morning about my hunch that this book is the key for a book cipher. Hopefully he and the team can be on the lookout for the missing note, and if they recover it, they could figure out what message this key cracks."

If such a message existed.

Greta dismissed the thought as quickly as it came. She was a positive person by nature. And they had a plan. There was nothing she liked more.

Chapter Eleven

Greta was working in the office early the following morning, catching up on email and her duties as library director before she was on tap to attend the library conference programming. She stepped outside the cramped space and behind the circulation desk to stretch her legs and touch base with Josie and Iris. A group of visiting librarians was touring the library, and Greta joined them.

"Is your children's area always so busy?" one asked her.

"Usually, yes," Greta said with a smile. While they didn't have a designated children's librarian like the larger branches, she, Iris, and Josie worked diligently to put together programming and interactive activities to keep kids—and their parents—engaged and returning.

"Incredible," the visiting librarian breathed. "I love how alive your space is."

"Speaking of being alive." A snooty-looking librarian piped up from the back of the group. "Any word on the woman in town who is very much unalive?"

Greta winced. Was it too much to hope that her colleagues had forgotten about that? If Fitz was here, Greta would tell him that she'd like to *shush* this *shush* of librarians, at least when they started asking about the murder investigation.

She took a deep breath. "Well, actually—"

"I have a working theory."

Greta turned to find Nathan slithering over. Why was he everywhere?

"Do tell."

"I want to hear it."

"Are you investigating?"

The chorus of curious librarians all spoke at once.

Nathan held up his hands, grinning. "Sure am. Though I'm not the only one. I saw Greta go into the police department earlier this morning."

Greta arched an eyebrow. Was he following her?

"I was meeting Nico for coffee at Mugs & Hugs," Nathan explained after taking in her questioning glare. "Anyway, I want to hear what she knows, too."

"I told you I'm staying out of it." Greta crossed her arms and her fingers.

Even though she didn't want Nathan to know her role in the investigation, she still hated lying on principle. She cast a quick glance to the shelf underneath the circulation desk where she'd stashed the box of Blythe's papers and the copies of the *Pride and Prejudice* pages. Chief Sorenson had appeared more swamped than usual this morning, trying to coordinate the efforts of the state CSI team that had descended on town to help fill in the gaps of the Larkspur police force's investigation, but he listened to her hypothesis about the book cipher. She planned to go through the box of Blythe's belongings again to see if they somehow missed the ciphertext.

"And I told you I didn't believe you. So, we're at an impasse." Nathan winked at her, and Greta's stomach twisted. He turned to the other librarians. "My theory, which is being backed up by a researcher slash author slash scholar," he added with emphasis, "is that Blythe Prescott, the deceased, uncovered clues that led her to believe that a cache of money was hidden by Dillinger and his gang on the property of Bobber's Bar. We have reason to suspect she approached the owner of the bar about her discovery."

"Ohh," one of the librarians cooed. "Did he kill her so he could try to find the hidden treasure himself?"

Nathan shrugged easily. "That's a definite possibility if you ask me."

The librarians murmured among themselves. Greta wanted to scream that no one had asked him when over Nathan's shoulder, movement caught her eye. Rob Hawler had entered the library and was standing nearby. His cheeks were flushed and his eyes were narrowed as he stared daggers into

Nathan's back.

"Let the police do their jobs and stay out of it, Nathan. It's not fair to jump to conclusions without evidence."

A bead of sweat dripped down Greta's spine as her mind flashed to the whiteboard she'd stuck in her coat closet last night after her friends had left her cabin. She needed to take her own advice.

Greta clapped her hands. "We should probably get going, though, right? Today's sessions are in Karrington. Does anyone need anything before they leave?"

The librarians said they were all set, and the group dispersed. Thankfully, Nathan didn't linger.

Greta exhaled and pivoted to the desk to gather her things for the day.

Rob caught her eye. He'd seated himself at a nearby table and was joined by a woman around his age. She had black silky hair, cut to shoulder length and pinned back with a simple clip. She wore tattered jeans and a plain white t-shirt and looked effortlessly chic. She covered Rob's clenched fist with her hand in a sort of caress. This must be Rob's girlfriend.

Greta glanced at her watch. She had a couple minutes before she needed to leave. She detoured to their table. "Hey, there. Anything I can help you with?"

Rob looked pensive, but he offered her a strained smile. "I think we're good. Thanks, though."

"No problem." Greta smiled in return. "I don't believe we've met, but I've seen you around. Rob Hawler, right? I'm Greta Plank, the library director here."

Rob shook her hand. "Nice to meet you. This is my girlfriend, Sadie Janowick."

Greta cocked her head to the side. "Any relation to Celeste Janowick?"

Sadie nodded. "She's my aunt."

"I adore her." Greta beamed. "It's a pleasure to meet you both." She turned serious. "How's your mom doing, Rob?"

Rob shifted in his seat. "She's alright. Still shaken over everything for sure."

"That's understandable." Greta paused. "I was talking to her right before she discovered Blythe. It was so nice of your parents to open up the bar for the librarians."

Rob sniffed. "I'm sure they're regretting it now."

Sadie shot him an uneasy glance, and he seemed to remember who he was talking to. "No offense," he added quickly. "I only mean that that librarian who was in here, what's his name?"

"Nathan," Greta supplied, hiding a grimace.

"Yeah. Him. He's causing all sorts of trouble. Pointing the finger at my parents. They didn't have anything to do with it!"

"Nathan has no authority." Greta tried to sound reassuring. "I wouldn't worry about him."

"He needs to mind his own business, or he's going to be sorry," Rob seethed.

"I'll try to talk to him again," Greta offered. Not that she had any sway where Nathan was concerned, but Rob was visibly upset. "I saw him talking to your dad at the bar yesterday at lunch. Has he bothered him since?"

"Not that I know of, but I'm sure it's only a matter of time."

"What does he want from your family?" Greta had heard Nathan's theory, but she wanted to know what Rob had to say.

"He's obsessed with the gangster trail. Him and that author. They think that's what Blythe was tied up with, too. But my family has nothing to do with any of that. That's what my dad told him. But he won't take his word for it."

"Sounds like Nathan." Greta offered Rob an understanding wince. "It's weird because your parents didn't know Blythe at all, right?"

"Right." Rob's response was hurried. "They'd seen her around but never talked to her much beyond a hello."

Except for the fight your dad had with her behind the bar.

"Well, I'm sorry about the mess with the librarians and for bringing them to your front door. Literally. I feel bad. Your mom said you've been such a rock for her. Said she'd have fallen apart without you and your dad."

"We're taking care of her, yeah."

"I'm glad you didn't have to be the one to stumble upon the body. Your mom said you two were together that day?"

It was a total leading question, and all Greta could do was pray Rob and Sadie didn't see through her. She put on her best innocent library face—basically, she made herself look like an open book. People found her approachable that way.

"Yep." Rob flipped his hand and linked his fingers with Sadie's. "We always hang out on Mondays, right, Sad?"

"Right." Sadie only met Greta's eye for a fraction of a second before she glanced down at her laptop.

Not wanting to push her luck, Greta excused herself. She glanced at the couple when she made it behind the circulation desk. They had their heads together and were whispering back and forth.

Greta held in a sigh. They were kids. She hoped they weren't doing anything to jeopardize their futures.

Chapter Twelve

When Greta got out of the afternoon session about how libraries can serve the underprivileged members of their communities, she had a message from Iris in their group text chain.

Iris: Touched base with Nico. He said he'd be glad to meet up tonight, so I called Cindi. Can you get here by 5:30?

Greta looked at her watch. The session had ended at four, so she had plenty of time to drive from Karrington to Larkspur.

Greta: Leaving here shortly!

Josie: Keep me posted. I'm scheduled to attend the evening programming in Larkspur. Maybe see you guys after.

Josie: Also, G, check your email. Forwarded you what Jake sent me about JuJu.

Greta: Thank you!!! See you soon, Iris.

She clicked out of the group text and over to her chain with McHenry. A new message was waiting for her, and her heart warmed.

McHenry: All done. Leaving Chicago in the next half hour. Can't wait to see you.

Greta: Ditto. Drive safely! XOXO

Greta pocketed her phone with a smile and went in search of Fitz. He was behind the reference desk, but he walked her back into his office and offered her a seat. They debriefed on the conference, and when the business items were out of the way, he asked, "Is Nathan giving you any more issues? I've been trying to figure out a way to tell him to leave without actually telling him to leave."

Greta chuckled. "No, he's fine. He hasn't bothered me personally, but he's giving the Hawler family a run for their money." She filled in Fitz on her conversation with Rob.

He hissed. "I don't like that he comes into our towns and acts like he owns them."

"You and me both," Greta sighed.

"You'll keep me posted if I can help with him or anything, right?"

"Not a lot to do. The conference is running itself," she said with a shrug.

Fitz doffed a pretend cap. "Thanks to our expert planning."

"Hear, hear. Now, you can be my reference when Cindi tries to get me fired."

Fitz laughed, but almost immediately sobered. "Wait. You don't think *she* could have been behind Blythe's death, do you? She did have that outburst."

"I thought of that, but no. I can't see it."

"Well, you know her better than I do," Fitz said. "Hopefully, we all get some answers soon."

"Amen." Greta stood. "I've got to run. I'm meeting with her and Nico to discuss the Little Bo Anniversary event."

"Good luck. I'm actually looking forward to coming. I might learn something that can impress my cohort or my professors."

"Your charm and good looks will be more than enough." Greta waved over her shoulder, smiling at Fitz's big, booming laugh.

She made the drive to Larkspur with plenty of time to spare.

"How do you want to play this?" Iris asked her as they walked into Mugs & Hugs to grab a coffee pick-me-up ahead of their meeting. Caffeine always helped Greta handle Cindi.

"Let's see what they say, what they both offer up, and then go from there."

As far as plans went, it wasn't much, but Greta was looking forward to some face time with Nico. She couldn't get a read on the guy. The fact that he was always with Nathan wasn't helping matters.

"Hey, ladies," Allison greeted them from behind the register. "What'll you have today?"

Greta placed her order for an iced hazelnut latte, and Iris asked for a honey-lavender cold brew.

"Coming right up."

They paid Allison and moved down the counter to wait on their drinks. Greta's gaze landed on the table she'd seen Blythe and Tuck seated on the night of Josie's engagement.

"Hey, Allison," she called. When Allison looked up, Greta gave her a description of Tuck. "You haven't seen him around lately, have you?"

Allison glanced toward the ceiling, culling her memory. "Not that I can recall, but I can keep an eye out now that I know you're looking for him. What's his deal?"

Greta shrugged. "I don't know, but he's connected to Blythe."

"You can count on me." Allison held out two to-go cups. "Here you go."

Greta and Iris took their drinks and walked outside into the late-day sunshine. A breeze kicked up, and there was a chill in the spring air. Greta was grateful she'd opted for navy blue pants today. "Oh! I almost forgot about Josie's email." She juggled her coffee and retrieved her cell phone, navigating to her email account. She clicked on the forwarded message. She held out her phone so Iris could read over Jake's email, too.

Hey Jos,

Your question about JuJu Vance is an interesting one. He's one of the lesser-known members of Dillinger's gang. In fact, all the research points to him being a late addition. There is some speculation about his loyalty, which could be why he was separated from the group when they fled Little Bohemia in 1934.

From what I've been able to determine, he was a loner, with no family. He was originally from the Midwest, which is likely how he fell in with the Dillinger crowd. But there is surprisingly little documented about the man. In cases such as these, the most likely way of learning more is to determine family history and lineage and determine if there has been any information passed down within the family that hasn't been shared with either historians or the general public. Sorry I'm not more assistance. I'm attaching the sources I found in case it's helpful to you.

Let me know what comes of this. I'm super intrigued.
  Talk soon,
  J

Greta finished reading and clicked over to the attachments. There was a marriage certificate for a Julian Vance and a Deborah McNamara.

"Not Viola Douglass. Interesting." Greta zoomed in on the signatures.

"So was the receipt we found in Blythe's box for a ring for Deborah or Viola?" Iris wondered out loud.

"I don't know. But that could be the difference between whether there's treasure buried in the backyard of Bobber's Bar or not."

"Speaking of Bobber's Bar's backyard, what do you say we meet Nico at the rental house and walk together with him back to the library?" Iris asked. "It might be the only time we get with him out from under the watchful eye of Cindi."

"Good thinking."

They changed courses and angled over to Bobber's Bar. They walked through the side yard, keeping a solemn silence as they bypassed the crime scene. Blythe's body had obviously been removed, but remnants of the tragedy remained. There was still yellow crime scene tape dangling from the trees it had been attached to, and a few orange cones were tipped on end and had been left behind.

Iris took a sip of her cold brew and knocked on the door. She waited a beat and then knocked again, calling out, "Nico? It's Iris, from the library."

"Did he say he'd be at home when you talked to him earlier?"

"He didn't mention any other plans." Iris frowned and knocked again.

"Maybe we missed him." Greta stepped to the side of the porch and peered through the front window. There was no drapery or blinds blocking her view, but inside was dark.

"What do you say we take a quick look around?" Iris held up her key ring.

Greta flinched in surprise. "You want to go inside?"

"Why not?" Iris was already putting a key in the deadbolt lock. "I'm basically like housekeeping at a hotel. Besides, it's my parents' place. If anyone asks, I'll say they needed me to find something. I made an adequate effort to reach the tenant first, so…" The lock unlatched and Iris turned the knob, shoving the door open. "After you."

"Who are you, and what have you done with my rule-following, unassuming friend?" Greta said on an exhale as she entered the desolate house first.

Iris stepped in behind her, shutting the door with a muted *snick*. "Same old me. But I feel like I need to take matters into my own hands from time to time. What a perfect opportunity."

Greta turned and looked back at her friend. Iris gave her a nonchalant shrug, but Greta had to wonder how she was handling Josie's engagement when, less than a year ago, her own happily ever after blew up in her face.

Iris would be the first to say it was for the best, but Greta knew from her experience with Nathan that even when things worked out for the best, it didn't necessarily take the sting away from being duped.

Greta let her eyes adjust to the dim light of the building's interior. A look around revealed Nico was a messy tenant. There were papers strewn all over the coffee table and three half-empty mugs lined up along the edge. She walked over to the table. "Since we're seizing the day, let's look for anything about JuJu Vance."

The two of them glanced over the papers.

"These are definitely notes about his work." Iris read bullet points from a loose-leaf sheet. "Dillinger and the FBI. From BOI to FBI: The origins of the Federal Bureau of Investigation. Gangster's Paradise: Was the federal spending worth it?"

"Those are book proposals. Look." Greta pointed at the bottom corner of one of the more formal-looking typed sheets. "There's the name and address of his literary agent."

"Kerry Jefferson of The Steele Group," Iris read. "Nico must be getting ready to shop around a new book."

With everything that had happened, Greta had completely forgotten to look into Nico's publishing history. He said he needed redemption, but why?

Greta nudged some papers aside with her elbow to reveal a spiral-bound notebook. Written at the top was *B.P.'s Idea?? Does it have legs?* Beneath the heading was another notation, this one in a different colored ink, as if Nico had added to the page at a different time. It was a nine-digit number, underlined four times. Greta slipped her cell phone out of her purse and snapped a photo of it.

"What do you think that means?" Iris looked over her shoulder.

"Not sure. I'll google it later. Maybe it's a phone number." Greta moved from the living room into the small kitchen. A pile of dishes was in the sink. A laptop was set up on the kitchen table. Greta circled to get a better look, but the screen was black. Her knee bumped the leg of the table, nudging the computer out of sleep mode.

"Shoot," she said at the same time as Iris wiggled her eyebrows and said, "Nice." She looked closer. "Oh, but is it password protected? Darn."

Before Greta could respond, a push notification popped up on his screen from his email account."

Greta peered closer. The message was sent from Nathan with the subject line **Blythe's email???** Only the first line of the email text was shown in the notification, and all Greta could read before it disappeared was *Forward me what she sent you, and I'll look into it some more with my resources. This could be...*

Greta groaned when the notification dissolved.

"We know Nico and Blythe were communicating before he arrived," Iris noted.

"Right. Something she sent him must've been significant enough for him to want to tap into Nathan's library resources. But what?" Greta stared at the password-protected screen, as if she could will it to spit an answer back at her. When nothing else appeared after a minute, the screen went back to black. Greta sighed.

"Anything else we should look for while we're here?" Iris poked around the kitchen. "I'm going to have to tell my parents to hire professional cleaners when he's done with this place," she added with a hint of disgust.

"We've overstayed our welcome. Cindi will be waiting for us. Let's get out of—"

CHAPTER TWELVE

The sound of a key being inserted into the front door lock had Greta slamming her mouth shut.

Chapter Thirteen

Iris turned wide eyes on Greta. "What do we do?"

"Hide," Greta whispered. She looked around the cramped kitchen for anywhere she could go and be out of sight.

The creak of the front door reached her ear and Iris grabbed her wrist, hauling her toward a door in the far corner of the kitchen. She tugged it open and pulled Greta behind her. The two of them balanced precariously on the top steps of the basement staircase.

Greta clutched Iris's upper arms to keep her balance, but she didn't dare say a word. It was dark in the stairwell, and Greta's other senses roared to life. The damp smell of basement air reached her, and she twitched her nose. She stilled at the sound of scuffling feet on the other side of the basement door. Greta held her breath as the footsteps stopped, and the scrape of a chair against the floor told her Nico was sitting down at the table. Had he forgotten about their meeting? Greta squinted at her wristwatch. They were dangerously close to standing Cindi up, and she dreaded the woman's wrath.

Nico started muttering under his breath. "This guy. Nosy busy body."

Greta and Iris exchanged a look, and even in the semi-darkness of the staircase, Greta could make out Iris's raised brow. "Nathan?" she mouthed.

Greta nodded. Was Nico having second thoughts about joining forces with the librarian? It wouldn't surprise her.

A moment later, Greta heard the tell-tale snap of a laptop being shut. The chair legs skated across the floor again, and footsteps receded. When the front door opened and closed, Greta let out her first breath in what felt like an hour.

"That was close." Iris cracked the door open.

Greta blinked against the light of the kitchen. "We should hurry, or we'll be late."

"Let's go out the back door." Iris pointed across the room to the cabin's other exit point.

Greta nodded, but her eye caught on another closed door to the left of the basement. There were a few streaks of dirt on the floor in front of it. "What's in there?"

"It's a tiny broom closet. I thought about wedging us in there, but I figured you'd prefer to be in a closet with McHenry. So, I picked the stairs." Iris wagged her brows.

"Very funny." Greta stuck out her tongue.

Iris laughed. "Come on."

They snuck outside and paused in the backyard, making sure that Nico didn't spot them before hustling back to the sidewalk.

"Remind me of this the next time I decide to take life by the horns." Iris's face was flushed. "I'm much more of a predictable beach read girl than I am an action and adventure novel girl."

"Don't sell yourself short. The character growth displayed in beach reads is top shelf. I'm glad we snooped. If for no other reason than to have found out that maybe there's trouble in paradise between Nico and Nathan."

"Yeah, but we don't know how much of Blythe's research she shared with Nico and how much he, in turn, shared with Nathan."

"True. He'd probably be glad to get his hands on the box Heath dropped off for us." Greta figured the contents of the box would fill in the blanks for the author, but she didn't know if that was necessarily a good thing.

They quickened their pace and got to the library only a couple minutes later. Librarians flitted about, heading to their final break-out sessions of the evening. Greta waved to Fitz and Josie, who ducked into one of the small meeting rooms.

Nico was studying some of the magazines they had on display in front of the floor-to-ceiling windows that lined the interior wall of the library. Greta and Iris walked over to him.

"Nico, long time no see," Greta said breezily.

Next to her, Iris snorted, but covered it with a cough. Cindi joined them and shot Iris a scowl. The four of them took seats at one of the workstation tables in the center of the library.

"Thanks for agreeing to a quick meeting," Greta said.

"We wanted to make sure you had everything ready to go for this weekend's programming." Iris tucked a strand of her hair behind her ears. "We're happy to help with any last-minute needs."

Cindi sniffed. "We've had to pivot since Blythe's passing. Such a shame." They sat in weighty silence for a beat before Cindi continued. "Her funeral will be Friday. Many of The Seekers are planning to attend to pay our respects, but it won't interfere with our program planned for Saturday."

"That's very nice of you," Greta offered.

"Did you ever figure out what Blythe was planning to present this weekend?" Iris asked, her face the picture of innocence.

Cindi frowned. "I don't know how we'll ever know now. That is, if there was something to her whole charade."

Nico cleared his throat. "She reached out to me about it earlier this month." Cindi sputtered. "She did?"

Greta scooched to the edge of her seat, waiting to see what else Nico would reveal.

"She didn't tell me much. But she believed she found evidence of hidden treasure buried in Larkspur and associated with the Little Bohemia Raid and the subsequent fleeing of Dillinger's gang."

Cindi sat back and crossed her arms. "What kind of treasure?"

Nico shrugged, averting his gaze. "I'm not exactly sure. I'm looking into it, but truthfully, it's like you said, Cindi. I'm pretty sure it was nothing. I doubt Blythe was actually onto anything worthwhile."

Cindi issued a self-satisfied snort. "Figures."

Iris drew her into conversation about the RSVPs that had come in for the event, but Greta hardly listened. Her mind was on Nico and Blythe.

Did Nico really believe that Blythe's discovery about Julian Vance was insignificant? It was difficult for Greta to tell. Did he come to town early to try to determine if what Blythe found had any merit? And if so, was it a coincidence that his primary source ended up dead?

Or was he the cause?

"It's a bit of a letdown, actually," Cindi was saying. "All these people coming out. I admit, even I was looking forward to hearing what Blythe had cooked up, as crackpot as it may have been. If the woman was one thing, it was entertaining."

"I'll still plan to give my presentation as we discussed," Nico assured her. "It'll focus on the history of the gangster hideouts in Northern Wisconsin and Minnesota. Not sure if I'm what you call entertaining, but I do carry a bit of author cred."

He gave a self-deprecating chuckle, and Cindi, seeming to remember herself, smoothed out her features.

"Right. Yes. That will be perfect. I'll give a brief spiel on the True Treasure Seekers Club and what we do. Then I'll introduce you." Cindi pulled out her phone and scanned the screen. "I've got to run. Are we done here?"

"Yes, ma'am." Greta fought the urge to salute.

"Good. I'll be in early tomorrow for the genealogy club's meeting. Make sure the desk and tables get wiped down in the meantime, Greta. This place is a disgrace. The dust bunnies are multiplying." Cindi rose and stalked off.

"Bunnies have a way of doing that," Greta grumbled to herself.

"Looks good in here to me," Nico said when Cindi was out of earshot.

Greta gave him a grateful smile.

Iris shifted the conversation. "How's your time in Larkspur been so far, Nico? Anything we can get for you? I hope the cabin has been okay."

"Everything's been perfect." Nico grimaced. "Aside from the murder."

"Blythe really didn't share anything with you about what she was working on?" Greta ventured. Maybe Nico would be more willing to show his hand now that Cindi was gone.

"Sadly, no." Nico glanced down, rubbing at an ink stain on the table.

"I overheard you at Bobber's Bar asking the owner about a man named JuJu Vance. Who's he?" Greta pressed.

Nico kept his focus on the table, and several seconds passed before he responded. "Turns out that lead was a dead end. I thought he might have been a significant player in the gangster era, but I was wrong."

"Oh." Greta wasn't sure she believed him. "That's too bad."

"Yeah." Nico pushed his chair out. "I should head back to my cabin. Thanks again for the hospitality."

Iris bobbed her head. The two librarians waited for him to leave before collecting their things.

"I wasn't the only one to notice how shifty he was being, was I?" Iris asked.

"Definitely not."

They walked to the library exit. Josie was on tap to lock up for the night after the librarians concluded their session.

"I can't figure out what's going on with him, but I feel like we're only getting the partial story where he's concerned." Greta pulled out her phone and ran a quick search for Nico Eddison. Most of the news articles that populated were from a couple years back, heralding Nico as an authority on twentieth century American history, with a focus on the Midwest. Further down the search page, Greta spotted an article about his most recent release. "Look at this." She held out her phone for Iris. "He self-published a book last year, and it got ripped to shreds for being a sham."

"Yikes." Iris read over her shoulder. "Looks like he took it out of circulation. He must've been trying to bury the error."

"That's why he feels like he needs to redeem himself." Greta pushed open the exterior door to the municipal complex, and a grin twitched at her lips.

McHenry was leaning up against her car, his strong figure cast in shadows of the April sunset.

"Well, well, well. Look who it is." Iris gave Greta a side hug. "Enjoy your night together. I'll see you in the morning. Later, McHenry!" She offered him a finger wave and cut over to where her car was parked.

McHenry smiled as Greta approached. "Hey, you."

Greta curled herself into his chest, inhaling deeply. "Welcome home."

"Glad to be back." McHenry pressed a kiss to her forehead.

"Are you exhausted?" Greta leaned out of his embrace. "Want to grab a drink?"

"I'd love that."

"Bobber's?" she asked.

McHenry studied her. "Are you trying to get me back to the scene of the crime?"

"Maybe."

He chuckled. "Let's go."

He looped his fingers with hers and turned them toward the bar. The night was quiet. It was only Wednesday, so the weekend crowd hadn't come out yet, and locals were in the throes of spring sports season at the high school on the outskirts of town.

"How'd everything go for you?" Greta asked.

"Pretty straightforward."

She exhaled. Straightforward was good. "I'm glad. I'm more glad you're back."

"Me too. Do I dare ask what you've been up to the past two days?"

They turned down the side street, and the glow from the windows of Bobber's Bar beckoned them forward. As they walked, she told him about the conference and what she'd just learned about Nico Eddison. When she mentioned her run-in with Tuck White and their roadside chat, McHenry's jaw tightened.

"I was never in any danger. I actually think I impressed him with my tire-changing abilities. I might have gotten more out of him if he hadn't spotted Rob Hawler." Greta frowned. "I can't figure out the connection there."

"Persons of interest interacting is always something to look into." McHenry cut her a look. "Something for the police to look into. Not a civilian. Even a civilian consultant."

Greta held up her hands in surrender. "Happy to let the professionals take over."

McHenry nodded and pulled open the bar door. The interior was empty aside from Rob Hawler, who was at the bar wiping down glassware. He glanced up when they entered, and nodded at them.

"Want to sit over here? It's more private." Greta angled her chin toward a two-person table beneath one of the bar's windows.

"Want me all to yourself, Miss Plank?" McHenry's low tone was teasing.

A familiar fizz rose in Greta's chest. Her boyfriend was a serious police detective, but she cherished getting to see this more playful side of him.

"Is that a problem?" She winked.

"I kind of like it." McHenry reached for her hand across the table. "I've missed you."

"I—"

Greta was interrupted by an angry voice from the kitchen. "I *swear,* even from the grave, that woman is haunting us."

Chapter Fourteen

Greta spun her head around and looked to the bar in time to see Rob darting through the door to the kitchen. The yelling subsided almost immediately.

"Ace Hawler isn't happy about something." McHenry pulled his hand back and crossed his arms over his broad chest, his focus on the kitchen door.

"I'd bet that something is Blythe Prescott. How could she be haunting him from the grave?"

"We'll need to have another conversation with him."

"Did he have an alibi for the time of Blythe's death?" Rob had told her Ace was in the kitchen, but Greta wasn't so sure.

"Not one that can be confirmed. At least, I don't think so." McHenry raked a hand through his hair. "I'm out of the loop on the investigation. A lot could have happened in the past two days."

Greta studied her boyfriend. There were more stress lines than usual around his eyes. His usually firm-lined jaw looked sharp enough to slice granite.

"What are you worried about?" she asked quietly.

His gaze bounced to her. "What do you mean?"

She tipped her head to the side. "Come on, Mark. I can read you. You're more tightly wound than usual. Is it the case? Or is there something you're not telling me about Chicago?"

McHenry pressed his lips together, his gaze boring into hers. After a couple seconds he sighed and reached for her hand across the table again. "Both, I guess."

"Talk to me." Greta slid forward in her seat. She was still trying to figure out how best to show up for her boyfriend. "I can handle it."

He squeezed her fingers. "You shouldn't have to. I hate that my job keeps ending up being the focus of our relationship."

Greta chewed on her lip. "Your work is a big part of who you are. I want to be supportive of it. Just like you let me prattle on and on about the library's budget and the new releases I'm excited about. Obviously, I don't like people getting murdered in Larkspur, but it's the reality we're living right now."

McHenry looked like he'd swallowed a lemon. "I wish I could wrap you in bubble wrap and keep you locked away."

Greta felt her eyes widen.

"That came out way creepier than I intended." McHenry rubbed his jaw. "What I mean is, I don't want you to get hurt, and I hate to think that your association with me could be putting you in danger."

"I'm my own woman, detective." Greta waved him off with her free hand. "Haven't I proven I can handle myself?"

"You have more than proven yourself to me. It's..."

He broke off, and Greta didn't like the look of uncertainty in his eyes when he glanced away from her. He met her gaze again, and she saw genuine anguish there.

"What?"

"This whole thing with my brother has really messed with me," McHenry admitted. "The people he got tangled up with in Chicago are awful. They hurt anyone who gets in their way, without a second thought. Being in that world again, I remembered why I've shied away from personal relationships. I'm..." He broke off and swallowed hard. Composing himself, he pinned her with a look that was loaded with tenderness and also a heavy helping of fear. "I'm afraid of losing you or of not being able to be there for you if something happens to me."

"Oh, Mark." Greta reached across the table and cupped his cheek. "I'm right here. I'm not going anywhere."

"I know, but we can't know what could happen—"

"Exactly. We can't know. All we have is today. Right now. We're here, together. There's nowhere else I'd rather be."

Greta studied her boyfriend as he seemed to fight some sort of interior battle with himself. The man she knew was so much a protector, she could see him cutting ties with her in an effort to keep her safe or shield her from the hard stuff that came along with his job. She didn't like the thought of that.

"Hey. Look at me." She waited for him to meet her gaze. "Promise me you'll be open with me about how I can best support you. If you need a sounding board for work stuff, I can be that for you. If you need space, that's okay too. Just don't shut me out or make a unilateral decision about our relationship because you think it's for the best. I'm a big girl. I get a say."

He nodded, but still looked unsure.

"Say you promise, Mark."

He sighed, shoulders slumping forward. "I promise."

"Good. Now, what do you want to drink?" Greta grabbed the beverage menus from the slot where they stood in the napkin holder.

"I was going to ask the same thing!" Suz bustled over to their table, a perma-grin pasted on her face. It was as fake as a forged Shakespeare folio. "What can I get for you both?"

"I'll take a glass of merlot, please." Greta tucked the menu away.

"Just an ice water for me." McHenry nodded at Suz before winking at Greta. "I'm mostly here for the company."

"Back in a jiffy." Suz smiled between them, but she didn't linger.

"Are you planning to go back to work after this?" Greta asked.

"Yeah, I need to get caught up."

"I feel bad that I'm prolonging your night."

"Don't." He reached for her hand. "I wanted to spend time with you."

Chapter Fifteen

Greta savored her glass of wine and her conversation with McHenry. They moved on from the weightiness of his honest admission about his feelings to more playful banter. After sitting in comfortable silence for a couple moments, Greta shifted in her seat, setting her empty glass on the edge of the table. "I think I should try to talk to Suz. See if she'll open up to me."

McHenry's brows formed a V-shape. "Regarding?"

"Everything. Ace's outburst before, for one. I might be able to learn something. But I think she'll be more likely to talk to me if I'm alone."

"Are you kicking me out?"

"Never. But you should fake like you have to take an important call, or something."

"What if I say no?"

"I'll pout." Greta turned her lips down into a frown.

McHenry pretended to pull a dagger from his heart. "Not that. Anything but Little Miss Sunshine pouting."

Greta laughed and nudged his knee under the table. The contact sent a tingle of heat up her spine.

He leaned over and kissed her, the press of his lips sure and solid like the man himself, and then he strode out of the bar.

Greta stared after him, and as the door swung closed on his retreating figure, she knew one thing for certain. She was in love with him. Now, she had to figure out how to tell him that. He'd been honest with her tonight. But he hadn't said the l-word. What if he didn't feel the same? What if he decided she was too much of a liability, always getting in his way with his work? What if—

"Did your date have to run?" Suz picked up her empty wine glass.

Greta nodded, shoving aside her relationship thoughts for the time being. "Can you sit for a minute? I'd love the company."

Suz glanced toward the kitchen, hesitating but eventually sinking into the seat McHenry had vacated.

"Is everything alright?" Greta asked.

"Yes. No." Suz's eyes welled with tears. "Look at me blubbering! I don't know what to do with myself."

Greta reached into her purse and produced a clean tissue, which she handed over.

"I don't mean to fall apart."

"You're allowed." Greta offered her a kind smile. "Does this have to do with Blythe?"

Suz blew her nose delicately. "What else?" she lamented. "I honestly can't remember life before this week. I never could have expected what a tizzy her death would throw me into. Throw us all into."

"I couldn't help but overhear Ace when we got here. He said she was haunting you from the grave? What was that about?"

Suz shifted her gaze. "I probably shouldn't say."

Greta waited.

After a long pause, Suz leaned in. "Our family had nothing to do with Blythe's death. You have to believe me."

Greta nodded at her to continue.

"But I wasn't completely honest when I spoke with you yesterday morning. Ace did have some contact with Blythe. She's been a thorn in his side about this place." Suz waved her arm around the dining room.

"About the bar? Why?"

"She wanted to buy the property."

Greta frowned. "What about her jewelry shop?"

"She wanted to expand. Said this was a perfect spot for her satellite location."

Greta flinched. "She wanted to take the bar and transform it into a retail space? Why wouldn't she pick literally any other open property in town?"

"Exactly what I said." Suz pointed at her. "This is our family's legacy. Ace inherited it from his father. Rob is set to take over for us. I don't know what got into Blythe, but she was insistent."

"She didn't ever explain why she wanted this place in particular?" A picture was forming in Greta's mind—a hypothesis of sorts. If Blythe was certain she found hidden treasure on these grounds, it made sense that she'd want to own the property—to reap the benefits of the discovery. Not only would ownership of the treasure fall to her, but the notoriety of the find was right up her alley. It would be a perfect marketing ploy. *Come shop for your diamond where a historic diamond was discovered.* Or something like that.

"I never talked to her much. Ace told me to leave her to him. He insists she didn't say more about her motivations for wanting to buy this place out from under us." Suz looked away.

Greta sensed a *but*. She waited, but Suz didn't continue. "Do you believe him?"

Suz sat up straight. "I trust my husband fully."

Greta nodded. She thought back to the argument she overheard Ace and Blythe having over the weekend. In light of this new information, she could piece together the gist of it. Blythe wanted this property. She threatened Ace about it.

Did he kill her to stop her from moving in on his family legacy? Did Blythe tell Ace more about her findings? If so, would he have killed her in order to swoop in and search for the hidden treasure himself?

What Greta needed to figure out was whether or not that treasure actually existed. It didn't make sense that someone would kill Blythe over a hidden treasure that wasn't confirmed. Did that mean the killer found the cache? Or that Blythe had?

Or was Blythe's murder completely unrelated to the gangster trail and buried treasure?

Greta had more questions than answers. She still didn't understand Ace's outburst when she'd arrived. "Why does Ace think Blythe is haunting him from the grave?"

Suz sighed. "She must've contacted the restaurant board on us. We got a tip from someone on the inside that we should expect a surprise health and safety inspection. So now we have to worry about that on top of everything."

"But you'll pass, won't you?" Greta looked around. The bar was tidy and well-run. She'd never had any issues with the food or the cleanliness of the facilities.

"Hopefully. I mean, we definitely should." Suz bit her lip. "But certain inspectors are finicky, and you never know. We've always passed in the past. Ace thinks Blythe was trying to sabotage us before she died. He caught her trying to take apart the guard rails on the ramp out back. Not having an ADA-accessible and safe entry point would be a major strike. So, yeah. Even though she's gone, Ace is convinced what she set in motion is playing out. And we're dealing with the brunt of it."

Greta digested this new bit of knowledge as Suz rose. "I should get back." She took a step for the kitchen but spun around and leaned in. "Please don't spread this around, Greta. I'm sure Ace will tell me I shouldn't have been out here running my mouth, but it's almost too much to bear. This cloud of dread is hovering, and I'm so ready to be rid of it."

Greta nodded. She'd make no promises, but she understood what Suz was saying. "It'll all work out. Hang in there."

After paying, Greta left the restaurant in search of McHenry. She didn't have to go far. He was leaning up against the side of the wooden exterior of the bar.

"You're still here." Greta joined him. "I thought you'd be at the station, catching up on work."

"You thought I'd let you walk back to the library alone?" McHenry said by way of response.

"I guess not," she said with a smile.

"What did you learn?" he asked as they strolled toward the library.

Greta shared what Suz had told her about Blythe's attempts to buy out the Hawlers and take possession of the bar.

"She doesn't know when the inspection will be, but she's obviously concerned about it. Judging from Ace's tone, I'd say he's more than concerned."

"Concerned enough to kill?" McHenry mused.

"Good question." They walked in silence, and Greta kicked a pebble down the sidewalk in front of her, lost in thought. "I should go back to Blythe's papers," she said after a minute. "There might be something there that I missed."

"You didn't tell me what you found out about the book."

"We think it's a book cipher, but we don't know what it'll decipher." Another perusal of the papers couldn't hurt anything. Greta was nothing if not thorough.

The library was dark as they approached, the conference having wrapped up for the evening. "I'll grab that box quick and take it home with me."

"How about if I grab it for you?"

"Detective, did you just flex your bicep?" Greta squeezed his upper arm where she had tucked her fingers for warmth.

"Maybe." McHenry's voice came out as a low rumble.

Greta sighed with contentment. She removed her hand from his muscle and unlocked the exterior door. McHenry followed her down the hallway toward the library entrance. Greta let them in and ducked behind the circulation desk. She peered underneath it, scanning the low shelf where she had stashed the box of papers and the photocopies of *Pride and Prejudice*.

"That's weird." She stood upright. "It's not here. Iris or Josie must've moved it."

She walked into the office the three librarians shared and scanned the small space. There weren't many places they could go with a box of that size, and Greta didn't see it anywhere.

She turned to the doorway, and McHenry was leaning against the frame. "Nothing?"

Greta shook her head. "I'll text them."

She shot off a message to their group chat, and waited for her friends to respond. Texts populated from both Iris and Josie in less than a minute. Neither of them had touched the box.

Greta: Did you see it today?

Iris: I haven't been behind the desk since this morning. I can't say for sure.

Josie: Don't know, either. I didn't pay much attention.

A swell of panic rose up Greta's throat. She looked up from her phone and met McHenry's penetrating stare. From the concerned creases in his forehead, he'd guessed what had happened, but Greta said what she was thinking anyway.

"Someone stole Blythe's papers and the copies of the book."

Chapter Sixteen

Greta and McHenry turned over the entire library. They checked the stacks, the children's area, all the meeting rooms, the bathrooms...everywhere.

"Could our janitor have thought it was garbage and thrown the box into the recycling?"

Greta's question was how McHenry ended up scooching himself up and into the large recycling dumpster in the back of the municipal building.

"Can you describe it?" He flung one leg over the side of the metal receptacle and dropped himself inside.

"It was a cardboard box filled with papers." Greta was sure she blushed when she added, "The outside said 'Bigger Is Better' in orange script with a giant diamond ring embossed onto the cardboard."

McHenry stood inside the bin. He was tall enough that Greta could still see his upper torso and head. He shuffled around, keeping his eyes on the contents at his feet. "If someone got rid of it today, it would be on the top of all of this. I'm not seeing anything." He looked around for another couple minutes before vaulting himself out of the recycling bin.

Greta's eyes flicked to the nearby garbage dumpster.

McHenry followed her gaze. "You want me to check there?" he asked, sounding resigned.

Greta winced. "No stone left unturned, right? But I should be the one to do it. It's my fault. I should have put these things somewhere more secure."

"Don't beat yourself up. Heath dropped those papers off for you without preamble. How could you have known they were significant enough for anyone to mess with?"

"But the book pages." Greta wanted to wail. "What if they get into the wrong hands?"

McHenry hoisted himself into the dumpster. He made a face at the stench of his surroundings, but set his head in a slow swivel, taking in the trash pile he was surrounded by. He shifted some garbage around. "It doesn't look like it's here."

Greta's shoulders slumped. "Now, what do we do?"

Her mind raced. Who would have taken Blythe's box? Someone who believed its content to be significant, that's who.

"Who knew I had it?" she posed the question out loud. She hadn't been vocal in her police work. Her friends were privy to the information, and she supposed anyone could have snooped in the library and discovered Blythe's papers.

Nico and Cindi had been there alone after hours yesterday. All the of the librarians were in and out today. She hadn't been around much to determine who else had been in the library, but basically her list of suspects was as long as *War and Peace*.

"I'll let Chief Sorenson know the latest development." McHenry had escaped the dumpster and gestured for her to head back inside. "For now, we should get some rest."

Greta eyed him. "Are *you* going to get some rest?"

McHenry didn't meet her gaze. "I've got some work to do. But you should go home. Sleep. You have two more days of the conference left, right? And then the weekend programming? I don't want you to run yourself into the ground."

"Ditto," Greta whispered, but she wasn't sure McHenry heard her.

After she locked up the library, he walked her to her car. "This isn't your fault, Greta."

She bit her lip. "Feels a little like it is, though." Greta couldn't believe the police had finally let her help—officially—and she'd gone and lost evidence.

McHenry leaned in and placed a light kiss on her lips.

Greta reached up and wanted to draw him in for a deeper embrace, but he backed away. "I smell rancid."

Greta sighed, settling into the driver's seat, defeated. "Also my fault."

McHenry clicked his tongue. "I'll always go dumpster diving for you."

She couldn't help but smile at that. Even when she was bungling things, McHenry was wading through the mess alongside her—in this case, literally. Did he love her? All signs pointed to yes. Her heart lifted. She waved to McHenry and made the quick drive back to her cabin on the lake.

Biff greeted her with a loud meow, and Greta bent to her knees and nuzzled his smooth fur. He pushed his head up against her chin and rubbed it back and forth before sauntering off to the kitchen. Greta deposited her keys on the hook inside the front door and wandered into the living room. She stopped at the hall closet and pulled out her suspect board.

Of the people they had come up with as persons of interest in the case, almost all of them had access to the box of papers. Granted, she hadn't seen Tuck or Heath in the library, but the latter knew she had the box. Perhaps he returned when he realized that it contained something valuable and stole it back. The former was privy to what Blythe had been working on. If Heath let slip that he'd given away Blythe's research, Tuck could have come in search of the papers.

The Hawlers were less likely suspects in the box theft, though not completely out of the question. Rob had been in the library with Sadie. Greta wasn't convinced the family didn't know more than they were letting on about the history of the gangster trail and its connections to their bar. If they learned that Blythe had evidence about a treasure on their property, it was a logical jump that they could have sought out the source material.

Nico and Cindi could have taken the box for the same reason.

Greta massaged her temples as Biff strolled into the living room and leapt onto the couch beside her.

"I don't know, Buddy. This investigative work is not for the faint of heart."

* * *

After a restless night of sleep, Greta woke on Thursday morning and put on one of her favorite dresses. It was a soft celery green color that popped against her golden-red, curly hair. She paired the dress with her go-to low-heeled booties and an oversized jacket. The air was chilly when she stepped out her front door, but the forecast promised sunshine. She would have loved to walk into work, but she needed her car to get back and forth to Karrington for the conference.

Greta arrived at the library early. She shut her eyes hard as she stepped behind the circulation desk and blinked them open, hoping to see the missing box where she last remembered it, but it wasn't there. She sighed as she walked into the office and sat down with a huff. Who took Blythe's research?

The question had rattled around in her head all through the night, but she was no closer to an answer than she had been when she and McHenry had scoured the premises. She stared into space, racking her brain as to what she should do next.

She couldn't know who stole the box. But she could be productive while she waited for the police to figure out what happened to it. She grabbed a nearby notepad and began scribbling down everything she could remember seeing in the box itself.

When Iris and Josie arrived a half an hour later, she had made a list.

Greta showed it to them to see if they could help her fill in any of the blanks.

Blythe's Research
(1) Viola Douglass's love letters to JuJu Vance
(2) Map of the Bobber's Bar grounds (crime scene?)
(3) Engagement ring purchase receipt

Josie wiggled her cell phone. "Did you get the email Jake sent me that I forwarded to you? I thought it was interesting that he included a marriage certificate for JuJu."

Greta nodded. "To a woman who wasn't Viola. Yeah, Iris and I noted the same discrepancy. What was her name again?"

Josie clicked around on her phone. "Deborah McNamara."

Greta added a point to her notes.

(4) Deborah McNamara (not in Blythe's research, but who is she?)

The three of them stared at the list. No one offered any answers. At this point, there were none.

"Ed and I were thinking about heading up to B'Jeweled later today for our, *ahem*, errand." Josie held out her left hand and studied her engagement ring. The square-cut diamond glittered in the low light of the office.

Greta smiled in spite of the circumstances. Her friend was getting married! All she wanted to do was get this investigation behind them so they could turn their attention to planning a wedding.

"Have you two set a date?" Iris asked.

"I've always wanted a fall wedding, so we're thinking early October. Six months is a fast turnaround, but—" Josie shrugged as if to say, *I couldn't care less.* "Anyway, it actually works out pretty well. It makes a lot of sense that we'd be shopping for wedding bands already if we're less than six months out from the big day."

"Tuck mentioned something about the secrets Heath was keeping behind closed doors. I'd love to get a look at his office space." Greta spoke slowly, a plan forming in her head. "Maybe I could meet you guys there, and while you're distracting Heath, I could do some digging."

Iris scrunched up her nose. "Is that safe? I can't go with you since I'm on for the evening portion of the conference tonight. I don't like the thought of you sleuthing alone."

Greta nodded. "I know. But Heath is a one-man show at this point. If he's tied up with Ed and Josie, then there is literally no chance that anyone else will be in the building to sneak up on me."

The more Greta thought about it, the more she liked the idea.

"You should run this past McHenry," Iris said.

Greta scowled. "He's not going to like it."

"Exactly." Iris dipped her chin. "He's a good counterbalance to you. At least promise me you'll tell him where you are and when you're there so that if something goes sideways, he can be your backup."

Greta sighed. She couldn't argue with that logic. Besides, if she wanted him to be open and honest with her, she had to return the favor. "Okay."

"Should I text you when we're on our way?" Josie asked. "Will you be coming from here or Karrington?"

"I need to touch base with Fitz about the end of the conference, so I'll be in Karrington. I'll plan to meet you there but remain unseen."

"Ed's friend—the jeweler," Josie clarified, "is free midafternoon, so we're all going to ride over together."

"Perfect. I'll text you if I have any issues getting inside." Greta was banking on there being some sort of back entrance. "I might need you to prop a door open."

"I'll ask to use the bathroom right when we get there and scope things out. I'll let you know what I find."

"You guys always have the investigative fun." Iris pouted. "I hate to miss this."

"But wasn't almost getting caught snooping at Nico's fun?" Greta wagged her eyebrows.

Iris shuddered. "On second thought, I'll leave you to it."

Greta laughed, and the librarians dispersed and set about their tasks. Cindi arrived shortly before they opened and let herself into the library. She was juggling a laptop computer, an oversized bag, and a stack of books.

Greta's stomach dropped when she realized the woman had free and total access to the space...even after hours. She'd known that. Cindi had told her so with her own mouth. But now, with the theft of Blythe's things in mind, Greta considered this knowledge in a different light. Maybe Cindi had found out about the box and taken it.

"Good morning, Cindi." Josie rolled a cart of books past the library board president.

"Yes, yes." Cindi scowled at having to pause in her stride to let Josie pass. "Move along. I've got tons to do."

"We have the large meeting room reserved for the genealogy club this morning." Iris pitched her voice with good cheer.

Greta had to applaud her team. They laid it on thick where Cindi was concerned. If the woman refused to appreciate them or show them any sort of warmth, it was on her. They were nothing but cordial.

"That'll do." Cindi shifted her load, and a book toppled to the ground.

Greta retrieved it for her. "Here. Why don't I take some of that off your hands?"

Before Cindi could protest, Greta plucked the rest of the books from her grasp and secured them in the notch above her hip.

Under her breath, Cindi grumbled something that sounded *thank you* adjacent, but Greta couldn't be sure. The woman spun on her heel and headed to the meeting room.

Greta followed behind her, her mind somersaulting.

Cindi pushed open the door to the dark room and hit the light switch with her elbow. She hoisted the bag onto the table and set the laptop down with a clatter. "You can leave those right here. That'll be all."

It was a clear dismissal, but Greta couldn't be swatted away so easily. "What's the genealogy club up to today?"

"We're looking into the family tree of Dillinger's gang as a tie-in to the program this weekend. Why do you even care?"

"Keeping tabs on the goings-on in the library is sort of my entire job." Greta tried to soften her words with a smile.

"It seems you keep forgetting about your day job in favor of your poor woman's Nancy Drew sleuthing efforts," Cindi spat.

Greta reared back. Sure, she hadn't kept out of Blythe's case as much as she intended, but that was because Chief Sorenson had recruited her to help. But she hadn't been spreading that information around. And she hadn't let it affect her library work.

"What do you mean? The conference has gone off without a hitch, and our Larkspur patrons have been well taken care of, too. I'd argue my team and I are doing a great job, despite a lot of extra distractions, given the circumstances."

Cindi hummed. "I had a long talk with Nathan, the library director from Green Bay." Cindi shot Greta a pointed look. "He told me you two used to date."

Greta tensed. She opened her mouth to defend and deflect, but Cindi continued.

"He also told me he's been looking into Blythe's death, and you have been too."

"Nathan is an unreliable narrator, Cindi. I wouldn't believe what he tells you. I'm fully committed to my work here."

Cindi sniffed. "We'll see. Now, if you'll excuse me. I need to get things organized before everyone else arrives."

Greta took a step toward the exit but stopped when an idea hit her. Call it her poor woman's Nancy Drew instinct. "Your club should try to find the family history of a man by the name of Julian Vance."

Greta watched Cindi closely for any signs of recognition; any twitch of her brows or tightening of her jaw. If she knew the name, Greta would know one of two things—either Nico or Nathan shared it with her—which she doubted, since Nico had left out that detail yesterday—or she'd been through Blythe's things and seen it in the deceased woman's notes. But Cindi's breathing pattern didn't falter. She stared back at Greta blankly.

"Why would we do that?"

"Josie's brother is a professor of twentieth-century American history. He mentioned the name when he was here. Said Julian Vance, or JuJu as he's sometimes referred to, is a lesser-known member of Dillinger's gang. I thought it might be a neat exercise for your club to look into him. Do some cutting-edge research, if you will."

While Greta could tell Cindi tried to downplay her excitement, the gleam in her eye told Greta she'd gotten the woman right where she wanted her.

"We'll see," was Cindi's noncommittal response.

"I'm sure if you map the family history of JuJu Vance, Josie's brother would love to hear about it." Greta waved over her shoulder. "Have a great meeting."

She allowed herself a satisfied smile as she strolled back to the desk. She was pretty sure Cindi hadn't heard the name Julian Vance before, and now, maybe she'd even find out something helpful to the case.

Chapter Seventeen

Greta wasn't sure how long she'd been busy working in her office when a light knock on the door jamb had her looking up from the computer.

"Sorry to bug you." Iris hooked her thumb over her shoulder. "Celeste is here, and she says she needs to speak to you. Urgently."

Greta cocked her head to the side. That was odd. Usually, Celeste and Dolores were her least needy patrons. "Be right there."

She saved the grant report she'd been drafting and joined Iris behind the desk. Celeste stood near the research station at the center point of the library. Her face was drawn, and her eyes were darting around. Greta hurried her way. "Celeste, what can I do for you?"

"Thank goodness." Celeste reached for Greta's wrist. "I need to talk to you. Privately," she added in a whisper.

"Okay." Greta spoke slowly. "What's up?"

"Not here." Celeste shook her head. "Can we step outside for a moment?"

Greta surveyed the library. Everything was well in hand, so she nodded. The two exited the municipal building in silence. Celeste didn't release her grip on Greta's arm until they were across the street, walking through the doors at Mugs & Hugs.

"You're scaring me, Celeste. What's going on?"

Celeste patted her palm against her forehead. "I've run into a bit of trouble."

"What? Are you hurt?" Greta scanned her body, but there were no signs of visible injuries.

"No. No. I'm fit as a fiddle." Celeste took a deep breath. "It's my niece."

"Your...niece?" The pieces clicked. "Sadie?"

Celeste pressed her lips together and nodded.

"I met her earlier this week. She was in the library."

Celeste dropped her gaze, and when she looked up again, her eyes were filled with a mixture of emotion—anger, concern, uncertainty, fear, doubt—Greta could read them all.

They had made it to the register, and each woman placed a coffee order with one of Allison's employees. Greta didn't push Celeste to talk further until they had procured their drinks and found a seat at a table in a secluded alcove.

"Sadie seems like a nice girl."

"She is." Celeste agreed. "A good girl. She's fallen head over heels for that boy. That's the problem."

"Rob Hawler?"

Celeste nodded curtly. "They've been together a year."

Greta took a sip of her latte. "Do Sadie's parents have concerns about the relationship?"

Celeste lifted a bony shoulder. "Not so much. He's mostly been a decent boyfriend. They sure spend a lot of time together. All day on Mondays, which I know Sadie's mother doesn't always appreciate." Celeste glanced around before leaning closer to Greta. "But that's just it."

Greta inched forward. "What is?"

"Sadie told the police she was with Rob on Monday, all day, like always."

"Okay."

"But she tells her mother everything. And her mother tells me everything. We're more like sisters than sisters-in-law." Celeste straightened one of the bracelets on her wrist. "Anyway. Sadie had a crisis of conscience because she wasn't actually with Rob all day on Monday."

"So she lied to the police," Greta said.

Celeste looked pained. "Yes, and that's not like Sadie. I'm convinced Rob put her up to this, and what I can't understand is why? Why lie unless he has something to hide?"

Greta cocked her head to the side, a memory of Rob's phone conversation after discovering Blythe's body flitting through her mind. *Cover for me.*

"Wouldn't it look better for Sadie if she wasn't with Rob? I mean, if he's up to no good, then better that she wasn't with him."

Celeste considered that for a beat. "I agree, but will the police see it that way? She lied to them. Doesn't that make her look guiltier in their eyes?"

"I don't know, but you should still go to the police."

Celeste looked pained. "My sister-in-law would kill me. This implicates Sadie now, and I won't have her reputation ruined because of some boy. That, and she'd never forgive me if she knew I was the one who squealed on her. You remember being twenty and in love, don't you?"

Greta shifted in her seat. She didn't. Her first serious relationship had been with Nathan, and she'd rather forget it in its entirety. Greta issued a noncommittal humming sound.

"Her judgment is skewed by her feelings for Rob. There has to be an explanation. *He's* the one that needs to come clean."

"What do you want me to do?" Greta swirled her straw around in her drink.

"I want you to talk to them. To both of them. You have a knack for this sort of thing, Greta. You're good at talking to suspects. *Not* that I think Sadie is a suspect. But you've done this before. Gotten the truth out of people."

Greta frowned. "I don't know that I—"

Celeste silenced her with a wave of her hand, bracelets clanging. "You're the perfect person to stage an intervention. You're not family, but you're an authority figure."

"I wouldn't go that far," Greta mumbled.

"They'll listen to you," Celeste went on. "If you explain the seriousness of the situation to them, I'm sure they'll spill the beans about what they—or rather, Rob—was up to."

"You're sure you want to know?" Greta asked quietly. What if Sadie was messed up in something? How would her protective family react to the truth?

"Yes." Celeste nodded as if it was a done deal. "I can get the two of them somewhere where you'll be waiting. And you can take it from there."

"But what's my angle? How would I explain knowing any of this without admitting that you told me and, tangentially, that Sadie's mom told you?"

"There has to be a way."

Greta considered the facts, a murky plan forming. "I did happen to see Rob in Karrington on Monday morning. He was alone in his truck."

Celeste snapped her fingers. "See? That's perfect. That's your opening. All you need is to get the conversation started. I don't think it'll take much to crack Sadie. The poor girl is guilt-ridden, according to her mom. She needs someone neutral to tell her it's okay and for her to unload the truth. Maybe we stage it as a chance encounter."

Color had returned to Celeste's cheeks as the plan took shape. Greta was glad to see that, for her friend's sake, but she worried about how Rob would react if Sadie told the truth and basically called into question his alibi. Had Celeste thought about that? She hadn't heard anything about the youngest Hawler being violent or vindictive, but she didn't really know him.

She sighed. "I'll see what I can do. But I make no promises. I'm not going to push too hard. If this doesn't work, you need to go to the police with this information, Celeste. I can't, in good conscience, keep it to myself."

Celeste looked away before meeting Greta's eye again. "I understand. You have my word that if Rob and Sadie don't talk, I'll convince Sadie to go to the authorities, or I'll go myself."

Greta reached across the table and squeezed Celeste's hand. "You're a good aunt."

The woman let out a strangled chuckle. "My own kids all live out of state now. I've taken an avid interest in Sadie since she was a girl. I don't want to see anything happen to her."

"The best thing she can do is tell the truth, and hopefully, that'll inspire Rob to tell the truth."

And hopefully, there won't be too much fallout.

The two stood and walked together back to the library. Celeste bid Greta goodbye after she promised to be in touch to coordinate specifics. Greta had to hurry if she wanted to make it to Karrington in time to catch Fitz before the mid-morning program on the future of public libraries was set to begin.

The meeting room where the genealogy club was gathering was shut, so they must still be working. Greta would have to figure out a way to covertly ask Cindi later if they'd learned anything about JuJu Vance.

She said goodbye to Josie, promising she'd see her later, and headed back into the parking lot. She wished she had time to pop into the police station to see McHenry in person, but she'd have to settle for a phone call on her drive.

After navigating the quiet Larkspur streets and getting onto the highway, she used her car's voice recognition software to phone him.

McHenry answered on the second ring. "Morning, Greta."

"Hey." Greta heard the smile in her own voice. They exchanged pleasantries, and Greta tried not to be too deflated when McHenry said he hadn't made any progress in locating the missing box of Blythe's research.

"What about the book ciphertext? Any progress working that angle?" Greta asked.

"Chief Sorenson said his men have searched Blythe's home and office, but they haven't uncovered any paper with a sequence of numbers like you described. I'm afraid we've hit a dead-end with it."

Greta chewed on her lip. "It's odd that the ciphertext wasn't found near the cipher. What's one without the other?"

"True. Then again, if it was important information, Blythe could have decoded it, read the message, and disposed of the ciphertext so no one else would ever find out what the message read."

"Or, she could have passed it off to someone else who had the same copy of *Pride and Prejudice*. Maybe she worked out the code with her book, wrote the ciphertext, and passed it off." Greta fought the urge to bang her head against her steering wheel. Was there anything worse than a clue that couldn't be unraveled? It was like a book without the last chapter.

"Maybe it'll still turn up. Or someone will come forward with it." She tried to pitch her voice with more optimism than she felt. "You could still find it and figure out what it says."

"We could. Though we're more concerned with finding the killer than we are with figuring out the code."

Greta switched gears. "You said you searched Blythe's office?"

"We did, yeah. Earlier this week."

"What about Heath's office? Did they share a space?"

"We didn't have a warrant for Heath's office. They had separate spaces."

"Down that back hallway behind the show counter?" Greta tried to keep her tone innocent, but she was definitely angling for information about the layout of the back-office space at B'Jeweled.

"Yes." Judging from the stretched-out way he hissed his *s*, McHenry was understandably suspicious. "Why does that matter?"

Greta bit her lip. She wouldn't lie to him. That wasn't how their relationship worked. So, she told him about Josie and Ed's plans to shop around at B'Jeweled for wedding bands. "They're bringing a legit jeweler friend of Ed's, and we're pretty sure he'll be able to sniff out anything that's not above board."

McHenry was quiet. "That still doesn't explain why you were wringing me out for information about Blythe and Heath's offices."

"You're going to make me say it?" Greta figured he already knew what she had planned.

McHenry's sigh was bone-deep on the other end of the line. "Let me guess. You're planning to snoop around in the offices while Ed and Josie distract Heath out front."

"Yes." Greta explained all the reasons why it would work, and she wouldn't be in any danger. "Besides, won't it be good to have eyes on Heath's things? I don't need a warrant. I'm a civilian."

"Anything you find won't be admissible anyway."

"Right." That was a bummer, but Greta wasn't to be deterred. "Still, if I find anything noteworthy, it can help you all figure out some next steps. It's a good plan."

"I hate it."

"Don't hold back. Tell me how you feel."

"I'm serious, Greta. Heath does not strike me as a good guy. If he finds you snooping, there's no telling what he'll do. He could accuse you of trying to steal from him. You could get in big trouble."

"He won't find me, though. He's the only one working, and he'll be with Josie and Ed. We'll more than outnumber him, especially with Ed's friend along for the ride. I'll be completely safe."

McHenry stayed quiet for so long, Greta thought the call might've been dropped. "You still there?"

"I'm here," McHenry grumbled. "I don't suppose there's any way I can talk you out of this?"

Greta smiled at her dashboard. "I'm not being reckless, Mark. I promise."

"It's not you I'm worried about. It's Heath."

"I won't make a sound. I'll get in and out. I'll even text you when I'm entering and when I leave if it makes you feel any better."

There was a sudden influx of background noise on McHenry's end of the call.

"I'll let you go. Sounds busy there." Greta strained to try to hear who was talking and what they were saying.

"Be in touch, please." McHenry dropped his voice. "When this investigation is behind us, let's go somewhere together. Somewhere we can focus on us...not on criminal behavior and sussing out suspects."

Greta's stomach fluttered at the thought of one-on-one time with McHenry. Having her boyfriend all to herself sounded like a luxury she could get behind.

"I'd love that."

She wished him a good rest of his day and promised again to text him while she was at B'Jeweled.

She ended the call as she pulled into the parking lot at the Karrington Public Library. Other librarians were arriving at the same time, and Greta smiled and chatted with them as they all walked into the building together. Once inside, she walked over to Fitz's office.

He was behind his desk, glasses askew on his head and nose buried in a book.

She knocked gently on his door, and his head bounced up. "Greta, hi."

"Sorry to interrupt. You look deep in thought."

"My brain is about to explode." Fitz removed his glasses and rubbed his eyes.

"What's wrong?"

"Nothing. Nothing major. At least, I hope not." Fitz gestured to a framed photo on his desk. "Wick is under the weather."

"Oh no," Greta cooed. "What's wrong?"

Wick was Fitz's dog. He was a mixed breed who Fitz loved like his own child.

"I'm not sure. I'm taking him to the vet tonight to hopefully get that sorted out. I hope it's not serious, you know?"

"Let me know how he's doing if you think of it."

"I will." Fitz shot her a grateful smile, but then it fell.

"What else is on your mind?" Greta prompted.

"I'm also realizing how much work trying to get my PhD is going to be alongside librarian-ing."

Greta grimaced. She had no desire to go back to school. Getting her certification to be a library director a year and a half ago had been enough. "There's only one way to eat an elephant," she quipped.

"One bite at a time," they said together.

Fitz's lips curled into a smile. "I'll remember that."

He stood, and they walked toward the conference rooms. Greta waved to Wren, the library assistant she'd met earlier in the week.

"You've got a great staff here," she told Fitz.

"That's true. And we're hiring because we're already stretched to the limit, so I know there'll be plenty of help by the time I start school in the fall."

"They'll be able to pick up the slack while you're off taking over the world and becoming *Doctor* Fitz Atwood, a famous archivist at some fancy-schmancy research library. Don't forget the little guys when you make it big, okay?"

Fitz slung his arm over Greta's shoulder. "How could I ever forget you, Greta?"

She laughed, and her phone buzzed with a text from Josie.

Josie: Planning to be at B'Jeweled at 3:30. Does that work for you?

Greta typed out a quick reply.

Greta: Should be fine. I'll sneak out of here a little early. McHenry said there are two separate offices in the back and a second exit. Text me if you have issues propping it open.

If that happened, Greta would make up an excuse about seeing Ed's car in the parking lot and stopping by to say hi. She'd somehow talk her way behind the counter and do her sleuthing from that direction.

Josie: Done and done.

Greta stashed her phone. "Sorry about that."

"No problem. Everything okay?"

"Yep. All good." She would have to fill Fitz in later. There were librarians and their supersonic ears everywhere. She didn't want anyone to overhear her plans and report them to someone like Nathan.

Speaking of her ex…

"Why is he always the center of attention?" Fitz grumbled as she walked into the conference room to once again find Nathan holding court at a table near the front.

Greta sighed. "I don't know. We better see what he has to say today."

"Ah, good. Greta." Nathan stood and took a step toward her.

Fitz stepped closer to her side, crossing his arms over his chest. Greta loved the man for his protective streak, even if his scrawny, fifty-year-old hipster-styled body didn't look all that intimidating.

"What's up, Nathan?" Greta asked.

"I was telling everyone how I plan to do some hands-on investigating tonight."

Fitz tensed, and Greta could feel the blood pump faster through her veins. It felt like it was all rushing toward her head and pounding its way toward a migraine.

"What do you mean, 'hands-on'?" Fitz narrowed his gaze.

"Going back to the scene of the crime." Nathan rubbed his hands together. "Any interest in joining me, Greta? I could use someone who knows the lay of the land."

"No, thanks."

"Come on! It'll be fun."

"Unbelievable," Fitz mumbled under his breath. Raising his voice, he drew the room's attention. "We're going to get started, folks. Please, find your seats."

Greta went to move around Nathan, but he reached out and grabbed her by the elbow. Her blood thumped harder. "Nathan." Her tone was laced with warning.

Nathan held up his hands in the surrender pose. "I mean no harm. Seriously, join me tonight. Even bring your boyfriend, and we can all put our heads together."

Greta pressed her fingers to her temple and started massaging. There was no point in reasoning with Nathan when he got his mind set on something. "Look, I get that me trying to stop you is useless. So go ahead and do what you're going to do. But I'm not going to be a part of it, okay?"

Nathan sniffed. "Fine."

Greta blew out a long, calming breath as Nathan turned to find his seat.

She took her spot near the front next to Fitz and tried to turn her attention to the presenter. The session was titled *Libraries: Where We Are and Where We're Going*. Greta had been looking forward to it all week. She loved thinking about how public libraries could and should evolve to serve the needs of the communities they were in. She was always looking for new ideas and best practices that she could implement in Larkspur. But today, she couldn't focus. She took detailed notes on what was said, but if anyone had asked her anything about the content, she wouldn't have been able to recall it without reading the words straight from the page.

Her mind kept drifting to what trouble Nathan would get himself into when he started poking his nose where it didn't belong. And, she was wound up about her own scheduled sleuthing endeavor at B'Jeweled.

They had catered a working lunch for all the conference attendees at the library. Greta put on her best game face and made small-talk with the visiting librarians, listening to their thoughts on the week as a whole and what their key takeaways had been. She usually loved this sort of networking, and while she came away with a good deal of positive feedback, she could barely appreciate it because her mind was so taken with Blythe's murder

127

investigation.

She'd never been so happy to get a text from Josie that informed her they were en route to Karrington. It came through toward the end of the afternoon session on diversity and inclusion.

Greta leaned over and whispered in Fitz's ear. "I've got to cut out early. You good here?"

"Naturally," Fitz whispered back. "See you in the morning?"

"One more day to bring it home."

Fitz held out his closed fist and Greta tapped it with her own.

Fortunately, they were seated in the back of the conference room for this session, so she could slip out undetected. Nathan was still in attendance, and she took some solace in knowing that he hadn't gotten into any trouble...yet.

She toyed with the idea of texting McHenry to let someone on the Larkspur police force know to expect him snooping around. Maybe McHenry could position Officer Clarkson to stand guard over the crime scene. But that was ridiculous—a waste of good resources. Nathan shouldn't need to be babysat.

The last thing Greta wanted to text McHenry about was her ex. Instead, she pulled out her phone and sent him a quick message.

Greta: Heading to B'Jeweled. Hope the day's gone well there. XOXO

She slid her phone into her bag and made the quick drive across town. She parked in a cluster of cars housed in stalls in front of the community college that was next to the jewelry shop.

Now, all she had to do was wait.

She fished out her phone and found a new message from McHenry.

McHenry: Let the record show I am still fully against this idea.

Greta smiled.

Greta: Your disapproval is documented for posterity.

Greta: But so is your willingness to let your girlfriend follow her whims. The record will also show you are supportive, not stifling, and basically the best.

McHenry: At least I have that.

McHenry: Keep me posted.

Chapter Eighteen

Greta spotted Ed's truck a moment later. He parked in a spot right in front of B'Jeweled.

He got out and opened the door for Josie. She hopped out and was followed by a man who looked scholarly in a pair of wire glasses and a button-up, collared shirt.

Josie's gaze flicked over to where Greta was parked.

Greta gave her a small wave, but Josie didn't show any sort of response, which was probably for the best.

They walked through the doors of B'Jeweled, disappearing from her view.

Greta kept her eyes on the building, and her head nearly hit the roof of her car when her phone vibrated a couple minutes later.

Josie: Back door is propped open with my glasses case. Grab it for me so I don't have to leave it behind.

Greta: You got it. Good luck with Heath.

Josie: Already don't like the guy. Good luck to YOU.

Greta clutched her phone in her hand after making sure she turned on *Do Not Disturb* mode. The last thing she wanted was a phone call or alert giving her away. She got out of her car and realized right away she had a problem.

Since B'Jeweled was in a strip mall, there wasn't any way to get around the back of the building without crossing in front of the large windows. She looked up at the signage for Karrington Community College, and a loose plan formed. She walked toward the entrance to the facility and opened the door.

Once inside, she took a beat to acclimate herself to her surroundings and proceeded to march toward the back of the building. If she acted like she belonged there, she hoped no one would stop and question her. She kept her eyes straight ahead. Students and teachers milled about in the common area.

She exhaled and picked up her pace once she was in a hallway that she hoped led straight to the back of the building. The hallway appeared to be lined with offices, most of which were empty, though there was light coming from the last one on the right side. Greta slowed and casually passed by, overhearing a couple fragments of a conversation between someone she guessed to be a professor and his student.

"Relax. You have a month before finals. You'll get everything done."

"But what if—"

Before Greta could hear the concerns of the harried student, she pushed open the rear door of the community college. She let out a breath when no alarm sounded.

Glancing left and right, Greta was thrilled to see the alleyway behind the strip mall was deserted.

"Chalking that up as a major win." She scampered over to the rear entrance to B'Jeweled, and sure enough, a hard-sided glasses case was propping the door open for her. Greta stuck her foot in the door and snatched up the case. She held it in her left hand as she slipped inside, making sure to hold the door so it didn't echo more than a dull click when it closed behind her. Greta blew out another silent breath. She paused to listen, and after only a moment, Heath's nasally voice reached her.

"I have several options that'll look stunning with that beautiful diamond. Let's start over here."

Good. They were just beginning. Greta took two paces down the hallway and peeked into the first room she came to. The lights were out, and the blinds were drawn, so she clicked the flashlight icon on her cell phone and directed the beam to the floor. Once she was fully inside the darkened room, she swung her light up and scanned the space. There were unlit twinkle lights tacked to the four corners of the ceiling. A white feathered rug was spread out below a wood desk in the center of the room, and along the back wall, a line of floor-to-ceiling bookcases was decorated to perfection with books, files, and décor accents of pale pink. Blythe's office.

Greta started with the bookshelves. She took her time, carefully scanning the titles from top to bottom. Interestingly, Blythe's collection of books made her out to be a much more contemporary reader than the copy of *Pride and Prejudice* would indicate. She had titles from all the heavy hitters in the romance genre, including Emily Henry, Colleen Hoover, and Abby Jimenez. A shelf over, she had a variety of history books. Greta spotted *Public Enemies* by Bryan Burrough as well as several biographies of John Dillinger and Baby Face Nelson. Nearby there were stacks of cookbooks, which seemed out of place in a jewelry shop office library, but maybe Blythe did her meal planning here. Below the cookbooks were business textbooks. Many had the sticker on them from Karrington Community College. They looked relatively new. Greta took one off the shelf and flipped open the cover. A sheet of paper fell out. Greta bent and retrieved it from where it had fluttered to the floor. It was a syllabus for a course on franchising, and it was for the current year.

So, Blythe had been a student as well as a business owner. She enjoyed steamy contemporary romance novels, cooking, and gangsters. The woman contained multitudes; Greta had to give her that.

Greta glanced over her shoulder. There was no way she'd have time to go through all the books on these shelves and search for the ciphertext that went with the book cipher. She took down a few and shook them from the spine. But nothing loose fell out. She turned her attention to the desk, which was mostly emptied. She padded to the door and listened again.

"I'd like to see some more. I'm an outdoorsy guy, so I need something that'll withstand the elements," Ed was saying.

Greta gulped. If they had already moved on from Josie's wedding band to Ed's, she was running out of time. She flicked her gaze across the hallway to where a door was closed. That had to be Heath's office. There was a light peeking out of the cracks around the door, and Greta held her breath as she darted across the hallway and tried the knob. She held in a curse when she found it locked. Now, what could she do?

She looked left and right, rising up on her tip-toes and feeling along the top of the door frame for any sort of key, but there was nothing. She crouched down and studied the knob. It appeared to be a basic door handle—one that she'd seen on bathroom and bedroom doors in builder-grade homes. Was it weird that Heath didn't have an actual key-lock on his office door? Yes. But Greta wasn't complaining.

She reached up and pulled out the bobby pin that was holding the curls off the side of her face. It was a sturdier one that was a little thicker than most. She bent it flat and inserted one of the ends into the hole in the knob, wiggling it around ever so slightly and trying to get it to catch on the internal mechanism. When she felt resistance, she flicked her wrist, and the latch gave.

Greta twirled the knob again, and this time, she was in. She stifled the urge to let out a cheer, instead pocketing her trusty bobby pin and ducking into the room. She pulled the door closed behind her and looked around. It was definitely Heath's office. Whereas Blythe's space had been all feminine touches and airy tones, this office was cramped with dark wood furniture and black accents. It mirrored Blythe's office with the same back wall of bookshelves, though admittedly less well-decorated. There were hardly any books. A couple files were stacked haphazardly in different corners of the shelves. Greta crossed the room and plucked one down, flipping through the papers. It only took her a moment to figure out what she was looking at. These were authenticity statements on the gems B'Jeweled was selling. Greta held one up to the light, and the seal of authenticity was plainly visible in the bottom corner of the page.

Maybe Tuck and the disgruntled customer had it all wrong. These papers seemed authentic to her layman's eye. Then again, she had absolutely no background. Hopefully, Ed's friend could tell them for sure. She abandoned the shelves in favor of the desk. The surface was littered with papers, and Greta was overwhelmed by the mess. She started shuffling some around, looking for anything notable, when raised voices had her freezing in place.

"It's no problem at all. I've got it right here." Heath sounded too close for comfort.

Greta looked frantically around the small office for a place to hide.

"It's not necessary." Josie's panicked voice reached her next. "We can always come back for it."

"Nonsense. You're here now." Heath's voice grew even louder as he approached the office. "Let me grab it for you to look at."

Greta did the only thing she could think to do in the moment. She dove underneath the desk, pulled the chair in as tightly as she could, and pressed herself into the corner as the door swung open.

Heath cranked on the knob a couple times. "Thought I locked this," he muttered.

Greta pressed her lips together, wishing she had an invisibility cloak.

"Where is it? Where is it?" Heath's lower legs appeared in Greta's line of sight. He was facing the bookshelf. "Aha!"

At his exclamation, Greta's body jolted, and she held her breath, praying he didn't notice the creak of his desk board against her weight.

The sound of ruffling papers reached her ear as a droplet of sweat trickled down her back.

Some more crinkling and then the light slap of a file being tossed back onto the shelf, and Heath walked out of the office. He didn't close the door, so Greta could hear his steps retreating down the hall and toward the showroom. "I've got it right here. The diamonds on this band are very valuable."

Greta scrambled out from her hiding place and shoved some errant curls behind her ear. Her time was running out. She pulled open the drawer nearest to her and didn't see much of interest besides office supplies. She moved onto the other side of the desk, and there were only Post-it Notes. The bottom drawer was empty, aside from a single key. Greta palmed it greedily. There was a thin drawer directly in front of the desk chair, and it had a lock on it. She tried it, and sure enough, the key slipped seamlessly into the lock, and the drawer pulled open.

Greta winced as the wood-on-wood track groaned. Her eyes perused the contents in a heartbeat. A notepad with a name and phone number written on it. A blank manila folder. And a pile of receipts—the old-fashioned, carbon copy kind. Greta opened the camera app on her phone and took a photo of the name and phone number. She flipped through the receipts. They all appeared to be from the same man. Greta took photos of the top four before shoving them back where she'd found them.

She could tell by the murmur of voices out front that Ed and Josie were getting close to being done with their shopping spree.

Greta flipped open the beige folder, not expecting to find much, and barely suppressed a gasp. Her hands shook as she brought her phone up and snapped another burst of photos.

Divorce papers.

She leaned closer and read the top of one of the forms. Blythe's name was listed as the sole petitioner. There was another form with the numerical code FA-4119V at the top. The signature line was blank at the bottom.

Greta had no idea what it all meant. She was no lawyer, but she happened to know someone who was. She'd be giving her mother a call as soon as she escaped from the bowels of B'Jeweled.

Speaking of, she needed to scoot before Heath came back and discovered her snooping in his office. Greta took one last glance through the paperwork before slipping it into the folder. She replaced everything in the desk as she'd found it, locked the drawer, and stowed the key. She padded over to the door and hesitated. There was still conversation coming from the showroom, so she slunk into the hallway, leaving the door open behind her.

It took her less than ten strides to make it to the rear exit. She pushed open the exterior door and dodged outside, squinting against the late afternoon setting sun even as she turned back to make sure the latch of the door didn't click too loudly.

"Victory." Greta whispered the word on an exhale. She just had to make it back through the community college without drawing attention.

Before she could pivot, a hand clamped around her upper arm.

Greta gasped, all the blood rushing from her head to her toes.

A male voice spoke from behind her. "Care to tell me what's going on here?"

Chapter Nineteen

Greta craned her neck around and looked into the beady eyes of Tuck White.

"Tuck," she squeaked. "What are you doing here?"

"I asked you first, flat tire lady."

Greta wasn't sure if she should be offended by the moniker, but now wasn't the time to unpack it. Tuck released her arm, and she shook it out, desperately trying to come up with an excuse.

She cleared her throat. "My friends are in the front shopping for rings. I...I had to use the restroom, so I came to the back of the store, and then I felt light-headed, so I slipped out here for some fresh air." She pressed a delayed palm to her forehead.

Tuck's eyebrows were slanted down. "How come I saw you next door, then?"

Greta's shoulders slumped. "You were at the community college?"

"I'm a student there. Imagine my surprise when I came out of my professor's office and saw you scurrying down the hallway and out the rear exit. I thought I recognized you from our little roadside chat. I followed you over here, and now here we are. Sorry, I don't buy the *my friends are shopping for rings* angle." Tuck crossed his arms. "Spill."

Greta tipped her chin up. "My friends *are* shopping for rings. But you're right, I wasn't with them."

Tuck glanced over her shoulder at the backside of B'Jeweled. "We'll grab a bite to eat, and you can tell me what's going on."

"I don't think I—"

He held up a hand, silencing her protests. "Or I could go talk to Heath about how I found you breaking and entering. I'm sure he would appreciate my concern for my former place of employment."

Greta gritted her teeth. "Fine."

"Come on. The Mexican place across the way is good." He reached for her elbow and steered her to the community college. He used his student ID to let them in through the backdoor.

Tuck nodded at a few people as he led her through the college. It was busier than Greta expected since it was nearing the dinner hour.

As she side-stepped another group of students, Tuck read her mind. "This place offers lots of evening and weekend classes for those of us who work full time and are trying to further our education."

Greta nodded. She appreciated that.

Tuck held the front door open for her and pointed her to the right, away from B'Jeweled. "It's that way. They have two-for-one margaritas on Thursdays."

They walked to the restaurant, which was called Los Frijoles.

"This place is known for its beans?" Greta was immediately skeptical.

"Don't knock it til you try it."

"I doubt it'll compare to Everything's Coming Up Tacos. Have you been?"

"In Larkspur?" Tuck nodded. "Amazing queso."

"Right? The best." Greta pulled out her phone and sent off a text to Josie and then to McHenry explaining where she was and who she was with.

McHenry's response was swift.

McHenry: I'm tied up in a meeting, but I can come there after if you need me to.

Greta: Pretty sure Tuck is harmless. We're in a full restaurant...I'm not worried, but thank you.

Josie's text came a second later.

Josie: We're hungry. We'll head that way to eat and keep watch...just in case.

Greta took a screenshot of Josie's message and sent it to McHenry.

Greta: I'll be well looked after.

McHenry's response made her cheeks heat.

McHenry: Tell that Tuck character you have a boyfriend.

Greta: Jealousy looks good on you, detective. <winking face emoji> <kissing face emoji>

McHenry: Yeah, yeah. Call me on your way home.

Greta pocketed her phone when the waitress arrived.

Tuck placed an order for a margarita, and Greta did the same.

When the waitress walked away, he leaned back on his side of the booth. "Alright, flat tire lady. Tell me what gives."

Greta mirrored his pose. "First of all, my name is Greta. Second of all, why should I tell you anything?"

"Because I told you Heath is bad news and that bad business is going on at B'Jeweled. The next thing I know, I see you sneaking around there. What are you, some sort of undercover cop?"

Greta huffed. "Hardly. I'm a librarian in Larkspur."

Tuck crossed his arms. "Where'd you learn to change a tire like that? One of your books?"

"No." Greta scowled. "My dad taught me. I could have taught you, too, if you weren't so anxious to run off after Rob Hawler."

Tuck's eyes widened like a cartoon. "What? I...how?"

Greta was silent as the waitress returned with their drinks. She ordered a plate of fish tacos and took a long sip of her margarita, glancing at Tuck over the top of her drink while he placed his order. The door opened with a whoosh behind her, and Greta turned to see Ed and Josie enter with the jewelry expert. She couldn't wait to hear what, if anything, they'd discovered. But for now, she needed to pump Tuck for some information. Knowing her friends had her back made her bolder.

When the waitress left them, Greta spoke. "I recognized Rob's truck. It's not the first time I've seen him cruise through Karrington, either. How do you two know each other?"

Tuck chewed on his bottom lip. It was apparent he was trying to figure out how much he wanted to say. Greta had shown some of her cards earlier than she would have liked, but the shock factor of putting Rob's name out there seemed to work.

Tuck slumped forward. "Blythe introduced us." His voice cracked when he said Blythe's name.

Greta's heart squeezed with empathy. It seemed like the two had been close. She wanted to offer her sympathies, but she needed to stay focused on getting information from him. She took another sip of her drink, letting the moment settle between them before asking, "Rob knew Blythe?"

Tuck nodded. "The three of us had connected several times about the research Blythe was doing."

"What sort of research?"

Tuck tugged on his collar. "She was researching buried treasure that was left in the Larkspur vicinity by her ancestors. Ever heard of Julian Vance?"

Greta stuffed a chip loaded down with salsa in her mouth to calm her racing heart. She officially had confirmation of what Blythe was up to. She willed up the courage to lie. "I hadn't heard of him before."

Before this week, she added to herself.

"He buried a diamond ring in Larkspur when he was fleeing Northern Wisconsin after the Little Bohemia Lodge raid in 1934." Tuck watched her carefully.

Greta nodded at this. "I've heard about the events up in Manitowish Waters. We're having a whole program about the Little Bo raid at the library this weekend in honor of the anniversary."

"Blythe was dead-set on presenting her findings at that very program." Tuck released a weary exhale. "Now she's just dead."

Painful, but true.

Greta let the reality of that hang in the air between them as she munched on another chip.

"Was Blythe certain there was actually a buried diamond ring in Larkspur?" Greta asked after she swallowed.

Tuck nodded. "She had proof."

"What sort of proof?"

"Apparently, she found old family documents that proved it."

"Blythe is a relative of Julian Vance?" Greta asked. This was news. She forced herself to sit still.

"Yeah, distantly. She found a connection between her, Julian, and his wife, a woman by the name of Deborah McNamara. Then she found documentation of an engagement ring Julian had purchased. But the specs of the ring listed didn't match the one that's been passed down in her family. She said she had figured out coordinates for where the missing ring is buried."

Greta sat up straighter. This felt like the kind of information she would have kept with her research papers. Greta had seen the receipt for the ring and the rough sketch of a map with the X on it. That drawing seemed to indicate that the location of the ring was behind Bobber's Bar, but there was nothing mentioning actual coordinates. Had Greta missed it? Or had Heath known about it and taken it out of the box he'd given to the library? And how did Blythe know the ring was buried in Larkspur? What if JuJu had given it to Viola, the woman from the love letters? Could Blythe, like Cindi suspected, have been on a wild goose chase?

"How do you know all this?" she asked Tuck.

"Blythe told me everything except the coordinates."

"Do you have any idea where the ring is buried?" If Tuck was the only other person to know about the buried treasure, he had to be considered a top suspect.

"I have a hunch." Tuck took a drink of his margarita, and Greta could tell he wasn't going to say more on that subject.

"Did she share her findings with anyone else? What about her husband?" she added.

"Heck no. Blythe didn't tell any of this to Heath. That guy would have tried to take all the credit for himself and manipulate the findings for his own benefit." Tuck's face transformed into one of pensive thought. "She did hint at it to Rob Hawler. About the diamond, I mean. It was all part of her attempts to win him over."

The waitress returned with their food, and Greta waited until she finished checking in on them and walked away before diving back into the conversation.

"What was she trying to win Rob over to?"

"Her proposition."

Greta arched a brow.

"Blythe wanted Rob to convince his parents to sell her the Bobber's Bar property."

"Why?"

Tuck arched his eyebrows. "Not entirely sure, but if I had to guess, I'd say it has something to do with the coordinates she discovered." He looked at her meaningfully.

She widened her eyes, pretending this was the first she was hearing any of this information. What she had learned was that Tuck knew enough to know the ring was likely buried at Bobber's. Interesting.

Greta considered this alongside what she already knew. "Rob's mom, Suz told me the bar is their family legacy. I can't imagine Rob would be too keen to part with his inheritance."

"He seemed open to the idea initially. Blythe was thrilled. But then he changed his tune. And Blythe was..." He broke off, as if searching for the word.

"Not thrilled?" Greta offered.

"To say the least."

"Do Ace and Suz Hawler know any of this?" Greta knew that they did, but she wanted to keep Tuck talking.

He nodded. "When Blythe couldn't make any progress with Rob, she went straight to Ace. He didn't want to hear from her."

"Did you ever approach them? The Hawlers seemed less than thrilled to see you in their bar the other day." Greta was trying to sort out all the main players in this case. But the picture in her head was foggy at best.

"Blythe and I ate at Bobber's together a few times, so they probably associate me with her. But I've never spoken to them myself."

Greta twisted her lips to the side. "Do you think the Hawlers would have gone so far as to harm Blythe to keep her from messing with the bar?"

Tuck shrugged. "I don't think Rob has it in him, to be honest. But I don't know his parents well enough to say."

They lapsed into silence, alternatively eating their meals—which, she had to admit, were delicious—and sipping on their drinks. Greta wondered what was in it for Rob. Why had he seriously considered Blythe's proposal initially? What made him change his tune?

She stared at Tuck, and he eventually met her gaze.

"What?" he asked.

Greta blinked, shaking her head slightly. "I'm curious. Blythe obviously confided in you. How come?"

Tuck's eyes glazed with sadness. "She was like my big sister. We met, taking night classes at the community college last year, and then she offered me a job. I think the further Blythe got into the research she was doing, and the more a plan formed to take B'Jeweled to the next level, the more she needed a confidant. I was her friend," he added with a shrug. "There was something about her. I guess I needed a friend, too. Blythe was easy to talk to. She didn't judge a person. I appreciated that."

Greta took note of the wane lines bracketing Tuck's eyes and the sad droop of his mouth.

"I'm sorry for your loss," she said quietly. Even as she offered her sympathy, she couldn't help but hold Tuck in suspicion. If she confided in him, perhaps greed got the best of him, and he wanted the ring for himself. Choosing her next words carefully, she added, "Can you tell me any more about Heath?"

Tuck sniffed. "Not much more to say. Guy's a total schemer."

Greta wiped her hands on her napkin and folded them in her lap. "Have you told the police any of this?"

Tuck stiffened. "Cops give me the creeps."

Greta fought an eye roll. That was hardly an excuse to withhold pertinent information. "You should tell them what you know." She thought for a moment. "Heath is throwing you under the bus. If you don't speak up for yourself, you might wind up in trouble."

Tuck's eyes narrowed. "I'm not afraid of Heath. He's the one who had motive to kill Blythe. She wanted to move on without him. In fact"—Tuck glanced around and leaned in—"she served him with divorce papers the week before she was killed."

Greta feigned shock. "How did he take that?"

141

"Not well. He punched a hole through the door to his office." Tuck let out a single snort. "I was there. It wasn't pretty."

So, Heath was a loose cannon from a physical standpoint, too. Interesting. That tidbit made him a realistic candidate for thunking Blythe over the head with a garden shovel.

He also must have replaced his door with a generic one, which would explain the lack of lock and key feature. It smelt like someone was covering their tracks.

Out loud, she said, "This is the type of information the police need to know. It sounds like Blythe was a good friend to you. Don't you want justice for her?"

"'Course, I do." Tuck shifted in his seat, brushing his finger through the condensation droplets from his now-empty margarita glass. "It's just the thought of spending any sort of time with law enforcement is not something I'm thrilled about. I had some," he paused, "*issues* as a teen. Shoplifting, actually," he added with a grimace. "Heath must've found out somehow, because he started dropping hints about how I couldn't be trusted."

That must've been what Heath was referring to. Greta wasn't sure which of the men to believe at this point, but her gut was telling her Tuck was the more honest of the two.

Greta waited, using silence to her benefit. Her patience was rewarded when a couple moments later, Tuck met her gaze again.

"But you're right. I'll talk to the cops."

Greta exhaled. "Good."

"There's something else."

She nodded for him to continue.

"I think Blythe was having an affair."

Greta pressed her lips together. "What makes you say that?"

"She started getting these notes at the office. They'd show up in plain white envelopes. I didn't see what most of them said, but I glanced at one, and it was a sequence of random numbers. Really weird."

Greta swallowed down a yelp. *The code!*

"You think they were from a lover? What makes you say that?"

142

"A gut feeling, I guess. Blythe would always get excited when one arrived. Usually, it was slid under the back door when we opened in the morning. There was never any information on the envelope, but she would clutch them to her chest like they were her most precious possession. I caught her pouring over them on several occasions when it was her and I at work. She'd always stuff the letters into her desk drawer when I came around, though."

"Did you ask her about them?"

Tuck nodded. "She said she'd tell me about him when the time was right."

"Him?"

Tuck nodded again. "That's why I assumed it was another man. I figured she wanted to be free of Heath before she went public with her new relationship."

"Makes sense," Greta mused.

It also muddied the waters. If Blythe was having an affair, whoever she was seeing would need to be added to the suspect board, if for no other reason than because they were an unknown entity.

"You need to go to the authorities with all of this," Greta said when Tuck didn't continue. Her mind was reeling. Had the cops discovered the hidden envelopes during their search? Could they already be in evidence? She doubted it. If they had, she would have heard about it from Chief Sorenson or McHenry. They knew to look for something matching that very description as the partner to the book cipher.

That they hadn't mentioned it led Greta to believe Blythe had hidden the envelopes with the code somewhere else. But where? She wouldn't have taken them home. McHenry said they had searched the home she shared with Heath, and Greta doubted Blythe would want her love letters, coded or not, to be in any type of shared space with her husband.

So, the envelopes were another mystery.

"I'll talk to them," Tuck sat up straighter, then. "You've milked me for all the information I'm worth. Now I want to know what you were doing inside B'Jeweled."

Greta should have come up with an excuse while she was stuffing her face with tacos, but she found herself woefully underprepared to answer Tuck's question. She decided to stay as close to the truth as she could manage.

"I wasn't lying. My friends were actually ring shopping. I remembered what you said about Heath, and I thought I'd use their presence as a diversion to see if I could figure out what he had going on. I was looking for incriminating evidence that his jewelry sales weren't above board."

Tuck leaned in closer. "Did you find anything?"

"The authenticity paperwork I saw looked legit. But I'm not an expert." She eyed Josie across the restaurant. What, if anything, had they found out?

"You should mention your concerns about Heath when you talk to the police," she added pointedly. Hopefully, his account of the events leading up to Blythe's death would move the needle in favor of justice.

Chapter Twenty

Tuck must've been satisfied with Greta's excuse for being in Heath's office. He left the restaurant after they settled the bill.

"That looked intense," Josie said when Greta joined them. She glanced to the restaurant's door, as if worried Tuck would return. "What happened?"

"He startled me as I was escaping from B'Jeweled. Demanded to have dinner to hear what I was up to. I ended up getting way more information out of him than he got out of me." Greta filled in Josie, Ed, and the jewelry expert, Larry, on everything from the divorce papers she'd discovered to Tuck's admission that Blythe was having an affair.

"He actually saw the coded notes?" Ed sounded skeptical. "You sure that wasn't him spinning a story?"

"How would he know to do that?" Josie countered.

"Maybe he was in on her scheme, and the two of them were actually the ones communicating in code."

Greta thought over Ed's hypothesis. "It's possible, but why would Tuck tell me about it if he were in on it? It doesn't make sense. If he knew the coordinates for the treasure, he wouldn't tell me that they existed. He would go after it on his own and get what he wanted."

The table lapsed into silence until Greta spoke again. "What did you guys find out?"

"Heath is so sleazy." Josie's tone was dry.

"Guy's the worst," Ed agreed.

"Being the worst doesn't automatically mean he's a corrupt businessman, though. Or a murderer. Did you get anything concrete?" Greta let her gaze bounce to Larry, who, to this point, had been sitting on the edge of the booth observing the back and forth between her and her friends with great interest.

He sat up straighter. "It's difficult to say without an actual sample of a gemstone to look at, but judging by the authenticity papers alone, I think there's something off with the diamonds he showed us."

Greta sucked in a breath. "Can you be sure?"

"No. Not without more information," Larry said. "But it's a good bet." He pulled out a folder. "See this documentation?"

Greta nodded, scanning authenticity papers that looked like the ones she had seen in Heath's office.

"The appraiser listed here looks good at face value, and his credentials and web presence would probably be enough for your everyday shopper to think he was above board, but he's lacking the certification within the industry that all appraisers are supposed to have."

"Basically, he's got the wrong acronyms behind his name," Josie put in. "Larry said jewelry appraisers are supposed to have xyz credentials, and he has wyz."

"My guess is the guy's a phony." Larry was about to return the paperwork to his bag, but Greta put her hand on top of it, stopping him. She peered more closely at the name of the appraiser on the bottom of the sheet. "That's the same name Heath had scribbled on a sheet of paper in his desk drawer, along with a phone number."

Larry looked thoughtful. "It wouldn't surprise me that Heath would have his phony appraiser on speed dial. If he needs a new authenticity document worked up quick, he wouldn't want to wait long."

Greta tipped her chin. "What next? Is there any way to prove this, or does Heath keep getting away with defrauding people?" She put her palm to her forehead. "Oh, gosh. I didn't even think about the disgruntled customer I saw the first time I went into B'Jeweled. If he, or anyone else, discovered they'd been cheated and they thought it was Blythe behind the scheme, they could have tracked her down and taken out their anger on her."

Larry looked a little green, and Greta had to wonder if he was regretting his willingness to help them out tonight.

Ed slapped him on the back. "You did good, man. We'll let the authorities take it from here."

Greta rose from the booth. "Let's hope Tuck makes good on his promise to share all he knows with the cops. If he doesn't, I will. The police need to take a closer look at Heath."

Josie slung her bag over her shoulder. "This did make me excited to go actual wedding ring shopping. Even if Heath is a total dirtball."

"I wanted to punch the guy." Ed tucked Josie to his side. "He has quite the wandering eye."

Greta knew that from experience.

Larry puffed up his chest a bit at this. "You know I'll be happy to help you with all your wedding ring needs."

He and the happy couple fell into step as they left the restaurant. Greta trailed behind them and made a promise that when it was time to shop for jewelry, she'd patronize Larry, too. The man did them a solid tonight, lending his time and expertise to their sleuthing efforts.

She told her friends she'd see them in the morning and pulled up her mom's contact on her phone before starting her car. She waited for her cell to sync with her car's speakers and hit dial.

"Hi, G!" Her mom's cheerful voice sounded after only one ring. "How's it going?"

"Can't complain. I was hoping to pick your brain about divorce."

The silence on the other end of the line made Greta realize that her statement was a giant plot twist.

"Divorce?" her mom repeated slowly, her voice rising in question at the end.

Louisa Plank, Greta's mom, was a lawyer with over thirty years of experience. She worked first in Chicago as a defense attorney before retreating to the Wisconsin Northwoods for a quieter career as the neighboring town of Churchill's one and only lawyer in residence.

Greta brought her up to speed on what she had discovered and why she was looking into Blythe's death. "The police actually asked me for help this time. Can you believe that?"

"I can. You're a great resource," Louisa said staunchly. "Can't say I like the thought of you snooping in a potential killer's back office, though."

Greta sighed. Everyone was making a big deal out of that. She supposed she should be grateful to have so many people looking out for her.

"I wasn't alone," she pointed out. "Josie and Ed had my back. Anyway, I'm wondering how this all works. If Blythe served Heath with papers, but the form she gave him was left unsigned, where is the process at?"

"Well, now, let's think about this." Her mom launched into a giant spiel about divorce proceedings from state to state and what Wisconsin law said. "What exactly did you see?"

"There was a form with some letters and numbers on the top. I can text you a picture when I'm not driving. I think it said, 'Admission of Service.'"

Her mom hummed. "You said that one was blank?"

"Yeah."

"That would mean that this Heath character didn't acknowledge that he'd been served papers. At least he hadn't done so before his wife was killed."

"Walk me through what would have happened, if there hadn't been a murder."

Louisa cleared her throat. "Well, somehow, Heath would have had to acknowledge receipt. If he refused, the authorities may have gotten involved. After that, if there were any stipulations from either end, or if Heath wanted to make a counterclaim, he could have done so. Temporary orders would have been established, and the one hundred twenty-day waiting period would go into effect before anything would become final."

"So, it's not like a person can file for divorce and be granted it immediately?"

"No. The courts want to ensure there's enough time for mediation. If children are involved, this is when a custody arrangement would be finalized. And you have to have time for asset distribution."

"Got it." Greta fell silent. The more she thought about it, the more she had to admit that Heath killing Blythe immediately after being served divorce papers didn't make a ton of sense. He would have had time to figure out his next steps, and he wouldn't have needed to do anything rash. Blythe wasn't going to be able to dislodge from their relationship immediately.

Then again, if he panicked—which the mode of killing lent itself to—he could have lost it and killed Blythe in a fit of rage. Based on what Tuck said about the door situation at B'Jeweled, it wasn't so far-fetched.

"Would there be a record of the divorce proceedings, if Heath hadn't filled out the admission paperwork?" Greta asked.

"Blythe would've had to file all her paperwork with the circuit court, so yes. There would be a paper trail of the divorce."

Greta mulled that over. Blythe owned B'Jeweled. If she divorced him, she'd take the business. If he was selling shoddy gems and taking some sort of illegal cut, he would lose his income source or be exposed as a fraud. "I wonder if Heath knew that."

"Divorce proceedings are a complicated process. Until you're in it, many folks don't know what it all entails."

Greta nodded, though her mom couldn't see her. "I'm wondering if Heath was up to something shady that a divorce would bring to light. He might've silenced her for good to try to keep his secrets secret."

Louisa's voice lowered. "That thought makes me shudder."

"You and me both." Greta gripped the steering wheel tighter before forcing herself to relax her hands. "This is helpful, Mom. Thanks."

The two passed the rest of Greta's drive home, discussing how the library conference was going and details for the upcoming weekend. When Greta pulled into her driveway, she said goodbye.

In the distance, thunder rumbled, and Greta shivered. There was a bite in the April evening air. Winter held on a little extra at night. Greta hurried inside, grateful to flip on the lights in her cabin and feel the warmth of the space seep into her bones.

"Hiya, buddy." She bent and stroked Biff. When lightning flashed through the large, glass sliding door that led to Greta's deck, Biff scampered away. Greta discarded her things and, after grabbing a drink of water, took the suspect board from her closet. She added details about Tuck and Heath and, under the suspect column, she added *Blythe's boyfriend?*

Her phone rang, and Greta scrambled to retrieve it from her bag before it was too late.

"McHenry. Hi!"

"Hey, are you home?"

"I am."

"Care for any company?"

"I'd love some." Greta smiled. "Come on over."

"See you in a minute." McHenry disconnected the call, and Greta went into the kitchen to fix a quick snack plate for the two of them to share.

Outside, the skies opened up, and rain poured down, pelting her driveway and making everything out of Greta's kitchen window look distorted—like she was peering at it through an improperly focused lens.

While she was at the sink, headlights cut through the spring thunderstorm. She went to the front door to let McHenry in, but her cell phone jangled from where she left it in the living room.

She opened the front door and waved to McHenry before darting back into the living room. She checked the screen and didn't recognize the number, so she silenced the ringtone.

McHenry shuffled inside, soaking wet. "I'm making a mess of your floors," he said by way of greeting.

"Don't worry about it. Let me grab you some towels. Come on in."

McHenry toed off his shoes and stood in the kitchen while Greta flitted about.

Her phone started up again, and she checked the caller ID. It was the same number. She squinted at it. "I should make sure it's not one of the librarians who needs me for something."

McHenry motioned for her to answer.

She clicked *accept* on her home screen. "Hello?"

There was a cacophony of sound on the other end of the line, and it took Greta a moment to realize she was listening to a combination of wind and rain.

"Greta? Greta. Hey. It's me."

Greta pressed her phone more firmly to her ear. She could barely make out the voice on the other end. "Who is this?"

"Greta? Can you hear me? It's Nathan. I'm—"

He cut out, and Greta moaned. "Nathan. What is it? Where are you?"

"Bob—I found—come he—show—"

"Nathan, you're breaking up. I'm sorry. I don't understand."

"Hur—This is big, and I—"

Greta pulled her phone away from her ear to see if the call had dropped completely. Her screen showed the call was still active.

"You're at Bobber's Bar?" she asked, trying again. "Why don't you go back to the cabins? It's miserable outside."

"I know, but you've got to see this. I—"

With that, there was dead silence in Greta's ear. It was as if Nathan had hung up. She stared at her phone as McHenry reemerged from the bathroom where he'd gone to towel off.

She must've been scowling because he immediately asked, "What's wrong?"

"That was Nathan. He's outside at Bobber's Bar. He said he had something he wanted to show me."

He frowned. "In this weather?"

"I know. It's weird. And why is he calling me? I've told him I don't want anything to do with him." Greta stared at her phone, half waiting for Nathan to call back.

When her phone didn't ring after a couple seconds, she looked over to McHenry. The longer strands of his hair were sticking up off the top of his head, like he had ruffled them with the towel and not bothered to smooth them out.

Greta walked over to him and tousled his hair with her hand. He let her before grabbing her wrist in a gentle grip and squeezing.

"You look concerned," she said.

"I am. We should drive over to Bobber's and see for ourselves. I don't like this."

Greta peered up at McHenry. He had small dark circles under his eyes, and she would guess the last thing he wanted to do was go back out in the elements, but he was already looping their fingers together and tugging her to the door. "Come on. I'll drive."

They made the trip back into town in under five minutes, even with the torrential rain still pouring down.

McHenry parked in the lot outside Bobber's Bar. They sprinted inside, trying to dodge the quarter-sized raindrops.

When the door slammed behind them, Rob glanced up from the bar. Greta looked around, but she didn't see any sign of Nathan. She approached Rob, grimacing at the trail of puddles she left in her wake. McHenry followed closely behind her.

"Quite the storm we're having out there." Rob nodded toward the window as lighting cracked across the sky.

"Sure is. Have you seen Nathan in here tonight," Greta asked.

Rob shook his head, frowning. "Not since dinner time. He was in with that author. What's his name?"

"Nico," Greta supplied.

"Right. Him. The two of them ate together, but then they left, and I haven't seen them since. Sorry."

"No problem. Thanks." Greta and McHenry turned and retraced their waterlogged steps to the door.

Greta lingered in the entryway, not wanting to sprint into the storm without a game plan. "Maybe we should check at Nico's cabin?"

"I'll go. You stay here where it's dry."

"Absolutely not," Greta argued. "I'm going with you."

McHenry nodded and grabbed her hand. They took off at a brisk pace around the side of Bobber's Bar. The rain pelted Greta in the face and she squinted against the sting of it. The front porch stoop at Nico's cabin was illuminated by a single outdoor light. As Greta and McHenry drew closer, Greta's gaze bounced toward the windows for any sign of the two men inside, but the cabin looked dark.

McHenry's breath hitched next to her, and he muttered a curse.

"What is it?" Greta snapped her gaze to his, but he was picking up his pace, staring straight ahead at the side of the porch stoop.

Greta followed his line of vision and soon understood McHenry's urgency.

There was a limp figure slumped against the porch. McHenry pulled her to a stop a few feet off, but it was impossible to mistake the immobile mass of Nathan.

Chapter Twenty-One

Greta's scream was stolen from her lips and tossed away in the wind.

McHenry sprinted forward, keeping a firm grip on her. With his opposite hand, he placed his fingers to Nathan's neck. "He's got a pulse! It's faint, but it's there."

Greta fumbled for her phone and dialed 9-1-1 as McHenry knelt beside Nathan, listening for respiration. When the dispatcher picked up, she relayed where she was and what was going on as best she could in the elements.

"Hang on, Nathan," she muttered as she waited for the ambulance to arrive.

His face was slick with rain, and his hair matted to his forehead. He wasn't wearing a jacket, and his short-sleeved Polo shirt was soaked through. His lips had turned a purplish-blueish hue, and if she hadn't had McHenry's reassurance that he was still alive, Greta would have been convinced otherwise. She scanned the grounds, but it was impossible to see beyond the muted glow of the single porch light. It seemed to be trained on Nathan's body, highlighting the dreadful state he was in.

Greta's gaze caught on something white in Nathan's left hand. "Mark, look."

He glanced up at her, and she pointed to Nathan's clenched fingers.

McHenry shifted and carefully pried Nathan's fist open to reveal a fragment of a sheet of paper. He stood and held it close to his chest, trying to shield it from the rain.

"What is it?" Greta shouted over the wind.

"Not sure. It's only a corner." McHenry cupped the paper with his hand, as if he was cradling a baby animal that he was trying to keep protected.

She inched closer to his side, pressing herself into him and trying to salvage the paper before it turned to mush in the rain. She peeked at the front of it, and though the ink was starting to blur, the gist of the content was unmistakable based on the pattern and sequence of numbers outlined.

Her gaze collided with McHenry's, and in his eyes, she saw a flicker of fear. "It's part of the ciphertext for the book code."

His nod was grim. Nathan was likely hurt because of it—the very piece of intel Greta had been tasked with uncovering.

Before Greta could dwell on that, Officer Clarkson arrived from the police station followed quickly by the EMTs. They administered supplemental oxygen and got Nathan loaded into the back of the ambulance.

"He's got a puncture wound on his upper arm," McHenry said to one of the technicians, shooting a glance at Officer Clarkson.

Greta sucked in a breath. Could that mean Nathan was drugged? She placed her palm against her forehead, feeling lightheaded. Who did this to him? Would he recover? And what had he been trying to tell her over the phone? Whatever it was, was it the reason he was lying on the brink of death?

Greta didn't realize she was trembling until McHenry strode over and wrapped her in his arms. He was drenched, but she sunk into his embrace.

"Let's get you inside." He turned her to the bar.

"B-but the scene." Greta's teeth chattered. "Don't you need to p-process things here?"

"Clarkson has things under control for now." Over her head, McHenry looked to the junior officer, who produced an evidence bag which McHenry slipped the ripped code into, before he steered her toward the back entrance. The lights of the emergency vehicles had drawn the attention of those in the kitchen, and Rob poked his head out the back door.

"What's going on?" He held the door open for McHenry to usher Greta inside. "Are you alright?"

"We're fine." McHenry walked Greta toward a stool that was positioned against the nearside wall. "There's been another attack out back. I need to go check on things. Get her something warm to drink as soon as possible. Please," he added, voice strained.

Rob's eyebrows shot up, but he quickly nodded and turned to Greta. "Tea or coffee?"

Greta would love nothing more than the bitter taste of coffee right now, but if she had a cup at this hour, she'd be up all night. At this point, she was going to need all the help sleeping she could get. "Tea would be g-great. Non-caffeinated if you have it."

"On it."

Suz bustled into the kitchen. "Greta, oh my stars. What happened? What do you need?"

McHenry gave Greta's shoulder a squeeze and disappeared outside. Greta missed his presence instantly, but she tugged her shoulders back and blew out a breath. She explained what they had found near the cabin behind the bar, leaving out the fact that Nathan had called her before the attack and the discovery of the code in his hand.

A thought hit Greta. He might have been on the phone with her *when* he was attacked. If whoever hurt him overheard him talking to her, would they come for her next? They might, if they thought he shared pertinent information with her.

Greta darted a gaze around. Could the Hawlers have been behind Nathan's attack? Neither Suz's nor Rob's clothes appeared wet. Their shoes weren't caked with mud like hers were. But they could have easily shed them and changed before she and McHenry arrived, after attacking Nathan. Both of the Hawlers wore baseball caps, likely for sanitary purposes in the kitchen, but she couldn't tell if their hair was damp from the rain. And where was Ace? Could his family be covering for him?

Suz took the mug of tea Rob had prepared and thrust it into Greta's hands. "That should help you warm up a bit, honey. What a fright you had!"

Greta nodded, unsure what to say. Her mind was whipping from one thought to the next. She took a tentative sip, bracing her lips against the heat of the liquid.

"Thank you for this." She held up the mug slightly. "It was a shock."

"Did you know that guy well?" Rob gestured to the back entrance. "Nathan, or whatever his name is...was?" He waited for her to confirm or deny Nathan's status.

"Is. He had a pulse when they loaded him up. They were headed to the hospital."

Suz clasped her hands together over her chest, and relief washed over her face, dulling the stress lines in her forehead.

"That's good." Rob turned and started wiping down the kitchen counters. "What was he doing out there?" he asked over his shoulder.

"I have no idea."

"But you were looking for him?" Rob eyed her again.

Greta took another sip of tea, buying herself time to formulate a generic answer. "We were. He called me, but we had a bad connection. All I made out was that he was here."

"Here, at the bar?" Suz's eyes went wide.

"I heard him say Bobber's, but the rest was static. We figured we'd pop over and see for ourselves. And then we found him...like that." Greta shuddered. If they hadn't come, it might have been too late. Nathan might have succumbed to the drugs. She blinked against the thought. He wasn't her favorite person—far from it—but she didn't wish him dead.

She cleared her mind, focusing instead on a missing piece of the Nathan puzzle. She raised her voice to catch Rob's attention. He had moved to the far side of the kitchen. "You said he was in with Nico earlier?"

"They had dinner," Rob said.

Greta hummed. Where was the author now? Was it a pure coincidence that Nathan was found right outside the cabin where Nico was staying? Or did Nico have something to do with Nathan's current state?

Red and blue lights shone through the kitchen's high windows and the transom on the kitchen's back door. Greta hated that McHenry was out in the storm, dealing with yet another catastrophe. But what could she do?

"Rob?" a feminine voice called from the front of the bar, and a moment later, the kitchen door swung inward, and Sadie appeared. She was wearing a raincoat and oversized rain boots. Grass and mud were splattered along the bottoms. Her eyes were saucers as she scanned the room. "What's going on?"

Rob walked over to his girlfriend and dropped a kiss against her forehead. "That librarian, Nathan, was injured out back."

Sadie looked horrified as she shucked off her jacket. "Injured how?"

"I'm not entirely sure. He was unconscious, though, I think." Rob glanced at Greta for clarification, but she didn't respond. She wasn't about to give details on what she had seen before McHenry gave her permission.

An unwelcome thought hit her. Could Sadie have been behind Nathan's attack? Had she been nearby and used the excuse of coming to see Rob at work to cover her tracks? Greta took a minute and assessed Sadie's composure. She wasn't shaky. Her eyes weren't darting around. Other than her soiled rain gear, she looked completely put together. Greta let out a sigh of relief that Sadie wasn't acting guilty.

"That's terrible. I hope he'll be okay." Sadie's voice was kind.

"I'm going to go tidy up behind the bar." Suz stopped by Sadie and gave her a brief hug. "Help yourself to something to drink, dear."

"Thanks, Mrs. Hawler." Sadie smiled, and then Suz was gone, and Greta found herself alone with Rob and Sadie. Her whole body was exhausted. Her limbs hung heavy, and her head felt thick with a combination of worry and confusion.

Outside, the storm continued to rage, with rain beating against the exterior walls of the bar and providing a steady hum of white noise. Greta sipped her tea and observed the couple. Sadie was quiet as Rob wiped down the work surfaces in the kitchen.

Eventually, he tossed his dishcloth in the laundry bin and swiveled his attention to the two of them.

"I like your bumper sticker," Greta said.

By way of an icebreaker, it wasn't much, but given her mental state, Greta patted herself on the back for not coming right out and asking him to tell her the truth about where he was on Monday.

Rob chuckled. "The bigfoot one?" When Greta nodded, he smiled. "It's an inside joke between my dad and me from way back when he was teaching me to drive."

"I don't think I know this story." Sadie's shoulders dropped from up closer to her ears, and a small smile touched her lips.

"My dad was afraid I was going to turn into a reckless driver. He was always reminding me to cover the brake and drive defensively. I was more concerned with how fast I could go on these back country roads. One time, when we were out in the middle of nowhere practicing, I told him, 'I won't brake for anyone but bigfoot out here.'" Rob shook his head wryly. "I was so proud of myself for the one-liner that I had a bumper sticker made up. Stuck it on the back of the truck I'd be driving in all my teenage, angsty glory. But my dad was definitely onto something. I learned my lesson the first time I got into a fender bender."

Greta smiled behind her cup. Rob delivered his story with the exact right mixture of humility and humor.

"I always feel safe when you drive these days." Sadie squeezed Rob's bicep.

"What can I say? I'm a changed man."

The three of them laughed, and as silence descended, Greta decided to go for it. She kept her voice nonchalant. "I saw your truck in Karrington earlier this week. Had myself a good laugh when I saw the bumper sticker, and then put it together that it was you when I saw the same truck parked back here. Monday, I think it was."

The mood in the kitchen shifted almost tangibly. Rob stiffened, and Sadie's cheeks paled.

"You sure it was me?" Rob rubbed against the peach fuzz on his jawline. "I don't think I was in Karrington on Monday."

Greta hummed. "Well, you told me the bumper sticker is basically one of a kind, and I saw it in Karrington on Monday afternoon. Right outside B'Jeweled, actually. You know, the place Blythe Prescott owned."

Judging by the way her knuckles had turned white, Sadie was gripping Rob's bicep with full force.

"Robbie." She whispered his name, pleading.

He shook his head firmly at her before cutting a suspicious look to Greta. "Why do you care?"

"I want to know what you were doing with Blythe on the day she died. But if you don't want to tell me, that's fine. I assume you already told the police. They're the ones who need this information so they can put a clear picture of Blythe's day together. I'm just a curious civilian, so don't mind me."

"I wasn't with Blythe on the day she died." Rob raised his voice, but when Sadie whimpered next to him, he sighed. "At least not at B'Jeweled."

"If not there, then where?"

Rob shot a look at the door leading to the bar and front end of the restaurant. "I was at the Karrington Community College," he said, his voice low. "Blythe and I had a class together on Monday, so I saw her there, but that's it. I certainly didn't kill her if that's what you're implying."

Greta held up her hand. "I didn't say anything about that." She flicked her gaze to Sadie, who had started trembling. "Are you okay, Sadie?"

"I'm fine," Sadie squeaked. "I hate lying," she added in a whisper.

"Aw, babe, I'm sorry." Rob wrapped Sadie in a hug.

"What did you lie about?" Greta asked when the two pulled apart.

Rob kept Sadie tucked under his arm. "It's all my fault. My parents think I spend Mondays with Sadie." He looked to the door, like he was afraid his mom would reappear at any minute. "I don't want them to know I'm taking classes."

"Why not?"

"Because I'm getting an associate's degree in history." He looked at her expectantly.

It didn't take Greta long to connect the dots. "Which is not restaurant management," she said.

"Exactly. My mom and dad are dead set on me taking over for them here at Bobber's, but that's not what I want to do. It'll break their hearts when I tell them, and I haven't had the guts to do it yet." Rob sighed. "So, I'm taking classes, and Sadie's been covering for me. When everything went down on Monday, I called her and told her to act like she did every Monday."

"But wouldn't school be a solid alibi for you either way?"

"Yeah, but I didn't need my secret coming out with all of this going down. My parents are stressed enough as it is."

160

Greta thought about that. She had several follow-up questions, but she didn't know where to begin.

"Rob's been working so hard. I'm really proud of him, and I didn't want to be the one to spoil his plans or tip his parents off before he was ready to tell them the truth. But lying to the police has been eating me alive," Sadie admitted.

"You need to fix that," Greta said matter-of-factly.

Rob grimaced. "I know. I know. I will. I swear I had nothing to do with what happened to Blythe."

"But you were in classes with her?"

Rob nodded.

"And with Tuck White?"

Rob's eyes flashed. "How did you...how do you—?" He cut himself off. "How?"

"I've run into him a couple times. He said he was a student at the community college, too. With Blythe. Tuck also said she talked to you about purchasing this property." Greta hadn't known how Blythe had gotten a hold of Rob to make her pitch, but it made sense now.

Rob looked a little like a frightened bunny, searching for an escape from a circling bald eagle. In this case, she was the eagle, and she wasn't going to let him out of her sight until she had answers.

"She brought it up to me, yeah. But I told her she'd have to talk to my parents. I have no say in this business. Not yet, anyway."

"She did talk to your parents, then?"

Rob shifted his weight between his legs. "I don't know," he hedged.

Greta stared him down with her best mean librarian glower. She didn't use it much, but it did the job.

"Fine. I overheard her talking to my dad over the weekend. She was threatening him. He didn't know I was still around, and I slipped out of the kitchen before he came in from out back after confronting her." Rob's skin had faded paler as he spoke.

Greta let her voice soften. "You're worried your dad might have had something to do with Blythe's death."

"He would never. At least I don't think..." Rob swallowed. "But..."

Sadie wrapped her arm around Rob's waist. "But your dad loves this business, and you think he might've done anything to save it. No one had eyes on him when Blythe was killed. But like I've told you a million times, it's not your problem to solve. You should let the police handle it."

Rob's eyes flashed, and he took a step away from Sadie. "He's my dad, Sad. It's awful of me to think that he could have done this. It's all my fault, anyway. If I hadn't crossed paths with Blythe at school, she wouldn't have had easy access to our family. I was trying to be a good friend and make people like me. I invited her here to our property on more than one occasion. She said she was always intrigued by old supper clubs here in the Northwoods and the history associated with them. I got caught up in the conversation. When she started talking about gangsters and buried treasure being nearby, I was fascinated. She asked me a bunch of questions, but I didn't think anything of it, and I couldn't tell her much. I don't really know the history of this place. Something I plan to change now." He shook his head. "Either way, I brought the trouble to our door."

"You had no idea what she was after," Sadie reminded him.

But Rob dragged a hand through his hair, leaving it stuck in all directions. "I entertained her proposition to buy the place. At least, at first. Thought it might soften the blow of my news if I brought my parents a willing buyer straight off." Rob started pacing. "But then I realized it was my parents' business, not mine. I had no right to go behind their back like that. I told Blythe as much. She got angry. She renewed her efforts to get her claws in around here. She started making complaints to the health department."

"Your mom told me about that. Your parents run a good business. They'll pass their next inspection fine," Greta said.

"Still." Rob's face was marked with stress lines. "Blythe might not have even pursued her treasure hunt in the first place if it wasn't for me handing her the keys to the kingdom without any resistance. It's all my fault."

Greta doubted that Blythe would have given up so easily. Not when the woman knew from her genealogy research she had gangster ties in her bloodline. She would have sought information regardless of whether or not she ran into Rob. From the little she knew about Blythe, the woman was like a bloodhound. She wanted the glory and the excitement that came with the hunt.

"If I may," Greta said after clearing her throat. "None of this is your fault. The truth is always the right course. Tell the police what you know. Trust your dad's innocence, and let the chips fall where they may."

Before Rob could say anything in response, Suz bustled back into the kitchen. "Greta, that detective of yours is out front. He said he's ready to take you home."

Greta rose from her seat, placing the teacup on the counter. She offered Rob and Sadie what she hoped was an encouraging look and followed Suz into the dining room.

McHenry made quick work of shuttling her outside into his car. When the driver's door slammed behind him, McHenry turned in the seat. "We got word that Nathan is stable. He's unconscious, and they don't know when he'll wake up. I haven't heard about brain activity yet, but they'll check that, I'm sure."

Greta blew out a breath. In other words, there was no telling *if* he would wake up, and if he did, no one knew if he would remember who attacked him. "How did this happen?"

"He got himself into the mess," McHenry said quietly.

He was right. Nathan stuck his nose where it didn't belong. No one deserved to be hurt like that, but if Nathan hadn't pushed, he wouldn't have found himself unconscious at the hospital.

"This is why I don't like you around active cases, Greta." McHenry's voice was pleading.

"I know. I get it." She did. She didn't want to wind up like Nathan any more than McHenry wanted to see her hurt.

He pulled into her driveway and put the car in park. "Are you going to be okay here tonight by yourself? I know you and Nathan weren't close, but you had a history with him."

Greta placed her hand on his forearm. "I'll be fine. Thank you for taking care of me. Mostly, it's you I'm concerned about. You have to run headlong into scenarios that could land you in the hospital like Nathan." *Or worse.* Greta tried hard not to think about that part of McHenry's job, but it was difficult not to on nights like tonight.

"This is what I'm trained for," he said matter-of-factly.

"I know. I trust you. I do." Greta leaned over the console and kissed McHenry. "I'll be at the library in the morning. Stop by?"

"I'll bring the coffee." A hint of a smile tugged at McHenry's lips.

She smiled back and went to get out of the car. "Oh." She stopped and turned back to him. "I'm hoping Rob Hawler comes to you, but if not, someone should probably press him on his alibi. He didn't do it, but he wasn't where he said he was."

McHenry's jaw clenched. "I'm sick and tired of people not telling the truth."

"I know. But he's only a kid. His girlfriend, too. Try not to be too hard on them."

McHenry sighed, but he gave one nod in response. Greta pecked him once more on the cheek before running up to her door.

Once inside, she got Biff settled and took a hot shower. She returned to the living room wearing flannel pajamas. She'd yet to put them up for the approaching warm-weather season. In Wisconsin, you never knew when you needed your winter sleepwear.

Greta paced her small living room, chewing on the corner of her lip. She could barely keep track of all the moving parts of this case, between the Hawler family, Heath, Tuck, and Nico. Biff watched her walk back and forth, jumping up onto the back of the couch and mirroring her movements. When Greta finally plopped down with a huff, he darted out of the room.

She grabbed for her cell phone and typed a quick message to Josie and Iris.

Greta: Nathan was attacked tonight outside Bobber's Bar. We're not sure why.

Josie: What?

Iris: Is he okay?

Greta: Unconscious last I heard. At the hospital in Karrington.

Greta: He tried to tell me something over the phone, but our connection was bad because of the storm.

Josie: What now?

Greta: McHenry is freaked about my involvement.

Greta: I'm a little freaked myself, to be honest.

Iris: Understandable.

Greta pressed her lips into her mouth over and over as she thought about next steps.

Greta: The police will get in touch with Nathan's wife. I'm sure she'll come here. Maybe you can walk with her through his cabin over at Ed's, Jos?

Josie: What am I looking for?

Greta let her head fall back. That was the question this entire case hinged on. Had Nathan found what Blythe was looking for? Or at least directions for how to find it? Is that what the murderer didn't want him to uncover?

Greta: Not sure. He was holding a shred of the coded sequence. Maybe look for Blythe's box of research with the photocopied pages?

Greta: I'm grasping at straws, I know. <shrugging woman emoji>

Josie: Nah. I got you. I'll talk to Ed and we'll make sure one of us shows Nathan's wife around the place so we can get eyes on his things.

Greta didn't like the thought of exploiting Nathan's personal space, but at this point, she guessed he'd be glad for someone to figure out who did this to him. If they could find out what he knew, then they would be one step closer to closing the book on the case.

Chapter Twenty-Two

Rain continued the next morning, and the windows of the library were foggy. Greta could barely make out Main Street from where she stood behind the circulation desk, checking in titles. The library wasn't officially open for another forty-five minutes, but she'd called an emergency meeting with Fitz to talk about how to handle Nathan's attack.

Currently, her librarian comrade was pacing in front of her, dragging a hand through his hair. "What do we do? Cancel?"

Greta didn't answer him right away. There was definitely a pall on the day, and her spirits were low. Blythe's funeral was scheduled for that morning; Nathan was still unconscious, according to an early morning text from McHenry, and the weather mirrored her mood perfectly.

"This is a disaster." Fitz let his hands fall to his sides with a slap. "No one is going to remember anything about this conference but the murder that kicked it off and the attack on one of our own. Our reputations are basically ruined, Greta. *Ruined.*"

Greta had grown accustomed to Fitz's dramatics, but at this point, she couldn't care less what people thought of her. A year ago, Greta would have doubled down and worked tirelessly to prove herself if she thought the librarian community didn't hold her in high esteem, but she'd grown more confident in who she was and surrounded herself with people who cared about her well-being enough to know that things outside of her control didn't define her.

Still, she'd like to salvage the event if at all possible. "Let's plan to finish out the day. Everyone's still in town, so we may as well, right?"

A rap on the library door drew their attention.

A woman dressed in a sharp-looking black sheath dress with four-inch pumps and a slate-colored trench coat hanging open and falling to just above her knee waved back.

Greta cut out from behind the desk and flipped the lock, opening the door enough to smile out at the woman. "We're actually closed for another thirty minutes."

The woman stepped forward. "I know. I'm looking for Nico Eddison. It's urgent."

"I haven't seen him today." Greta blinked up at the woman who was at least six inches taller than her, especially since Greta was wearing flats with her pencil-legged pants and white-blouse ensemble.

"But you have seen him? This week, I mean." The woman's eyes scanned Greta's face with such alacrity, Greta wondered if she thought Nico was hiding in one of her pores.

"He's here for our event tomorrow."

The woman scoffed. "I should have known where to look."

"I'm sorry. Who are you?" Greta couldn't keep the confusion from her tone.

The woman thrust out a hand. "I'm Kerry Jefferson. Nico's literary agent. The man has been avoiding me all month."

Greta shook the proffered hand, digesting Kerry's words.

"Why would he be avoiding you?" Fitz joined the two women.

Kerry let out a mirthless chuckle. "Why? Because thanks to his abysmal last release, his career is imploding. He's in denial, and he doesn't want to hear tough truths from me. We need another book idea, and we need it *stat*, or all his credibility is going to be shot for the foreseeable future, and he can kiss his career goodbye. His previous publisher is this close to dropping him altogether."

Greta's mind flashed to the list of topics she and Iris had seen when they'd snooped around Nico's rental. He must not have shared his new material with his agent yet.

"Why is he in such dire straits?" Greta asked. She had only a cursory understanding of the publishing industry, but it was difficult to believe that one bad book ruined an author for life. All major authors had duds somewhere along the line. Most loyal readers were gracious enough to offer a second chance.

Kerry groaned and motioned to a chair. "May I sit?" She didn't wait for a response before she blew by Greta and slumped into one of the wooden seats at the library's research station.

Greta gaped at Fitz. He shrugged in return. They joined Kerry, who was massaging her temples. "Nico's last project more than tanked. It reduced his credibility as a historian and researcher.

"He wrote about the recent history of crypto-currency. But the main guy he interviewed as his *credible source*"—she made air quotes—"is being sued for heading a pump and dump scheme that scammed a bunch of people. I tried to talk Nico out of hitching his horse to this guy's wagon, but he wouldn't listen to me. He said writing about something that's recent history would make him a trailblazer. He stubbornly self-published that book without my blessing. His plans backfired." Her expression was completely forlorn. "I've worked tirelessly to mitigate the damage, and I'd say I've done a bang-up job for the most part."

Greta had to agree. Her research had only revealed a couple of news articles about Nico's self-published release, and even those didn't have a ton of detail. No one who was coordinating the Little Bo event had questioned his credibility. Perhaps they should have been more discerning.

"In case it wasn't obvious, if Nico's career is shot, then mine is, too," Kerry continued. "He's my biggest client. I've poured all my time and resources into helping him thrive, and this is how he repays me. By disappearing!"

"Maybe I can help you find him. Let me make a call."

Greta returned to the circulation desk and glanced at the library personnel directory, finding Cindi's phone number easily.

She dialed and held her breath. Cindi answered after a couple rings.

"Cindi, hi. This is Greta Plank calling from the library."

"What is it, Greta?"

"I'm wondering if you've seen Nico this morning, or if you know what his plans are for today?"

"I'm not his babysitter," Cindi snapped.

Greta took that as a no. "His agent is here looking for him. There might be an issue with his next project, and she'd like to get a hold of him."

Over the phone, Greta heard the unmistakable sound of the bell above the door of Mugs & Hugs.

"You're in luck, then." Cindi's voice grew distant as she called out, "Nico! Just the man I was looking for."

Greta looked over at Kerry. "He's at the café across the street."

Kerry bolted upright. "Don't tell him I'm coming," she shouted as she sprinted for the exit.

At the same time, Greta overheard Cindi say, "Your agent is here, and she's looking for you. What? Where are you going? Nico!"

"Cindi! Don't tip him off," Greta said through the phone.

From the sounds of things, it was too late.

"The nerve of that man, after I've been nothing but hospitable to him." Cindi's voice grew louder as she returned the phone to her mouth. "He sprinted out of here, Greta. I don't know what to tell you."

Greta sighed. "Okay. Thanks for your help."

Not.

"I'll be by later this afternoon to get things organized for tomorrow." Cindi shifted into work mode. "I trust you'll have my materials prepared."

"Absolutely." Greta tried to sound enthusiastic. She couldn't help but wonder if Nico would even show up for his presentation the next day if he was so dead-set on avoiding his agent. She chose not to think about that at the moment.

Cindi hung up without saying goodbye.

Greta exhaled and turned to Fitz. "I've said it before, and I'll say it again. There's never a dull moment around here."

Fitz nodded as McHenry strode into the library. As promised, he carried an extra to-go cup from Mugs & Hugs. Greta reached for it like a lifeline.

"Happier to see the coffee than me, huh?"

"Untrue." Greta sniffed the hazelnut aroma wafting out of the small opening in the lid. "It's a tie."

McHenry's lips twitched, and she met him on the far side of the circulation desk, going up on her tiptoes to place a quick kiss on his cheek. "Thank you for this, though. Seriously. We've already had our fair share of drama around here today, and we haven't even opened."

She and Fitz took turns telling McHenry about Nico's agent's arrival and what Kerry had told them about the state of Nico's writing affairs and finances.

McHenry frowned. "What a mess."

Fitz agreed. "Hopefully, you have a backup plan for tomorrow's programming."

"My backup plan is Cindi boring the crowd by talking for the entirety of the allotted time." Both Fitz and McHenry chuckled, but Greta wasn't kidding. With Blythe dead and Nico seemingly unreliable, she was out of options.

One problem at a time, though. Today, she had to navigate a librarian conference while one of their own lay in a hospital bed.

"Any news on Nathan?" she asked McHenry.

"No change. His wife got here. I spoke to her at the hospital late last night. The doctors told her they were doing everything they could for Nathan, but he was injected with Ketamine, and his body is having a difficult time metabolizing the amount of the drug he's been exposed to."

"Ketamine." Fitz stuck up his nose. "Like the club drug, Special K?"

Greta arched her brow at him, but Fitz shrugged in return. "What? Some of my friends got wild in college."

McHenry cleared his throat. "That's the same drug, yes. It can be used recreationally, but it's also used as a horse tranquilizer and in some medical settings. We're running under the assumption that someone injected him with the hopes of keeping him quiet."

"They tried to kill him with it." Greta hated the thought.

McHenry dipped his head in agreement. "It looks that way. Since we stumbled upon Nathan and the EMTs were able to administer counteractive treatment sooner rather than later, he's got a chance to survive it. One of the side-effects of a Ketamine overdose is amnesia, though, so there's no telling what he'll remember or how his brain will react when he wakes up."

"What a nightmare." Fitz shuddered. "I don't like the man, but that sounds awful."

The three of them stood silently, staring at the floor. Greta took a long sip of her latte to give herself something to do with her hands and to try to quell the nausea that was fighting its way into the back of her throat.

"I'll give you two a minute." Fitz gestured to the large meeting room at the back of the library. "I'm going to make sure the conference room is set up for the morning session on continuing ed."

"I'll meet you there in a bit," Greta said with a wave. She turned to McHenry. "Did Nathan's wife say anything that could help with the case? Did he tell her anything about what he was doing with regard to Blythe's death?"

McHenry shook his head. "She was completely in the dark."

Greta shouldn't be surprised, but the disappointment was still swift. "What about his cabin? Have the police searched it?"

"We walked through with Heather, his wife," McHenry clarified. "Josie was there, too."

McHenry shot her a suspicious look, and Greta felt a blush color her cheeks.

"Right," Greta said. "Josie said she would make sure Heather got what was needed. She's been helping Ed out more and more."

"Mmmhmm. She seemed especially curious about the paperwork strewn about."

Greta gasped. "Did you find anything helpful?"

"Handwritten notes that looked like research on Julian Vance."

"In Nathan's handwriting or Blythe's? Did he steal her box?"

"It was Nathan's handwriting, as confirmed by Heather."

Greta's shoulders slumped forward.

McHenry reached out a palm and gave her a quick squeeze. "We'll figure it out. If the killer went to such great lengths to hurt someone else, they must feel the walls closing in on them."

"What about the scrap of paper we found? Did you manage to decode any of it?"

"Officer Clarkson is setting to work on the code as we speak. We won't be able to figure out much, but any little bit would help, and hopefully, it'll shed some light on who Blythe was communicating with."

"Where did Nathan find it, though?" That's what Greta couldn't stop thinking about. It wasn't in Blythe's box of research. She was pretty sure it wasn't hidden at B'Jeweled, since both she and the police had searched the place. The letters Tuck had told her he'd seen must have been stowed somewhere, and somehow, Nathan stumbled upon them.

She wasn't sure if she should call him lucky, given his present state, but what she wouldn't give to get eyes on the prize.

McHenry checked his watch. "I've got to run. Rob Hawler made an appointment for this morning."

Greta perked up. "That's good. I hope you'll hear him out."

"I always do."

"Has Tuck White come by?"

McHenry nodded. "He's working with us to expose Heath Prescott's shady dealings at B'Jeweled. The state police have taken that angle of the case and run with it. They plan to bust Heath for fraud as soon as they have proof that he's passing off fake jewels as real ones."

"Good." Greta thought back to the man she'd seen in B'Jeweled the first day she'd stopped by. If others could be spared the financial and emotional toll of shoddy jewelry, all the better.

"Drinks tonight at my place when you're done?" McHenry asked. "We should celebrate the end of the WLO conference."

Greta sighed. Tonight seemed forever away when she had to face down the remainder of the day, but at least she had something to look forward to. "I'd love that."

McHenry placed a lingering kiss on her lips. Greta would have sunk further into it, but Josie and Iris showed up and started making smooching noises the moment they saw the couple.

Greta broke the kiss, her cheeks heating. She secretly loved that McHenry didn't move out of her personal space. She smiled up at him. "See you later?"

"Have a good day, Miss Plank." He winked, and her whole body felt warm. "Can't wait, Detective," she called after him.

Chapter Twenty-Three

"Y ou guys are cute." Josie wagged her eyebrows as she and Iris walked behind the desk. Josie gave them a quick run-down of her time in Nathan's cabin. She reiterated everything McHenry had shared, and Greta wished they'd discovered more.

"McHenry is meeting with Rob. Pretty sure he didn't do it, but his parents are still a question mark. Them, and Nico." Greta told her friends about his agent's arrival.

"It's suspicious that Nathan was found outside Nico's cabin." Iris tapped the circulation desk.

"Nico was the last person seen with Nathan," Greta told her.

Iris crossed her arms over her chest. "In that case, I bet he's hiding something."

"I didn't even ask McHenry if he had a chance to talk to him last night." Greta checked the clock on the wall. The morning sun had begun to warm the exterior windows, erasing the layer of fog, and through the panes, Greta could see a group of librarians walking toward the library.

"Time to open for the day, and then I've got to get back to the librarians." Greta propped the doors. When she returned to the circulation desk, she leaned toward Iris. "We may need to borrow your parents' key to Nico's cabin to search it again, don't you think?"

Iris's eyes widened. "I told you to talk me out of that if I ever tried it again, not suggest it."

Greta let loose a soft chuckle. "I know. But I feel like this whole thing has to hinge on Nico and something to do with his research"—she paused—"or lack thereof."

Nico's agent, Kerry slumped into the library followed by a *shush* of librarians, who quickly approached the desk and pegged Greta with a million questions.

"Did you hear?"

"How is he?"

"Do you think he'll recover?"

"Who did this to him?"

"Serves him right, I'd say."

"He may be annoying, but he didn't deserve this."

Greta held up her hands. "Fitz is waiting in the conference room. Let's all head that way, and we'll debrief together."

The librarians scuttled along, but Kerry remained, standing limply to the side of the research station. "Nico's gone."

Greta frowned and quickly introduced her to Josie and Iris.

"I'm sure he's not gone for good," Iris soothed. "All of his things are here. He wouldn't leave town without clearing out of his cabin."

"The presentation is tomorrow too. He's been completely on board with it," Josie said. "Maybe he panicked when he heard you were here. I'm sure when he cools off, he'll come around."

Kerry's postured drooped even further. "I've been pretty aggressive. He stopped answering my calls and texts earlier this week. I shudder to think how his missed call log makes me look. Like a deranged ex-girlfriend or something."

Greta tried to look supportive. "Make yourself at home here. Nico will turn up. Iris and Josie can help you if you need anything, but I've got to run."

Greta made her way to the conference room, pausing at a cracked door to one of the meeting rooms. She poked her head inside. "Anyone in here?"

The room was empty, but there was an intricate diagram written on large sheets of poster board tacked to the adjacent wall. She stepped forward, triggering the motion sensor lights. "Wow," she said on an exhale. It was a family tree, and Julian Vance was at its center.

"Hold on, hold on! She'll be here shortly, and we'll get started." Fitz's strained voice reached Greta's ear, and she whispered a curse under her breath. She snapped a series of photos of the tree. She'd dissect it later.

Pocketing her phone, Greta exited the room and shut the door. She hurried to the large conference room, where every pair of librarian eyes bounced to her.

Greta gulped. She tried to exude confidence as she stood behind the podium at the front of the room. She'd stick to the facts. It was all she could do. And hadn't she advised Rob that the truth was always the right course?

"Good morning, everyone. As I'm sure most of you have heard, Nathan was found injured last night. It appears he was attacked near Bobber's Bar." A ripple of shock flowed through the room. "He's unconscious, but alive, and his wife is with him now. I'm afraid I don't have any more information to share at this time."

"His attack has something to do with the woman who died earlier this week, doesn't it?" One of Nathan's colleagues from Green Bay spoke from the back of the room.

"I truly don't know." Greta was dying to ask the room if anyone knew what Nathan was doing last night, but she didn't want to step on the toes of the police, and she didn't want to speculate, so instead, she said, "If anyone has any information that would be helpful in figuring out who did this to Nathan or what he was doing last night, I'd encourage you to go talk to the police immediately. Their offices are right down the hall. Otherwise, we're going to continue for the day."

Greta's attention was trained on the table of Green Bay librarians, many of whom she used to work with, as she introduced the first speaker of the morning. They were Nathan's crew, and if he'd let anyone in on his plans for the previous evening, it would've been them. Their heads were together as Greta turned over the mic to a seasoned librarian from the Madison area who was set to talk about continuing education.

Greta stepped to the side of the room and leaned against the wall nearest to the exit, where Fitz was standing. When one of the Green Bay librarians stood and caught her eye, Greta dipped her chin and motioned for her to follow her outside.

"Is everything alright?" she asked the woman. Her name was Diane, and she worked as a children's librarian at Nathan's branch. Greta remembered her as a straight shooter. Gruff, but kind.

"I'm going to go tell the police what I know, or at least what Nathan said to me yesterday. It's been bugging me."

Greta nodded. She was bursting to ask what it was, but she refrained. "The authorities would appreciate any and all tips, I'm sure. This is quite the puzzle."

Diane snorted. "Funny word choice. Nathan said he was sure he was going to find the missing piece of the puzzle last night."

"What puzzle?"

"He's been going on and on about how the dead woman, what was her name?"

"Blythe," Greta supplied.

"Right. Blythe. He said he found out she was using a book cipher to decode secret messages. He made it his goal to figure out the puzzle."

"How did he know that?" Greta rifled back through her mind. Had she told Nathan about the *Pride and Prejudice* book? No. She mentioned it at the crime scene, explaining that she'd met Heath when she tried to return Blythe's book, but at that point, she had no idea it was a book cipher. Since then, she'd been careful to avoid reading Nathan in. So, who let it slip?

"He was bragging to us yesterday how he overheard your Chief of Police here on the phone with someone talking about a book cipher. He pieced together the information from what he heard on the call."

Greta's heart sank.

"He also said *you* were working on the cipher." Diane raised her eyebrows.

Greta wouldn't lie. "The police asked me to look into it, but once I figured out it was a cipher, that was pretty much all I could help them with. They didn't have access to the ciphertext sequence."

Diane nibbled on her lip. "I wonder if that's what Nathan thought he could find yesterday. He said something about how he thought Nico held the key."

That was in line with Greta's suspicions, too. Now, she was dying to get back inside Nico's cabin. "Telling all of this to the police is a smart call. If you go out of the library and turn left, you'll run into the back door of the police station. You can't miss it."

Diane squared her shoulders and set off.

Greta slipped into the conference room again, and Fitz arched his eyebrows.

Greta pressed her lips together and held up a finger, signaling him to give her a minute. She'd fill him in when they weren't in a room full of librarians.

Chapter Twenty-Four

When the group broke for lunch, Greta made sure everyone was taken care of, reminding them to be in Karrington for the closing session in a couple hours. Next, she touched base with Josie and Iris, who said Kerry had left to check into a hotel in Karrington.

"Are you remembering that I have this afternoon off?" Josie asked. "I'm volunteering over at the high school, and then I promised Ed I would go for a sunset canoe ride with him."

Greta smiled. "Yep. Have a great night."

"I'll be manning the desk while you wrap up the conference, but here." Iris wedged a key off her key ring. "If the opportunity presents itself for you to"—she cleared her throat—"*clean* Nico's cabin, now you'll have access."

Greta palmed the key. "Thank you both. Thanks for all your help covering this week. It's been a doozy."

"You can say that again." Josie pointed between the three of them. "When this is all over, I need your opinion on some wedding dresses."

Greta and Iris took turns gushing, and Greta left the library in a cheerful mood, despite the circumstances. She decided to pop into Mugs & Hugs to grab a mid-day pick-me-up from Allison before she made the trek to Karrington to bring the conference to its conclusion.

Greta walked across the parking lot, and a cool spring wind whipped her curls into her face. Fitz drove by her and tooted his horn. She waved and crossed the street.

Inside the café, the warm, yellow walls encircled her like a hug, and Greta's shoulders relaxed. She hadn't realized how tense the library conference

179

had made her until she had a moment to exhale. She inched further into the space, drawn by the scent of coffee, chocolate, and, today, bacon. Greta looked to the chalkboard signage near the register, and sure enough, Allison's special for her lunchtime patrons was her hallmark bacon, lettuce, tomato, and avocado sandwich with homemade sweet potato chips. Greta's mouth watered.

She wove her way through the half-full dining room to the stools positioned near the register and pastry case. She scooted into a seat at the empty bar and looped her bag over her knee.

A server came by, and Greta placed her order for the special. She changed things up and ordered a honey lavender iced latte to drink.

Her phone vibrated with a text message from McHenry.

McHenry: How'd the morning go?

Greta: Good! At Mugs & Hugs now grabbing coffee and lunch.

McHenry: You mean coffee and a defining sense of self.

He included a GIF of Tom Hanks in *You've Got Mail* with the caption "Tall. Decaf. Cappuccino."

Greta couldn't help the grin that spread over her face. How did she get so lucky to find a boyfriend who was both considerate and strong. Perceptive and kind. And frequently referenced her favorite romcoms?

Greta: You know it.

She grinned and clicked to her photo app and scrolled through the group shots they'd gotten of the conference attendees. Greta was torn on what to post and share to social media, given that one of their own was lying in a hospital bed.

She swiped further back into her photo stream and zoomed in on the family tree pictures she'd quickly snapped.

Her eyes flew over the screen, taking in the lineage of Julian Vance as the genealogy club had determined it. Sure enough, they'd made the tie to Blythe Prescott through Julian's marriage to Deborah McNamara. Greta was impressed to see Viola Douglass's name listed as well. Apparently, she'd married into a family with the surname Brown. But, the genealogy club had also included the child Viola had with JuJu out of wedlock. Not for the first time did she wish she could look through Blythe's research again.

"Here you go, G." Greta jumped as Allison set her plate of food on the counter in front of her. "Whoa, sorry. Whatcha working on?"

"Gangster genealogy." Greta popped a chip into her mouth. It was still warm from the oven. "These are so good," she said around her bite. She handed her phone over to Allison. "Check this out."

Allison wiped her hands on the front of her navy blue and white polka-dotted apron. "What am I looking at?"

"JuJu Vance's family tree."

"He's the gangster?" Allison squinted at the tiny screen.

"The one who's buried treasure Blythe was convinced she'd find on the property behind Bobber's Bar. See how he was married here?" Greta pointed to one line of the tree. Allison nodded, and Greta scrolled to the right. "But he had a child with this woman."

Allison's eyes widened. "A child of an affair?"

Greta shrugged. "It's hard to say, but the years the genealogy club have worked out have that baby being born after JuJu married Deborah, so I'm guessing he was seeing this other woman, but something happened, and he ended up with his wife. The baby was born out of wedlock."

The genealogy club hadn't added any details below that particular offshoot, so Greta was speculating.

"That had to be tough on the woman. Can you imagine being a single mom in the early twentieth century? Total *Scarlet Letter* treatment, right? Even though it was a different time. Heck, it's still nearly impossible to be a single mom nowadays, but at least there isn't as much of a stigma."

Greta took the phone back from Allison. "Anyway, I don't know what to make of it, but it is interesting to know a bit more about JuJu Vance, since he's been at the center of all this hubbub this past week." She swiped through her photo app, coming across the divorce documents she had taken pictures of in Heath's office.

"Whoa, Greta…what have you been up to?" Allison motioned to the screen.

Greta winced and quietly filled her in on what she had discovered in Heath's office. Allison made a low whistle. "What a tangled web."

181

Greta agreed. She made a mental note to ask McHenry when the police would take the next steps to try to catch Blythe's husband in his business misdeeds. Her finger swiped once more, and she peered down at the screen.

Staring back at her was a sequence of numbers she'd forgotten about. She'd snapped the photo at Nico's cabin when she and Iris went inside to look around earlier in the week. At her sharp intake of breath, Allison arched a sculpted eyebrow. "What is it?"

"A potential clue I completely missed." Greta pulled up a search on her phone and toggled back and forth so she could type in the sequence of digits.

When the search results loaded, she sat back on her stool. "Why would Nico have jotted down the phone number for the Wisconsin Department of Health and Safety?"

"What?" Allison leaned forward, and Greta spun her phone back around.

"He must've been the one to call in the tip that put Bobber's Bar under the microscope," Greta said to herself, pieces clicking together. "Ace thought Blythe had done so before she died, but what if it was Nico after the fact? Maybe he was picking up where Blythe left off."

Allison looked at her like she had sprouted two extra heads. "I feel like I've missed something. Nico was in here earlier."

Greta bottled up her breath with excitement. "He didn't mention where he was going, did he?"

"Said he had plans to do some research this afternoon. Out of town."

"Huh." Greta thought that over. She would have figured all the research he wanted to do was right here in Larkspur. But maybe she could use the knowledge that Nico was out of the picture for the day to her advantage.

"Why are you so concerned with that author?"

"I think he might've murdered Blythe in an attempt to steal the glory of her discovery of a long-forgotten, or little-known, gangster treasure and use it as fodder for a book deal he desperately needs."

Allison's mouth formed a perfect O shape. "Where does Bobber's Bar's restaurant safety status fit into it?"

"Blythe was trying to intimidate the Hawlers into selling her the property. If Nico had the number for the Health and Safety Department," Greta mused aloud, "then maybe he was taking up the cause that Blythe started. He could have wanted the treasure for himself." Greta motioned to her plate, snatching another chip off of it. "Any chance I can get a to-go box for this? I want to go talk to Ace and Suz."

Allison spun around to grab a recyclable to-go container. "Here you go. Keep me posted."

Greta grabbed her lunch and tucked the box into her tote bag, promising Allison she would as she scuttled out of the café.

"Wait! Your coffee!" Allison called.

Greta turned and hesitated, already mourning the loss of caffeine. But she could hardly stash an iced latte in her tote bag when she went inside Bobber's, and they had a strict no-carry-in policy. "Can you keep it cold for me? I'll circle back."

Allison shot her a thumbs up.

The walk to Bobber's was a swift one, but Greta's heart sank when she took in the full parking lot. Her chances of talking to Ace and Suz were slim.

Her gaze pinged to Iris's family cabin in the backyard. It sat still and quiet. The key Iris had given her felt warm in Greta's pocket. She reached for it, making the split-second decision to take a look inside under the guise of bringing in some extra paper products for Nico. The napkins from Allison she had with her to-go box would be her proof if anyone questioned her. Did Nico need extra napkins? Probably not, but it was the best cover she could think of.

She looked left and right before ducking her head and speed-walking across the side yard of the bar and to the front door of the cabin. Her eyes landed on the spot where Nathan had struggled with and been victimized by the killer. She blinked and wedged the key in the door, stepping inside before she could think too hard about it.

The cabin looked much the same as she remembered it from earlier in the week. It was still a mess, with perhaps even more papers strewn about. Greta was determined to find the box of Blythe's research. If Nico knew enough to put pressure on the Hawlers, he must've been tipped off by either Blythe herself or by something of hers he'd come across.

She spun around the living room. "If I were a box of papers, where would I hide?"

Greta dropped to her knees and lifted the flaps on the bottom of each of the couches, peering underneath to see if Nico had wedged anything there. She came up empty in the living room, except for some dust bunnies. She moved on to the bedroom, checking underneath the four-poster bed and in the oversized closet.

She methodically went through the drawer in the end table next to the bed. All she found was that Nico had started and stopped a ton of book proposals, ripping pages out of a college-ruled notebook and leaving them strewn about his room and his living space. The man must've been beyond frustrated with his project and prospects.

Frustrated enough to kill and then try to move the dial on a set of restaurant owners to get his way? Greta couldn't be sure.

She walked into the kitchen and put her hands on her hips. It was suspiciously tidy. The dishes were put up; the table was wiped down. The laptop that had sat at one of the seats was gone, likely with Nico doing whatever research he was up to. Why was the rest of the place a disaster, but this room spick and span? Could Nico have cleaned up after a run-in with Nathan the previous night? Maybe they'd argued in the kitchen, things escalated, and they ended up out front. That was all conjecture, but Greta couldn't look past the anomaly of what she was seeing.

There would be time to ask questions later, though. Greta scanned the room and decided to start going through the drawers on the far side.

She was halfway through the bank of cabinets when she froze at the sound of voices directly outside.

"I have nothing to hide, I swear." Nico's voice held a hint of fear alongside a heavy dose of annoyance.

"We have a warrant to search this property." This, from a voice Greta didn't recognize. Must've been someone with the state team helping out with the murder investigation.

Greta's heartbeat sped up. She launched herself across the room as quickly as she could on wobbly legs, whipping open the door to the basement and stumbling inside as the front door of the cabin creaked open.

Greta exhaled and then scrunched up her nose. She looked around and got her bearings.

No, no, no!

In her haste, she'd dodged into the cleaning supply closet rather than the entry to the basement. She was surrounded by a kitchen broom, a mop and bucket, and hanging on the wall behind her was an antiquated set of hooks with a duster, a fly swatter, and some sort of old-timey wooden sign. It was hanging from a chain, and in chipped, stencil-painted letters, it read *No Diving.* The whole closet was coated in a thick layer of dust.

Don't sneeze. Don't sneeze.

Greta glanced down at her shoes, trying to focus on something other than the tickle in her nose. She frowned. There were footprints other than her own and fresh dirt on the dust-covered linoleum. Had someone else been in this closet recently? If so, why?

Greta blinked. Probably to grab cleaning gear. Hadn't she noticed the kitchen was spotless?

She settled into her spot to wait out this search, but dread pooled in her gut. Any police officer who was doing his or her due diligence would certainly not leave a stone unturned—or, in this case, a closet unopened. She was going to be found out. How was she going to talk herself out of this situation?

Greta slumped into the wall on the backside of the cramped closet space, and her neck connected with one of the prong hooks and jostled the duster. Greta squished up her nose, trying to stave off a sneeze as she spun as best she could, and put a hand on the cleaning tools to try to still them and prevent any further rattling. As she pulled her hand away, her finger got hooked in the chain of the old sign and before she could untangle herself, she had tugged it an inch downward. Greta gasped when, instead of the sign breaking off its peg hook, the whole hook shifted downward, and the back wall of the closet slid aside eight inches, revealing a darkened room beyond.

Chapter Twenty-Five

Her heart hammered hard enough that Greta could feel it in the back of her throat. She took a step forward, creeping into the darkness that backed into the unassuming cleaning closet. Did Iris and her family know they had access to a secret passageway? This was the stuff of a Nancy Drew novel.

As Greta inched forward into a wider cavity, the trick door slid shut behind her.

"Oh dear." Greta breathed heavily. Now what? She was grateful to have escaped being found, but how would she get back out?

"The only way out is through," she murmured to herself, taking a step farther into the darkness. That's when it dawned on her. She wasn't completely without resources. She wrenched open the tote bag at her side and dug out her cell phone from the bottom. Her fingers pawed clumsily at the screen until she managed to click on the flashlight.

She breathed a sigh of relief at the illumination, minor though it may be. She beamed her light around the small space. It was a room that was maybe double the size of the cleaning closet, but in the corner, a stairwell led down. Greta craned her ear to hear any noise from behind her, but then decided to see where the hidden staircase led.

The walls of the stairs were dried dirt, but it was a substantial passageway, wide enough for two medium-sized people to easily walk side-by-side up and down it. Greta's pulse skittered as she anticipated where it would lead.

At the bottom of the stairway, a corridor stretched out in one direction. Greta stopped and closed her eyes, visualizing where she was on the property and what direction this route would take her to. She was always terrible at directions, but she'd guess she was heading away from the cabin, perhaps toward Main Street? There was only one way to find out.

But first, Greta opened up a text message and fired off a note to McHenry.

Greta: I seem to have found myself in a passageway underneath Nico's cabin, in case I don't check in, maybe come looking for me. The hook in the cleaning closet will get you here. I—

She stopped typing. Had she been about to write *I love you*? She deleted the last *I* and clicked send, pulling up her string with Josie and Iris instead.

Greta: Iris, did you know there's a secret passageway underneath your parents' cabin. I'm down here. Not sure where it leads, but I'm about to find out.

She clicked send again, but didn't hold out much hope that her messages would make it to either McHenry or her girlfriends. Judging from the lack of bars at the top of the screen, her cell reception wasn't strong.

She pointed her phone's flashlight ahead and started to walk slowly forward. She scanned the walls of the passageway for any hints that anyone had been down there lately. There was nothing that showed any sign of life, at least not initially, but when the passageway veered to the right, Greta pulled up short. Up ahead was an alcove. In it sat two rickety-looking wooden chairs and a small table between them. Greta approached, shining her light on the table. Her breath caught in the back of her throat. Sitting face up on the table was a pile of envelopes. Next to one of them was a looseleaf sheet of paper with a sequence of numbers scratched on it. Instinctively, Greta reached forward to grab for it, but she pulled back. She didn't want her fingerprints obscuring evidence. She dug around in her bag and retrieved one of the napkins. She shook it open and used it to pick up the loose-leaf sheet. It was Blythe's love letter. Or the code. Or both. Greta wanted to cheer.

Wait until the police see this! It could crack the case wide open.

Greta moved to collect the rest of the envelopes when she froze at the sound of a footfall coming from the opposite direction.

Her blood turned to ice, and she smashed her flashlight to her thigh to douse the light. She pressed herself into the nearest wall and her ears perked up as she listened. The footsteps stopped and then receded, going back in the direction from which they'd come.

Greta waited, her pulse pounding. The sound of a door creaking met her ear, and she peeked out around the wall. The passageway was shrouded in darkness.

Greta scooped the envelopes into her tote bag. She didn't dare leave the coded messages behind. Someone might return before she could and take them away, and she'd miss her chance to figure out who Blythe was communicating with and what they were talking about.

Greta rushed along the darkened passageway, with one hand clutching her phone in front of her and one hand holding the damp wall for balance.

Her mind spun with possibilities. Nathan must've discovered the passage-way somehow. If he had a coded message in his possession when he was attacked last night, then he'd obviously found Blythe's stash down here. That must've been what he'd been calling Greta to try to tell her.

Greta hesitated when she came to another corner on the path. She peeked her head around, and the bottom of a set of stairs came into view about twenty yards ahead.

Her heart hammered as she jogged forward. Her foot caught on the bottom step, and she stumbled. Her knee hit the stairs, and her eyes landed on a scrap of paper a couple steps up. She picked it up and frowned. It was rectangular and filmy, like the backing that had been peeled off a sticker.

She held onto it and pounded up the stair treads. When she got to the top, it wasn't a normal door that she was met with but instead a square opening above her head. She pushed against it, but it wouldn't budge. Panic made spots explode in her vision. Tiny, twinkling stars that, under any other circumstances, she would have thought were pretty. But at that moment, she couldn't help but wonder if she was going to be stuck down there. Would the librarians come looking for her when she didn't show for the afternoon session? Surely, Fitz would know something was up if she wasn't there. Maybe her text messages would send since she was closer to ground level. Greta didn't take the time to check to see if she had a signal. She pawed at the door above her until she found the edge of the frame. Her heart lurched when her fingers connected with a small lip along one side. She tugged, and the door slid to the right.

Florescent light hit her eyes and Greta squinted against it, lifting her tote above her head and pushing it out onto the floor before hoisting her body through the opening. When she glanced up and took in her surroundings, her head kicked back of its own accord. She was standing in a bathroom stall. She pushed the door to the stall open and spotted a wall of urinals.

A men's bathroom, then.

Greta scurried for the door, heaving a giant sigh of relief when she made it to the hallway between the men's and women's bathrooms of Bobber's Bar.

She pressed her tote to her side, since she was still cradling the coded letters within it, and walked out into the crowded dining room. A look at the clock on her phone told her she still had forty minutes to get to Karrington. Time must've warped when she was underground, because it felt like a decade had passed. Instead, several small groups of librarians still milled around the restaurant. Both Rob and Ace were behind the bar. Greta didn't see Suz, but she assumed she was around somewhere. Nico sat at a table along the far wall, nursing what looked to be a lemonade. He had a scowl on his face, and Greta wondered what, if anything, the search warrant of his cabin revealed. Since he wasn't in police custody, the authorities must not have found anything too incriminating. The front door to Bobber's was swinging shut as Greta made it to the bar. Any one of these people could have been the one she almost ran into down in the secret passageway. That, or whoever it was could have left through the front door like it was nothing.

Greta's skin crawled, and her eyes darted around.

The discovery of the underground staircases and corridor between Nico's cabin and the bar added a whole other layer to Blythe's murder. Anyone she'd seen at the bar before Blythe was killed—the people she had brushed aside as suspects because they had an alibi—were now on the table as potential killers.

"I didn't see you come in, Greta."

She jumped as Suz appeared on her left. Greta forced a smile. "Hey, Suz.

189

I'm glad I caught you."

"What can I do for you?"

Greta studied the woman, whose complexion looked healthier than she'd seen it all week. "You feeling better?"

"Actually, yeah. Our family had a bit of a come-to-Jesus moment."

Greta cocked her head to the side.

"Rob told us he's been taking classes in Karrington. He's not sure he wants to take over the bar here full-time, and he was afraid to share with us his passion for history. I'm so glad he finally told us, though. Ace and I want to be supportive."

"That's wonderful news." Greta was glad to hear it. Truly, she was. She only hoped Ace didn't kill someone to try to protect a legacy his son didn't actually want.

"It inspired Ace to come clean with Rob, too."

"Oh?"

"He's been stressed with the ownership of this place for a while. We both have been. He's been trying to put up a good front for Rob, but behind closed doors, he's been miserable. So miserable that I told Ace we couldn't go on like this. We had to make a change."

"You're closing?" Greta blurted out.

Suz laughed. "No, no. Not a change that massive. We're looking into bringing on a business manager. Someone who can be here and cover for us when we want a night off. Ace and I haven't both had an evening when at least one of us wasn't working in years. Anyway, apparently, Blythe was trying to get Ace to sell, and when he told her he wasn't interested, she started trying to sabotage this place. Ace was panicking because he wanted to make a good impression on the folks he was looking into onboarding for the new managerial role. With the health and safety department breathing down our neck, Ace didn't like our chances of bringing in quality candidates."

"Are you sure it was Blythe who called Health and Safety on you guys?"

Suz frowned. "We assumed so, yes."

Greta hummed. She wouldn't bring up Nico, but she had her suspicions. Out loud she said, "I'm so glad you guys were able to talk it out."

Suz reached out a hand. "I hear I have you to thank."

"Me?"

"Rob told us you encouraged him to tell the truth." She glanced over her shoulder. "To us and the police," she added with a whisper.

Greta squeezed Suz's hand back and made her excuses. "I've got to get to Karrington before the afternoon session of our conference, but we should grab coffee together soon."

"I'd like that." Suz smiled and walked behind the bar.

Greta took out her phone, quickly tapping out messages to McHenry and the group chat with her friends.

Greta: All good here. I'm at Bobber's. I'll tell you all about my adventure later today. Stay tuned!

Josie: Wait, what?

Greta studied her phone. Her original message never sent.

Greta: Never mind!

Iris: ??? Glad you're all good.

Greta: Heading to Karrington now.

But first, she was going to make a pit stop.

Chapter Twenty-Six

Greta knocked on the door frame of McHenry's office five minutes later.

He looked up from a document he was studying and smiled at her. "Hey."

"Hey, yourself. Did you get my texts?" Judging from his relaxed posture and the fact he wasn't immediately chastising her for her jaunt through an underground passageway, Greta figured he hadn't.

McHenry shuffled some papers around on his desk and retrieved his phone, wincing. "Sorry. It's been on silent since my meeting with the state police. They got a warrant for Nico's cabin."

"I know."

McHenry pinned her with a look.

"Don't be mad." Greta held up her hands before digging into her bag. "I brought you something."

She used the napkin to drop the letters on McHenry's desk.

He looked down at them, and recognition dawned on his face. "These are Blythe's letters? The coded messages."

"I'm pretty sure."

"Greta, where did you get these? You didn't do anything illegal, did you?" He looked stricken.

"No. I mean, not really. They were in a public place I happened to stumble upon."

Literally.

She gave him a brief rundown of where she was and what happened.

McHenry's jaw hung slightly open before he snapped to attention. "Thank God you're okay. What am I going to do with you?"

"I didn't try to find a secret staircase, Mark."

"But you went snooping in Nico's house."

"I was there to do some housekeeping." Greta winced. That excuse sounded flimsier than Bible paper.

"I'm not even going to dignify that with a response. What if the other person in the tunnel wouldn't have turned around? What if they would have come at you?" McHenry blew out a long breath.

Greta squirmed. "I'm sorry. I didn't mean to push so hard. I just got ahead of myself. But it's fine. They didn't see me. There's no way they could have known it was me."

McHenry gave her a hard stare. "You're sure?"

She nodded. "Positive. I'm heading to Karrington, and I'll be with the librarians for the rest of the day. Nothing dangerous about that. I wanted to leave these letters with you first, though. Hopefully, you can decode them and figure this whole thing out, right?"

McHenry gave a single nod. "Officer Clarkson is on it."

Greta offered him a tentative smile. "I can't wait to hear what you guys find out. Also, I found this as I was leaving the passageway." She dropped the paper backing on his desk. "I think the person who was down there may have dropped it."

McHenry studied the wax-coated slip of paper. "Not much to go on, but thanks."

She stepped toward his desk and placed a firm kiss on his temple. "I'll see you later tonight."

"Don't go falling down any other secret passageways between now and then, okay?"

"I make no promises."

He shook his head, but his lips quirked.

Greta felt lighter as she drove to Karrington, knowing the coded messages were in the hands of the police.

She pulled into the Karrington Library parking lot with two minutes to spare. She sprinted inside and slid into a seat in the back row of the conference room right as Fitz was welcoming the group back together.

From the front of the room, he widened his eyes at her before continuing on with his spiel. When he turned the mic over, he took a seat next to her.

"What's on your face?"

"What do you mean?" Greta got out her cell phone and opened the camera app, turning the lens around so she could see herself. She grimaced. "Oh yuck." She had a swath of brown dirt along her left cheekbone. Why hadn't McHenry said something to her? She sighed.

"Your pants are splattered with mud or some other indeterminate brown substance. Do I want to know?" Fitz joked. "You look like you just spent time in the caves with Indiana Jones."

"You're not too far off. I found a secret tunnel."

"You *what*?" Fitz gaped.

"Tell you more later." Greta got out another napkin and used it to rub at her face, trying to erase the evidence of her morning adventure. When she got it as good as it was going to get, she sat back and tried to enjoy the final presentation of the week.

* * *

At the end of the night, the librarians took a large group photo, wherein Greta strategically angled herself so that her non-soiled cheek was visible. She smiled and made conversation with the librarians.

"It's been a great conference. Thanks for hosting us." Diane, the librarian from Green Bay who had gone to see the police earlier, gave Greta a side hug. "I hope everything gets sorted out around here. The police were busy this morning."

Greta took a deep breath. "I hope so too. I think they're close."

As the last of the librarians took their leave, Greta checked the time. It was after seven o'clock. She'd have to hurry to help Fitz get things put away around the library and make it back to Larkspur for her date with McHenry.

"Alright, captain," she said to Fitz when he approached from the door. "Put me to work."

"Chairs can be stacked and lined on that wall. The maintenance crew will take them from there."

Greta nodded and started piling up the chairs. She and Fitz debriefed about the conference as they worked. The overall consensus was that the event was a success, minus Blythe's death and Nathan's injury.

"Ow!" Greta wrenched her hand out from where it had gotten wedged between two chairs. Skin had been pulled away from her nailbed, and her finger was bleeding.

"I have band-aids in my office if you want to go grab one." Fitz glanced at her finger and then looked away. His skin had taken on a green hue. "I'd go with you, but I don't do well with blood."

Greta chuckled. "Don't worry. I'll get it taken care of and be back to help you in no time."

She left the conference room and hurried to the library. Wren, the library assistant who she met earlier in the week was behind the research desk.

"Workplace injury." Greta held up her hand. "I'm grabbing some band-aids from Fitz's office."

Wren came out from behind the desk. "Let me get the door for you." She stepped ahead of Greta and turned the knob.

Greta hit the light switch with her elbow. "Okay. Band-aids, where would they be?" She scanned Fitz's tidy space, not seeing a first aid kit.

"Maybe the closet?" Wren crossed the room and pulled open the accordion doors. "Here you go." She stood up on her tiptoes and reached for a box with a red cross on the front of it.

"Perfect." Greta studied her finger. Her right hand, which she'd been using to cradle the injured digit, was now covered in blood. "Do you think you can open it up for me?"

"Definitely." Wren set the first aid kit down on Fitz's desk. "Sit over here. I'll get you taken care of."

Greta did as she was told, and Wren made quick work of donning plastic gloves and getting out some gauze and a Band-Aid. "Fingers are the worst. So many blood vessels in there. Makes it look like you were the victim of a crime scene, doesn't it?"

"Totally." Greta's hand was throbbing. "You're good at this. Did you miss a calling as a nurse?"

"Nah. I'm the oldest sibling and a built-in babysitter for my parents. I've had to do my fair share of boo-boo fixes. But I've always wanted to have a career with books."

Greta nodded. "I can relate to that."

Since she had most of the blood cleaned up, Wren leaned forward to wrap a Band-Aid around Greta's finger. Her magnetic name tag was at Greta's eye level, and Greta sucked in a breath when she noticed the young woman's last name. *Douglass-Brown.*

That had to be a coincidence.

Right?

"There you go. You're all good as new." Wren stepped back and beamed.

Greta wiggled her finger, suddenly feeling sick to her stomach. "I don't feel so great," she admitted. "Maybe I lost more blood than I thought."

Wren's face showed instant concern. "Do you feel faint? Stay here. I'll grab a glass of water."

She jogged out of the office, and Greta let her head fall back, circling her neck and trying to think. Douglass was a common last name. There was no proof that just because Wren shared it with JuJu Vance's mistress, she was at all descended from the woman.

And yet…

"Here you go." Greta jumped at the sound of Wren's chipper voice. "I brought some reinforcements."

Tuck White appeared in the doorway to Fitz's office.

Greta didn't think it was possible for her head to spin any faster, but she'd been wrong before.

"Tuck?"

"Hey, Greta. How's the hand?"

"I'll be fine. What, uh, what are you doing here?"

"I'm a new hire." Tuck pointed to a stick-on nametag that he wore over the left breast pocket of his polo shirt. "Don't have the official nametag yet, but since I got canned at B'Jeweled, I had to find a job somewhere."

"We were hiring." Wren held out a water bottle for Greta.

"Wren and I went to high school together, and I saw her social media post about the job opening." Tuck smiled, and Greta's skin crawled. "The rest, as they say, is history."

"How…convenient. Thank you." Greta took the water bottle from Wren, opened the cap, and took a long slug, hoping to get rid of the pitchy tone of her voice. Tuck's stick-on nametag was about the size of the scrap of paper she'd found in the passageway. Her stomach pitched.

Wren tidied up the first aid kit. She walked back to the closet and returned it to the shelf.

Greta traced her movements over the water bottle, and her eye landed on a piece of cardboard wedged in the bottom of the closet, tucked between a file cabinet and the wall. One side was visible, and the orange font on the box was unmistakable. Greta could even make out the large, scripted letter B from the *Bigger Is Better* motto.

Greta's heart lurched. There were too many coincidences for her to brush them aside.

"Is it safe for me to come in here?"

Greta spun to find Fitz in the doorway, his hand over his eyes. He was peeking through slats in his fingers. Thank goodness. An ally.

Greta let out a nervous chuckle. "All cleaned up. Wren was a great help. And I got to say hi to your newest hire, Tuck."

Tuck waved from where he'd stepped back to allow Fitz to enter the office.

"Greta was a great patient. Just the slightest hint of light-headedness, but otherwise much less squirmy than my younger brothers used to be." Wren pulled the accordion doors of the closet closed and dusted her hands as if to say, *my job is done*.

Fitz grinned. "Your brothers were little monkeys."

Greta stood and tested her legs. Not too wobbly, which was a good sign. "You know her brothers?"

"Sure. Fitz is a long-time friend of my family," Wren said. "He and my dad knew each other when they were boys, and then they ended up being college roommates. Right, Fitz?"

"I met this one when she was in diapers." Fitz grinned, his gaze bouncing from Wren to Tuck. "And we're happy to have Tuck on board. Look at us now. A whole big, happy library family. I'm sharing my office space with Tuck to show him the ropes. He's interested in library work."

Fitz chucked both Tuck and Wren on the shoulders as they passed him, and they grinned as they headed out of the office.

"Holler if you have any more finger emergencies." Wren waved to Greta over her shoulder. "Otherwise, I'm going to teach Tuck how we shut things down for the night."

"Thanks," Greta said weakly.

Fitz spun on her when his employees were out of earshot. "You sure you're okay? You look a little pale."

"I'm fine." Greta felt a renewed wave of nausea wash over her as she thought back over the week. She could kick herself for not filling Fitz in on Tuck's connection to Blythe before today. And for not bringing him up to speed on Julian Vance's family tree. She'd been so focused on Nico, but now she had a nasty feeling Fitz had one, if not two, criminals working under him.

Somehow, Tuck must've snuck into the Larkspur Library and swiped the box of Blythe's research. Wren hadn't been around, so it had to be Tuck. She frowned. But how did he know it was there?

Unless...

A blurry hypothesis formed, but Greta didn't like it one bit. In any case, it was best for everyone not to make a scene right now. If anything, she needed backup. "I do need to get going, though. Is there anything else you need from me?"

"Nope. Should be all set. Why don't I walk you to your car?"

"Sure. Okay." Greta focused on keeping her breathing steady as Fitz led her by the elbow past Wren and Tuck and into the parking lot.

"Do you have your bag?" he asked once they made it outside.

"It's in the car." Greta pulled her keys out of the pocket of her blazer and unlocked the doors. "Thanks for everything, Fitz. For all of your help this week. Sorry I wasn't much help with cleanup."

"Nonsense. Sorry I couldn't help *you* clean up. Blood sends me running for the hills."

Greta pasted a smile on her face and nodded. "See you soon."

"Yep. Tomorrow!"

She cocked her head at Fitz.

"Did you think I'd miss the Little Bohemia Lodge presentation? After all the hubbub it's caused this week, you better believe I'm going to be there to see what gives. Is Nico still planning to speak?"

"Right. The presentation is tomorrow." Greta had forgotten it. She chose her next words carefully. "As for Nico, you didn't hear this from me, but the cops are looking into him. I think he's their top suspect."

Fitz's eyes grew wide. "Seriously? Jeesh. I saw him today at Bobber's." He shivered. "Hard to believe a killer can just be sitting in our midst, right?"

A trickle of sweat made a slow line down Greta's spine. "Totally. I'll see you tomorrow. Hopefully, the police will have an update for us then. Enjoy a relaxing night, Fitz." Greta swallowed. "You've earned it."

Fitz gave her air kisses on each cheek and closed the driver's door after she had settled into her seat. She offered him a smile and a wave as she drove carefully out of the parking lot.

Her head pounded with the force of a full-fledged migraine, mostly because she was trying to reconcile what she now knew.

How had she been so wrong?

She had taken Tuck at his word when he found her outside of B'Jeweled. She had dinner across from him, and she believed him when he told her about Blythe's affair. She shouldn't have let her guard down.

And what about Wren? Did she know about any of this? Or was she an innocent bystander caught in the wrong place at the wrong time? Greta culled through her memory, trying to recall what Wren had said that first afternoon. Was she part of the whole scheme? Greta's whole body trembled at the thought of how close she'd come, on several occasions, to the murderer.

"The ketamine," she whispered out loud to her dashboard. Her mind had been running rampant, and she'd made it out of the town limits of

Karrington. Now just one more winding country road to the highway between Karrington and Larkspur that would take her to McHenry. Hopefully Blythe's letters would provide the final pieces to the puzzle.

Greta tapped the button on her steering wheel to activate the voice recognition system. When it dinged, she said, "Call Mc—"

But the rest of McHenry's name was stolen from her lips on a scream when an engine roared behind her and headlights blinded. Before she could react, a truck rammed into the backside of her vehicle.

Greta gripped the steering wheel, fighting for control of her car. She hit the rumble strips at the center line and cranked the wheel back. She thought she had her bearings, but the truck behind her collided with her again and sent her car careening off the road, straight for the tree line.

Chapter Twenty-Seven

Greta regained consciousness and was aware of two things at once. Her head pounded, and she wasn't alone. Someone was shuffling around in her back seat. She cracked one eye open, but all she could see were the branches from an overgrown arbor vitae bush. She flicked her gaze to the left and gulped when she saw how close she had come to careening headlong into the immovable trunks of a line of pine trees.

"Where are they? Where did you put them? I know you have them, you good-for-nothing snoop."

Greta's stomach turned over at the sinister sound of a familiar voice. She kept her body limp and closed her eyes, pretending to be knocked out as hands grabbed her shoulders and shook her.

"Wake up, Greta. Wake up! You've ruined everything. Tell me where you put the letters!" A hand slapped across her face, but Greta didn't react. Instead, she let her jaw go slack.

"You nosy, annoying piece of work!" the voice yelled.

In the distance, the sound of emergency sirens reached Greta's ears. Hope surged in her chest, but she focused all her energy on keeping her body still and relaxed. If she showed any signs of coming to, she was sure the murderer would lash out. She had to wonder why he hadn't killed her already.

He cursed, and she felt him move away. A moment later, the sound of tires squealing reached her ears. Greta craned her neck to look behind her in time to see a black truck tearing off in the direction of Karrington.

She shifted in her seat as a police cruiser pulled up on the shoulder of the road she had skidded off of.

A cop hopped out and sprinted toward her. "Ma'am, can you hear me?"

"Yeah, I can hear you." Greta groaned as she tried to scooch herself upright in her seat. Her whole body throbbed.

"Stay still. I'll get you out of there." The cop spoke into his radio, giving the code for a traffic accident. "Help is on the way," he said to her when he hooked his radio back to his side. "Looks like you took a nasty skid."

"I was run off the road." Greta gritted her teeth.

The officer's eyes widened, and he looked around. "By who?"

"Someone I thought I could trust." Greta blinked back a wave of tears, the full reality of the situation and the stress of the day landing like a sucker punch to her jaw. "Can you do me a favor and get a hold of someone on the Larkspur police force?"

"Sure. Who?"

"Detective Mark McHenry."

Chapter Twenty-Eight

McHenry insisted upon taking her to the hospital in Karrington so she could be fully checked over for injuries, even though Greta swore she was fine.

"You could be bleeding internally."

Greta rolled her eyes. "I'm not."

"You could have a concussion."

"I passed the roadside concussion protocol test."

"Just let me have this, Greta."

McHenry looked at her with so much concern in his inky black eyes Greta relented and subjected herself to a myriad of tests.

Finally, after several hours and the assurance that aside from some severe bruising and face lacerations she was completely fine, McHenry drove her home.

Biff was waiting by the front door when he carried her inside.

"My legs aren't injured, Mark." Greta was only half protesting this level of his care. She quite liked seeing him put his biceps to good use, and she was so tired.

"I know." He settled her onto the couch and placed a kiss on her forehead. "But I like taking care of you."

Greta snuggled into the cushions as he left her for the kitchen. Cupboard doors banged, and the faucet turned on. McHenry returned a moment later with a glass of water and a plate of crackers.

"What else do you need?"

"Nothing." Greta took a bite of cracker. "Except you. Can you stay for a while?"

McHenry moved to the end of the couch, lifting her legs up and settling them on his lap. He started to massage the soles of her feet, and Greta's eyes fluttered closed. Her whole body felt like it had been put through a paper shredder. Not to mention the mental toll.

"You've had quite the day."

Greta had told him the entire story—everything from the details of discovering the secret passageway to the aftermath of getting run off the road—during their lengthy evening at the hospital. She didn't think she'd ever forget seeing McHenry striding toward her where she sat in the ambulance. He had the sort of hard look on his face that made the criminals he dealt with confess their misdeeds immediately, but the second he laid eyes on her, his expression softened.

Until he got closer and saw the cuts and bruises that marked her face.

Then he looked ready to rage against someone.

She nodded now, grateful he was here with her as she was still processing all that she'd learned to be true.

"Tell me what you found out in the letters," she said, keeping her eyes closed.

"A lot of back and forth about the history of the gangsters in this part of the state. Details on JuJu Vance's life. Basically what you'd expect from two people communicating about a research project."

"So, they weren't love letters at all."

"No."

Tuck had steered her in the wrong direction. Of course it made sense that the code would pertain to the thing Blythe cared most about—finding the treasure.

"We also got the coordinates." McHenry said it in such a casual way, Greta only hummed in response. But then her eyes flew open.

"Wait. What?"

He smirked, and she reached over and shoved his shoulder.

"Mark! Way to bury the lede. That's incredible. You can search for the ring, then?"

"We'll have to get some experts in here. We want everything to be above board and to maintain the historical integrity of whatever it is we find. Even if it is just the underground tunnel."

"Did you go down there this afternoon?"

"Yeah. We brought in an engineer to assess the safety of the structure."

"And?"

"Whoever built it knew what they were doing."

"It's wild to think about who could have used the hidden tunnel over the years, isn't it?" The history in the place made Greta a little tingly.

"Wild is one word for it." McHenry sighed before switching gears. "Now that you've identified who ran you off the road, I'll have the Karrington PD pick him up and bring him in for questioning."

Greta shook her head. "Don't do that. I have a better idea."

"Greta, we can't have a known criminal walking around like it's nothing."

"I know, but all the evidence we have right now is circumstantial, at least as he's connected to Blythe. Think about it. There is nothing that ties him to her murder or Nathan's attack. Even if you pick him up for the hit and run, since his truck will be damaged, that's one thing. But it would be my word against his for what he said about the letters. Your case is built on straw and not stone. You have to catch him in the act, and I have a plan."

McHenry stared at her as she detailed her idea. He blinked once when she was finished. "That might work."

* * *

The next morning, Greta positioned herself at the door to the Larkspur Library so she could welcome guests to the program. It was humbling to see the reactions to her bruised face. A lot of folks openly stared, some gasped, and others asked her what had happened. She downplayed the accident, saying she got into a fender bender but telling people it was nothing serious.

Josie sidled over to her. "You sure you're up for this?"

Greta gave a definitive nod. "I need to see it through."

Iris joined them and bobbed her head toward the main doors. "That's good, because our main players have arrived."

Greta looked out the window, and sure enough, Fitz, Wren, and Tuck walked toward the library.

"How'd you get them here?" Iris asked.

"I'll take credit for that," Josie said. "I texted Fitz this morning. Told him there'd been an accident, and we were short-staffed, so we could use some extra help. I invited him to bring his auxiliary staff. I may have suggested it would be a good learning experience for them. Especially for anyone interested in the history of the state."

Greta snorted. "A learning experience about criminal behavior, maybe."

"We *are* talking about notorious gangsters." Josie grinned. "What can I say, I can be very persuasive."

"I'm glad you pulled it off." Greta turned toward the door as the trio walked inside.

Fitz's reaction to the sight of her was as she'd expect from a friend. He looked shocked and disbelieving. He rushed to her side and grabbed her hand. "Greta. Oh my gosh. What happened?"

"Car accident on my way home last night."

Fitz turned to Josie. "Is this why you said you needed extra hands?"

"I didn't think Greta would make it in today. But she's a fighter, this one." Josie nudged her shoulder, and Greta smiled. Pretty soon, this would all be over. She was so grateful to have her team by her side as they brought to book a killer.

Tuck and Wren lingered behind Fitz. Their reactions to Greta were a little more subdued.

Tuck avoided eye contact.

Wren stared wide-eyed at her. "You could have used me to bandage up more than your finger, it looks like, Greta."

Greta let out a chuckle. "As it turned out, I guess you're right." She pivoted toward the library proper. "Come on in. We set up in the main space since we're expecting a big crowd."

They had shifted the tables against the wall, so the research area was clear. Collapsible chairs had been set up in rows facing a podium at the front of the room. Cindi was standing near the podium, with her back to the growing crowd. She was futzing with the large board at the front of the room.

Greta had called her early this morning and filled her in on what had happened and what they'd learned. Cindi was more than willing to play a part in bringing down a criminal. She always did like the spotlight. She turned and caught Greta's eye, giving her a subtle nod.

Greta nodded back. It was a relief, being on the same side as her nemesis for once.

"I'm going to go talk to my brother." Josie cut off from the group.

Fitz stared after her. "Her brother?"

"He's a research expert on twentieth-century American history. He took the red-eye from the East Coast to be here today after we had some changes to our programming."

"What kind of changes?" Wren plucked a program from the table where the Larkspur librarians had strategically placed them for guests to grab as they entered the library. "Living History: A New Discovery for the Wisconsin Gangster Trail," she read.

"What's all this?" Fitz shifted and leaned over Wren's shoulder to read the program for himself. He glanced at Greta, dropping his voice. "Did the police find Nico? Or is this his new project?"

"Nico's right over there." She gestured to where the author was talking to Kerry near the New Book shelves.

Tuck's eyes darted around. He looked like he wanted to cry. "Blythe would have wanted nothing more than to be here."

"It's true. It's too bad someone took that chance away from her. After all, much of this is the result of her findings." Greta let that thought hang in the air between them for a beat before clapping her hands. "If you all don't mind standing here to greet our guests, I have to put some finishing touches on our presentation."

She leaned in as if giving them insider information. "Blythe discovered a secret treasure."

"What?" Fitz breathed.

"Yep. A long-lost diamond ring," Greta whispered.

Wren clamped a hand over her mouth. "Are you serious?"

"Is it here?" Tuck asked, his eyes flashing.

"No. It's buried nearby. You'll never believe it's actually in an underground tunnel. The professionals are coming later this week to help with the excavation. Until then, we're leaving it undisturbed."

"Greta." Cindi waved her to the front of the room.

"If you'll excuse me. I've got to go get the show on the road. Thank you again for being here." Greta smiled at them before turning toward Cindi.

"Took you long enough," the board president murmured to her when she reached the front of the room.

Greta glanced at the microphone. "Is that thing on?"

"Not yet."

Greta nodded but still angled her body away from it. She wasn't taking any chances.

Josie joined them with Jake. "You think he bought it?"

Greta glanced over her shoulder to see Fitz, Wren, and Tuck with their heads pressed together. "We'll see."

"Well, let's get this party started." Cindi held her shoulders back. "Blythe may not have been my favorite person, but she deserves justice."

Greta took her seat off to the side with Josie and Iris. Jake and Nico sat in the front row, and as Greta scanned the library, she was pleased to see they had pulled in a full house. There were lots of Larkspur folks in the crowd, as well as several faces she didn't recognize. History buffs would travel, she guessed.

"Good afternoon. We're about to begin." Cindi called everyone to their places before introducing herself as president of the library board. "I'm thrilled to have you all here today as we honor the history of the great state of Wisconsin, particularly as it pertains to the Wisconsin Gangster Trail. With me today are two illustrious scholars. Gentlemen, please stand." Cindi swept her arm toward the front row as Jake and Nico rose and faced the crowd. "First, Dr. Jake Sinclair, a professor of history at Chesterton University." Jake waved, acknowledging the smattering of applause. "Second, we have Nico Eddison, an author specializing in gangster lore, particularly as it pertains to the Midwest." More clapping ensued, the most adamant of it coming from Kerry.

"Before Dr. Sinclair and Mr. Eddison take the stage, I want to draw your attention to the family tree your very own Larkspur Genealogy Club put together this week for a lesser-known comrade of John Dillinger, one Julian Vance." Cindi stepped to the boards that were covered with a sheet and dramatically ripped it off, revealing the family tree Greta had snapped photos of.

Everyone leaned forward to try to get a better look at the lineage, and Cindi started describing Julian Vance's family tree. "Julian, nicknamed 'JuJu' Vance, has direct ties to Larkspur. It's believed that when escaping the Little Bohemia Lodge during the FBI raid on April 22, 1934, he fled south and ended up here. We have acquired documents that prove that not only did JuJu stay here in Larkspur while he waited for some of the buzz to die down surrounding the raid, but he also hid something here that was very important to him. Something very valuable."

Greta scanned the crowd. They were hanging on Cindi's every word, which, Greta had to believe, was how the woman liked it.

As casually as she could, Greta shot a look to the back of the room.

Fitz was saying something to Wren, and then he coolly turned and walked out the library door.

"Fitz is on the move," Josie said from her seat next to Greta.

Greta gave a subtle nod. "We'll give it a minute."

They turned back to Cindi, who was pointing out the lineage flowing from Julian Vance and Viola Douglass. "I'd also like to draw your attention to this line. Julian had a child out of wedlock. This will be important for our story today. Now, without further ado, I'd like to turn it over to Dr. Sinclair and Mr. Eddison."

The two men rose, and Jake motioned for Nico to take the mic.

He stepped up and cleared his throat. "As Cindi said, my name is Nico Eddison. I was invited here by the True Treasure Seekers to share some of my research on Dillinger and his gang with you. Little did I know there would be some history made upon my arrival. Some of you knew the late

Blythe Prescott. She passed away unexpectedly this past Monday. In fact, she was killed for the research she'd been doing surrounding JuJu Vance."

Those in attendance emitted a collective gasp.

Nico nodded sadly. "Blythe had been in touch with me, and she was excited about a potential collaboration between the two of us. She said she had new information on a compatriot of Dillinger's, and she thought it would make for a good book. She was anxious to tell me more in person. Unfortunately, she didn't get that chance."

The crowd started murmuring amongst themselves.

"I've spent the past week attempting to piece together Blythe's research," Nico went on.

Greta had met with the author earlier that morning, explaining what she'd learned. Nico, for his part, came clean. As it turned out, Blythe had shared more of her research than Nico let on. He knew about the diamond and was trying to work his resources to figure out where it was buried. Blythe didn't share the coordinates with him. He had no idea he'd been living just above the ring for the past week while he was trying to compile his research. Talk about irony.

He admitted that he initially thought he could use Nathan's help, but quickly determined the librarian was a liability. The two had dinner the night of Nathan's attack, but then Nico left Bobber's and drove to Karrington to purchase some more notebooks and other materials. Nico maintained he didn't know how or why Nathan was outside his cabin or what landed him in the killer's crosshairs. He was shocked when Greta told him about the secret passageway.

He did admit that he didn't want to face Kerry, his agent, until he had something solid to pitch her. He apologized profusely for not being more forthcoming.

As for contacting the Health Department regarding Bobber's, Nico said it was all a misunderstanding. Blythe had told him something shady was going on at the bar and that she'd reached out to the Health Department. He didn't know what she was talking about or why the bar was relevant, but after he got to town and started looking into everything, Blythe's reference to Bobber's made Nico initially suspect Ace of her murder. He jotted down the number for the Health Department in his notes—the nine digits Greta had seen—and he'd called the department to follow up and see if Blythe had shared anything incriminating with them when she'd made her complaint. His intent in reaching out to the Health Department wasn't malicious, as Greta assumed, but was merely a fact-finding mission. All he learned was that there was an outstanding request for an inspection on the premises, but nobody could tell him anything more about Blythe, so he chalked it up as a dead end. Later he realized Blythe was likely trying to put extra pressure on Ace and Suz, maybe to make them crack and sell to her.

Greta concurred and had looped Nico in on what she'd learned from Rob. All in all, the only thing the author was guilty of was holding his cards close to his chest.

"It's been a challenge since her documents were stolen," Nico went on, explaining some of Blythe's research, coupled with his own, to the crowd. "But we do know Blythe had access to letters to Julian Vance from Viola Douglass. Love letters that we hope to retrieve so they can be archived and shared as part of this tumultuous story. For more on that, I'd like to turn it over to Professor Sinclair."

Jake stepped forward. "I fell into this research by chance. I happened to be in town the weekend before Blythe's untimely death, celebrating my sister's engagement." He flashed Josie a smile. "I overheard Blythe speaking with someone about John Dillinger while I was here. It's not every day you hear a random couple discussing a gangster from nearly one hundred years ago and one of the most polarizing figures in American history over a cup of coffee in small-town Wisconsin, am I right?" The crowd laughed. "Anyway, I went home and didn't think much of it, but when my sister reached out to me a couple days later and asked me to look into Julian Vance, I sort of fell down a rabbit hole. I've brought my research for you to view here, but before we get to that, there's a part of this story that's unfolding as we speak." Jake's gaze bounced to Greta, who nodded. He turned back to the microphone. "So, if you'll follow the librarians outside. We're going to go for a little cross-town walk."

Greta, Josie, and Iris rose and hurried to the library's exit. Wren and Tuck were quick to join them.

"What's going on?" Tuck was almost breathless. "Did you guys piece together Blythe's research? Did you find the coordinates?"

"Ah, ah, ah," Josie scolded. "You'll have to wait and see like everyone else."

"My great-great grandma is Viola Douglass-Brown." Wren looked shocked. "That has to be the same woman, right?"

"Did your family talk much about her?" Greta sidestepped the question, keeping a close eye on Wren.

"Not much at all." Wren shook her head. "I had no clue she was tied up with a gangster. She was married to a man named Harry. That's about all I knew. I'm going to have to ask my dad. He's the history buff among us. I'm sure he knows more. You'd think he would have told me."

"Not necessarily." Tuck offered. "Viola may have buried that part of her history if she moved on or if it was too painful. Maybe it didn't get passed down in the family."

Greta nodded.

"But my dad just gave me her diary to show to Fitz the other day. He said he found a distant cousin through his ancestry research who had the journal. Wait. Does Fitz know about Viola's connection to JuJu Vance?"

"Where *is* Fitz?" Tuck glanced past Greta and out the door. "He said he had to make a quick call, but I doubt he'd want to miss this."

"He'll be there," Greta said dryly. "Hey, Tuck. You know that nametag you were wearing yesterday?"

Tuck nodded. "What about it?"

"Did you peel it off the backing or did Fitz?"

"Fitz did. He handed it to me when I showed up for my shift, and I stuck it right on my shirt. Why?"

"That's what I figured. Come on."

Greta ignored the confused glances from Wren and Tuck. The attendees were waiting for instruction. Greta waved a hand over her shoulder and led them outside.

The spring afternoon sun shone above, sending its warm rays down on the large group as they cut across the parking lot. They passed Mugs & Hugs, and several café patrons joined the crowd, intrigued by such a mass of people traveling together.

"Where are you guys going?" Greta heard someone ask.

"To be a part of history," another person responded.

* * *

Greta led the group to the backyard of Bobber's Bar. Ace, Suz, and Rob were standing outside waiting for them, along with Sadie, who waved to Greta.

Suz stepped forward and spoke directly into Greta's ear. "He came in earlier and went straight for the bathroom. We pretended not to see him, so hopefully, he thinks he was home free. Detective McHenry followed a minute later."

Greta nodded. McHenry was going to go down the stairs after Fitz, and other officers would be entering from the stairway in Nico's cabin. They'd trap Fitz below ground. If they were lucky, he'd be in the act of trying to dig up a diamond ring.

She'd like to see him talk his way out of that one.

Fitz was a trusted colleague. Fitz was her friend. She couldn't imagine him as a killer, and yet, the pieces fit.

She shook herself out of her thoughts and started directing traffic, encouraging people to form a semi-circle around the open area in the backyard of Bobber's. She wasn't sure which direction the police would haul Fitz out from, but this way, they'd be able to witness it, and then move on with their discussion.

Cindi positioned herself at the front of the group and held up both of her hands. "Ladies and gentlemen, if I could have your attention. Quiet, please. We'll be continuing in one moment."

Commotion behind her had everyone craning their necks. Several uniformed police officers shuffled a combative Fitz out the front door of Nico's cabin.

"This is ridiculous. I haven't done anything wrong." His eyes were wild as he took note of the crowd. When he spotted Greta standing with Wren and Tuck, he looked murderous. "This is all your fault," he hollered. "You've ruined everything. I needed that ring. I needed it more than Blythe ever did. We had an agreement! We were going to wait to share our findings. She's the one who went back on our deal."

Next to Greta, Wren's jaw hung open. Tuck pressed his lips together in a hard line.

The cops led an agitated Fitz into the waiting squad car and closed the door on him after reading him his rights.

Jake stood next to Cindi and raised his voice. "That man is now a key piece in the history of the saga that is Julian Vance. He's also the man authorities believe to be responsible for the death of Blythe Prescott. I'd like to invite Greta Plank, the library director here in Larkspur, forward to fill in some of the pieces. Greta."

Greta walked forward and spun to face the group. Half of the crowd was turned and watching the retreating police car. McHenry exited the cabin and his onyx eyes found her blue ones. Greta's shoulders relaxed when he went to stand off to the side of the group, but still in her periphery.

When the crowd's focus returned to her, she took a deep breath and began. "This is a bittersweet moment for me and for us as a community. While I'm grateful that a person is in custody for the crime committed against Blythe Prescott, I wish it had never come to this. This uncovered piece of history came at a cost. Blythe was working with that man, Fitz Atwood, to piece together the history of JuJu Vance. They met at the Karrington Library and pooled their resources in a quest to find a long-lost engagement ring that was purchased by Julian Vance, which we believe he intended to give to Viola Douglass."

Wren gasped and covered her hand with her mouth. Greta forged onward.

"This is an educated guess at this point, but thanks to Professor Sinclair's research and Nico Eddison's resources, we were able to track the engagement ring Deborah McNamara wore for her whole life and compare it with the specs from the receipt Julian Vance had for the other ring in question. They don't match."

CHAPTER TWENTY-EIGHT

The crowd buzzed, and Greta waited to continue.

"We're working to determine the exact location of the ring. We've uncovered a secret passageway between this cabin"—Greta pointed—"and Bobber's Bar. This, we assume, was used by the original owners of the bar and cabin, to move back and forth between the two buildings. It was likely adopted by some of the gangsters when they needed a place to hide or a quick getaway."

More excited conversation.

"The owners of Bobber's, the Hawler family, have been nothing but gracious as we've worked to contact the Wisconsin Registrar of Historic Places to determine the best next steps for preserving and maintaining this piece of local history."

"When will you know if the ring is somewhere around here?" someone called out from the back of the crowd.

Jake stepped forward and turned, raising his voice in response. "We're working with professional excavators who'll come in and complete a thorough search based on the information we've gleaned. As soon as we have more information for the public, we'll share it with you."

Greta smiled at him. "Now, I'd like to open the floor for questions for our guest author, Nico Eddison."

Chapter Twenty-Nine

After sleeping like a rock on Saturday night, Greta rallied for Sunday morning mass. She swung into the library afterward to disassemble the chairs, podium, and microphone that they'd left in place following the Little Bohemia Lodge program.

Greta stacked the final chairs in the storage room. She returned to the main part of the library and jumped when Iris popped her head out of the office.

"There you are." Iris put her hands on her hips. "I saw your car in the parking lot on my way past."

"So, you snuck into the library to ambush me?" Greta said, half teasing as she put her palm to her heart. "You scared me half to death."

"Sorry," Iris winced. "How're you feeling? You should have waited to tear this all down. I could have helped you. Or we could have called Cindi back in. Lord knows the woman likes to be useful. I bet you're exhausted."

"A little," Greta admitted. "But I didn't want to deal with this tomorrow before we opened." Besides, being in the library had a calming effect on her. Something about being surrounded by stories never ceased to make her feel at peace. That, and she had half a thought that she might run into McHenry coming or going from the building, which was always an appealing option.

"If you're up for it, I'm meeting Josie and Ed at Mugs & Hugs. They're having breakfast with Jake before he flies out," Iris said. "I've come to extend the invitation, but I totally understand if you'd rather go home and rest."

The siren's call of Mugs & Hugs was too much to resist. "No, that sounds nice, actually."

She pulled out her phone and texted McHenry. He had worked all night and into the morning, checking in on Greta several times. She, too, spent the evening at her cabin going over what she knew, what she thought she knew, and what she guessed about Fitz and his motives. The picture of the events of the previous week had come into focus the more she looked into it.

Greta: Heading to the café. Feel free to join us if you can get away from work.

Once again, Greta's fingers hovered over the letters that would type out three simple words. But they weren't simple at all. She pocketed her phone before she could type anything else. If she was going to tell McHenry she loved him, she was going to say it to his face, not through a text.

That was the other item of importance she'd been circling around and around the previous night. She and McHenry had been dating for six months. She loved spending time with him, and when they weren't together, she found herself wishing they were. He was still quiet and reserved—some might call him broody—but getting to be on the receiving end of his care and being able to take care of him had quickly become something Greta craved.

She loved the man. That was the long and short of it.

But she also needed to find closure with Nathan once and for all. If only he would wake up.

Greta grabbed her tote from behind the desk and slung it over her shoulder. "Ready."

She and Iris left the library, locking up behind themselves. They made the short walk to Mugs & Hugs. Allison had the outdoor standing heaters blowing, erasing the chill from the early morning April air.

Jake and Josie were seated at a table on the front patio.

"Hey, guys." Josie waved them over. "It's such a beautiful day. Thought we'd take advantage of it and sit out here, but if it's too chilly, we can move inside."

Greta tugged her knit cardigan together in the front. "This is great," she assured Josie. "We'll order and join you."

Greta and Iris walked inside and made their way to the counter. Several café patrons gawked at Greta's face, and she tried her best not to flinch under their stares. Her scratches were starting to scab over and the bruising had turned from the deep purple of a new injury to the murky purplish-green with rims of yellow of an established injury. Her face resembled the marbled binding of a hardback book.

"I look awful," she said with a sigh while she and Iris waited in line at the counter.

"You do not," Iris replied staunchly. "You look like a woman who solved a murder investigation. That's more than any of these people can say."

Allison stood behind the register and greeted them with a smile when they made it to the front of the line. "Josie and Jake were in here a bit ago."

Iris nodded. "We're meeting them outside." She placed her order for a butter croissant and a hot blonde roast coffee with a splash of cream. Greta opted for a chocolate-on-chocolate muffin and her usual iced hazelnut latte.

"I'll walk that out for you when it's ready." Allison took Greta's credit card for payment. "You ladies go and get comfortable."

Greta took her returned card and stashed it in her wallet, dropping it into her tote before following Iris. She paused when she spotted Sadie and Rob seated at a table near the front door of the café.

Sadie waved her over. "Greta, hey. How're you holding up? We were just talking about you."

Greta stopped at their table. "Good things, I hope."

Both Rob and Sadie nodded eagerly, and Rob spoke. "I can't thank you enough for all you did for me and my family. We weren't as forthcoming as we could have been," he added, looking chagrined.

"It's alright. I'm glad the truth is out there."

"Blythe deserved that, if nothing else," Rob said quietly.

Sadie reached across the table and covered his hand supportively.

"Anyway." Rob cleared his throat. "My mom said she told you that I talked to them about my future. What I want and what I don't want?"

"She did. I'm glad to hear y'all are on the same page."

Rob sat up straighter. "We are, and what's even better is that my parents are cool with me taking the reins of a new endeavor."

Greta cocked her head to the side. "What kind of new endeavor?"

"Well, new but existing. I want to shine a light on the gangster history here in Larkspur. I spent last night looking into how the Little Bohemia Lodge in Manitowish Waters is sort of like a shrine to the events of 1934, but also still a functioning supper club. I figure, why can't we do something like that here, you know?"

Rob grew animated as he spoke, a spark of excitement lighting his eyes. "We're going to work with the state historical board and get a landmark set up here. Sort of a museum attached to the restaurant. I can put my history hat on and spearhead it, while also helping out at the Bar. It's a win-win for everyone."

"That sounds wonderful, Rob." Greta's spirits lifted at the young man's obvious enthusiasm.

"We have all sorts of plans. It'll be open for field trips for fourth grade Wisconsin history units, and we thought it would be a great place to offer writing or research retreats to historians or creatives of any sort," Sadie put in.

"Sadie is putting her marketing major to good use already, as you can see." Rob grinned with affection at his girlfriend.

Greta's heart ballooned at the sight of the young couple. "Sounds awesome. Please keep me in the loop, and if there's anything we at the library can do to help you get this off the ground, let us know."

"Absolutely. Actually, Josie's brother, Professor Sinclair, already offered to be a resource. Nico Eddison, too. And Wren, that library assistant from Karrington? Her dad reached out and wants to be looped in. He's been doing genealogy research and has the contact info for his relative, a direct descendant of JuJu and Viola. Everyone wants in on this. It's not every day a discovery like this gets made in your backyard." Rob was practically vibrating, but then he checked himself. "That is, if there is, in fact, a diamond buried back there. We'll have to wait and see on that."

"Right. Time will tell, I guess." Greta offered him an encouraging smile. "You two take care. I'm sure I'll see you around."

As she excused herself, she ran into Allison, who was bringing a platter of drinks and food to their table outside. Greta held the door for her and followed her to the patio, taking her seat next to Iris.

"All good?" Iris asked.

"Yeah. Definitely." Greta filled everyone in on Rob's plans.

"That's brilliant," Josie said.

"There's a lot of research to be done and information to be documented. It'll be a years-long project, I'm sure," Jake said.

"He said he talked to you," Greta responded.

Jake swallowed a drink of his iced tea. "He did. I think it's a great initiative, and I'm happy to support it in any way I can. I was actually thinking about taking a sabbatical and coming out here to do some research. Nico and I might collaborate on a book."

"You know we'd love to have you and the fam around," Josie said. "Especially with the wedding coming up."

Greta beamed at Josie. Now that the murder investigation was behind them, they could turn their attention to happier things. Like planning the happiest day of Josie's life thus far.

Still, she wasn't quite ready to put the case to rest. Not when she'd stayed up half the night trying to tie up the loose ends.

"Isn't it a little wild to think about how something that happened almost a hundred years ago could make so many waves today?" she said. "Think of all the people whose lives were affected by the events of that night back in 1934. Fitz and Blythe, most recently."

A shadow fell over her side, and Greta glanced up to see McHenry staring down at her. "Mark, hey!" She moved to stand, but he placed a gentle hand on her shoulder.

"You sit." He kept his hand resting there as he greeted the rest of the group. "Did I hear you mention Fitz?" he asked.

"Did he talk?"

McHenry nodded. "You first," he said. "Then I'll tell you what I know."

Greta blew out a breath. "My best guess is that Fitz wanted to use the discovery of Julian Vance's lost engagement ring—and the man's life as a whole—as the source for his PhD dissertation." At the blank stares of her friends, she clarified, "He was going back to school this fall to get his doctorate in history. His plan was to become an archivist and work at a major national library."

Jake let out a low whistle. "Lofty goal."

"I know. Fitz talked to me about how it would be a lot to juggle his library career with his studies. Truthfully, I wasn't sure how he was going to pull it off. But knowing what I know now, I think his ace in the hole was Julian Vance."

"How did he find out about Vance in the first place?" Iris had her chin resting on her palm as she listened to Greta. "Did Blythe tell him about the guy? Seems like she wouldn't have, especially since she wouldn't even tell Tuck specifics."

"My hunch was that Fitz found out through Wren's family. The two were teasing at the library on Friday. Fitz said something about how he knew Wren when she was in diapers. Wren connected me with her folks. While she didn't know her ancestor had gangster ties, her father did. He told me that he'd discussed Viola with Fitz back in college, and he'd shared with him some old family documents, most recently a diary, knowing how much of a history buff he is. Fitz was looking into Julian Vance and his connection to Viola Douglass. I'm guessing his research led him to connect with Blythe, who was doing her own digging from the direction of Deborah McNamara's side of the tree."

"Whoa," Allison said. The whole circle nodded.

"When Fitz overheard Blythe's argument with Cindi last weekend at the library, he must've gotten the sense she was going to go public with their findings," Greta concluded.

McHenry shifted behind her. "Fitz told us the two had agreed to keep what they'd learned about Julian Vance under wraps. Fitz wanted it to be fresh information for his PhD program. He told us that Blythe had initially agreed to be a contributor to his research, but then the lure of instant fame and the gratification of being the one to break the big news at the event at the library, in front of a renowned author like Nico, was too appealing."

"When Blythe was fighting with Cindi at the library last weekend, she said, 'No one, and I mean no one, is going to steal this from me.'" Greta shook her head. "She wasn't really talking to Cindi, though. At least not entirely. She was also sending a message to Fitz, who was standing right there."

"Makes sense." McHenry's expression was grim. "The two got into an argument about it behind Bobber's, and the rest is history. Fitz claims he didn't try to kill Blythe. His temper flared, and then he panicked and fled the scene when he drew blood."

The group sat silently, each undoubtedly lost in their own thoughts about the week.

"I want to know what the deal was with the coded letters and the *Pride and Prejudice* book cipher," Josie said. "In hindsight, it seems a little unnecessary that Fitz and Blythe were communicating in that way."

"It definitely threw me off when Tuck suggested the letters were love letters," Greta admitted. "Really, they were Fitz and Blythe's secret way of discussing their research."

"Fitz told us Blythe didn't want her husband to know anything about what she was looking into or the potential monetary value that could be associated with it," McHenry told them. "Fitz suggested the book cipher plan. They each had the same version of *Pride and Prejudice*, and Fitz took it as a point of pride to use a book that mentioned his name."

"Wait. What?" Jake shot a quizzical look around the circle.

"It's Fitzwilliam Darcy." Josie looked at her brother with exasperation. "Come on, Jakey. I've taught you better than that."

Jake held up his arms. "I'm more well-versed in non-fiction, I guess."

McHenry continued. "Fitz maintains he's the one who discovered the coordinates for the buried diamond in an old letter he came into possession of from Wren's family. He shared the coordinates with Blythe during one of their final correspondences. She had been the one to discover the underground tunnel when snooping around the bar. Putting the two pieces of intel together, they thought they'd isolated the spot of the hidden treasure. Fitz maintains that he had the right to the diamond since he had the coordinates and he was the one researching Viola's side of the family tree. He argued that Blythe was going to steal it out from under him."

"Still didn't give him a right to kill her, though," Josie said staunchly. She held up her hand and studied her own diamond ring.

"I can't help but wonder why JuJu Vance ended up with Deborah Mc-Namara and not Viola Douglass," Greta said. It had been nagging at her. "The letters we saw in Blythe's box of research proved that Viola was madly in love with him. And since he'd bought her a ring, the feelings must've been mutual. But the dates on those letters were so close to the date on the marriage certificate you found, Jake, between JuJu and Deborah. It's sad to think something happened to tear Viola and JuJu apart."

"And send him straight into a relationship with another woman," Iris said, squishing up her features.

"We may never know," Jake put in. "But I do think that would be a neat angle to research for the book."

Josie twisted her ring and glanced longingly to the parking lot.

"Hey, where's Ed?" Greta asked, realizing Iris said he would be joining them for breakfast.

"He'll be here shortly. He was waiting at the cabins for Nathan's wife to finish up clearing out his things, and then he'll lock up and head this way." Josie sighed, dropping her shoulders. "I can't wait to see him. Does that make me completely ridiculous? All this talk of diamond rings and lovers being torn apart and torrid family histories makes me a little desperate for my man."

"You're not ridiculous," Iris assured her with a kind smile. "You got yourself a good one."

Allison asked Josie where she was at with her wedding plans, and the conversation shifted.

Greta tried to pay attention, but she was distracted by McHenry's proximity. A flush of heat crawled up her neck when he swished his thumb back and forth across her shoulder blade.

"You've been busy researching the night away," he said, crouching so he was talking right into her ear.

"Guilty," Greta said with a wry smile. "Now you've heard what I've deduced.

Anything I missed or that you care to share?"

"You've pretty much figured everything out. I'm not surprised." His voice held an undercurrent of admiration. "The main reason I'm here is because I wanted to let you know some good news. Nathan is awake."

Chapter Thirty

Greta followed McHenry down a squeaky corridor on the fourth floor of the Karrington Hospital. He turned and reached out a hand for her. She gladly took it and relished the feel of him squeezing her palm three times.

"You sure you're up for this?"

It was later on Sunday afternoon. Her friends had dispersed from their debriefing at Mugs & Hugs, and McHenry offered to drive her to Karrington.

"I'm good," she assured him. "Thanks for coming with me."

McHenry pulled up short next to a closed door. "This is him."

He knocked twice, and a scratchy voice called out, "Come in."

McHenry opened the door and allowed Greta to walk inside in front of him.

Nathan was propped up in a bed with wires connected to IVs in his arms and a breathing cannula in his nose. His eyes bugged when they landed on her.

"Greta. Whoa. What happened to you?"

"Car accident," she said simply. She didn't want to get into it.

He motioned to a chair near the window. "Please. Go ahead and sit."

"No, thanks. I'm good." Greta shifted her weight.

McHenry stepped a fraction of an inch closer to her, and she appreciated the small show of support and solidarity.

"Right. I…" Nathan dropped his eyes to his lap and started picking at his fingernail. "I didn't expect to see you."

Greta took a deep breath. "When Mark told me you were awake, I wanted

225

to come and check on you. Mostly to say how sorry I am that you went through this here in Larkspur. I feel partially responsible."

It felt good to say it. She was in charge of the library conference, and to have something happen to any of the librarians in attendance on her watch was making Greta feel all sorts of guilt.

Nathan's gaze boomeranged up to hers. "None of this was your fault. I got too big for my own britches, as the saying goes." He forced a tight smile. "Believe me when I say my wife chewed me out for my recklessness. Scared her half to death when I was in a coma, I think."

Greta glanced at the door. "Where is she?"

"I told her to go and get something to eat. Hospital food wasn't cutting it, and it's hard sitting here with me all day, so it's good for her to get out. She'll be back within the hour, I'd guess."

Greta nodded. "Good. I'm glad she's here with you. I'm glad you're alright."

She meant it. She held her shoulders back a little more firmly, pleased with herself for how far she'd come.

"What happened that night outside Nico's cabin? You must've found the coded letters." It was a loose end Greta hadn't yet worked out. How did he find the passageway?

"It was dumb luck, actually. I was in Nico's cabin." Nathan looked sheepish. "He left for Karrington after our dinner, and I thought I'd poke around. I could tell he knew more than he was telling me, and I wanted to take a peek at some of the paperwork in his cabin to fill in the blanks. The cabin is a mess, and I couldn't make out anything worthwhile in all of Nico's scribbles. But I did tidy up the kitchen as best I could. Figured it was some minor penance for snooping." He shrugged. "Anyway, when I was putting the broom back in the closet, I spotted that old wooden *No Diving* sign. I went to see if I could get it down from where it hung on the hook, and I accidentally opened the door to the passageway. I followed it down and discovered the stash of coded letters."

Nathan flicked his gaze to McHenry's again. "I knew about the book cipher because I overheard your police chief talking to someone on the phone about it. I was thrilled to find what I did, so I grabbed one letter as evidence and headed back the way I came. I called you"—Nathan looked to Greta—"and hoped you could come to the cabin so I could show you what I'd found. I was planning to go to the police with the letter. Truly."

Greta nodded. "Did you see Fitz before he attacked you?"

"Yeah." Nathan shook his head like he was warding off a bad memory. "He came out of nowhere. I was standing on Nico's porch, trying to talk to you on the phone, when all of a sudden, the door to the cabin opened behind me. Scared me out of my mind."

Greta shivered. "So what? Was Fitz in the passageway and he followed you?"

"That's what we were able to get out of him, yes." McHenry crossed his arms. "He'd entered the passageway from Bobber's Bar, and when he heard someone approaching, he hid. He saw you, Nathan, take a letter and retreat, and he followed you. He snatched the coded letter and attempted to silence you for good with the ketamine."

Greta gulped. "Where did he get that stuff? And why was he carrying it around?"

McHenry shrugged. "He felt like the walls were closing in on him. He was carrying around the syringe for a worst-case scenario of needing to take someone else out to cover his tracks. Nathan was the one who came up against him."

It wasn't lost on Greta that it easily could have been her.

"We were able to determine he swiped the Ketamine from his veterinarian's office," McHenry continued.

Greta nodded. Hadn't Fitz told her that Wick, his dog, had needed to be seen for an ongoing issue?

"Fitz had some sort of a connection with one of the vet techs and was able to weasel his way into the area with the locked-up medications and sedatives. We're not sure when exactly he snatched the drugs or how he figured out the code to unlock the safe, but he did."

The three stood in silence until Nathan cleared his throat.

"As soon as the doctors clear me, we'll head back to Green Bay, and then I'll be out of your hair for good." He gave Greta a wry grin. "I'm sorry for all the trouble I caused."

It wasn't a direct apology for stringing her along and dating her as a married man, but it was honestly more than she expected from Nathan. Perhaps his near-death experience would encourage him to reflect on his behavior and change his ways going forward. She'd like to believe it would.

Greta summoned a smile in return. "I hope you'll be back on your feet in no time. If you need anything while you're in town, you or your wife can find me at the library."

"And you have my card as well," McHenry said, placing his hand on the small of Greta's back. "Shall we?"

Greta smiled up at him. "Yep. I'm ready."

They said goodbye to Nathan, and as they turned the corner and walked the hallway away from his hospital room, Greta slipped her hand into McHenry's. She leaned into his side, touching her cheek to his upper arm. "Thanks again for coming with me."

McHenry grunted and glanced down at her. "Always."

Greta smiled to herself as they strolled toward the hospital exit. Once they made it out into the sunshine, McHenry pulled her to a stop before dropping her hand and running his fingers through his hair, looking suddenly distraught.

She arched her eyebrows. "Everything okay?"

His gaze pierced her, and he pressed his lips together.

"Mark, what is it?" Greta reached up and traced her fingers along the hard lines of his jaw. "Talk to me."

He exhaled. "There's probably a better way to do this. A better place, too." He motioned to the hospital building. "You deserve fancy and charming and romantic, and I'm just a gruff cop. But I don't want to wait any longer, so I'm just going to say it. I'm in love with you, Greta. Your warmth, your kindness, your tenacity. All of you."

Tears sprung into the corners of her eyes, and Greta opened her mouth to respond, but McHenry wasn't finished.

"I don't know much, but I do know that life is short, and we don't know what tomorrow will bring, so I don't want to go another day without you knowing how I feel. I realize I'm not an easy man to love. I'm quiet and stubborn, and I work too much. But I will do whatever I can to support your dreams and be the partner you deserve. I'm in this with you for the long haul. If you'll have me."

If she'd have him? As if there was any question!

Greta stood up on her tiptoes and kissed him in response, relishing the feel of his strong arms wrapping around her and holding her close. His heart pounded beneath his shirt, and Greta smiled against his mouth. With Mark, she felt safe—like she could fly and not be afraid of falling because she knew he would catch her.

She leaned away, just enough to look him in the eye. "I love you too. I've been wanting to say that to you for a while now. You are the best man I've ever known. You put up with me, and you make me feel cherished. I'm so thankful you accused me of murder last year. Who would have thought we'd wind up here?"

McHenry's eyes crinkled with his smile, and Greta's stomach swooped.

"We may not know what's coming next, but I know one thing," she said.

He kissed her forehead. "What's that?" he murmured against her skin.

"I'm ready for the next chapter."

Chapter Thirty-One

Several Weeks Later

T he backyard of Bobber's Bar was unrecognizable. Locals were milling around, mixing and mingling with guests who were in town for the main event. Chairs were lined in neat rows. Streamers were hanging from the eaves of the bar, softening the log exterior with rainbow colors. The summer sun beat down, and Greta was grateful for the shade the oversized aspen and pine trees provided.

"I can't believe today is finally here." Iris approached Greta. Anthony was with her. He was a reporter who they'd met in the fall under less-than-ideal circumstances. He turned out to be a great guy, and he was making frequent visits to Larkspur, which Greta attributed to both his roots in the area, and also his budding relationship with Iris. Iris was glowing, and nobody deserved it more. Greta was delighted for the fledgling couple.

"It's been a long time coming," Greta agreed. She glanced at the *For Sale* sign in the yard in front of Iris's parents' cabin. "Your mom and dad still feeling good about selling?"

Iris nodded. "It made the most sense. They don't have an interest in the gangster history of their property, and since it was determined the site of the buried diamond—"

"Alleged site," Greta cut in.

"Right. Well, you know," Iris shrugged. "Since it's not technically on their property, they didn't see any real need to hang onto the place for monetary value or anything. They were more than happy to accept the offer from the Hawlers."

Greta's gaze pinged to Rob, who was standing near the cabin. "He's completely invested in this project."

"Josie told me he and Jake communicate almost daily about the plans for the museum."

"Speaking of Josie, is she here yet?" Greta looked behind her toward the rapidly filling parking lot.

Iris swiveled her head around. "Not sure."

Instead of spotting Josie, Greta saw Cindi get out of her vehicle, smoothing down the front of her khaki pants. She caught Greta's eye and marched toward her.

"Well, here we are, ladies. Anthony." Cindi nodded and placed her hands on her hips, surveying the scene. "An exciting day for Larkspur."

"It really is," Greta agreed.

"You know"—Cindi pinned her with a glare—"I think we could have avoided all that hullabaloo in springtime if, when Heath gave you the box of Blythe's research, you had turned it over to me. Like he instructed," she added huffily.

Greta fought an eye roll. Ever since Blythe's research papers had been discovered at Fitz's house and Greta was called in to confirm they were, in fact, the documents Heath had given to the library, she and Cindi had been over this topic again and again.

"I've said I'm sorry, Cindi. I hope you can forgive me."

Cindi sniffed. "I'm just saying I could have accomplished more with my True Treasure Seekers *and* genealogy club resources than you did, and everyone would have been better off."

Greta gave her an indulgent nod. "I'll definitely keep that in mind for next time."

She closed her eyes briefly, saying a silent prayer there wouldn't be a next time.

Heath, for his part, had officially been charged with fraud. The state police came through and were able to prove he was passing fake diamonds off as real ones.

The papers he dropped at the library were actually on display in Iris's parents' house. Even though the sale hadn't gone through yet, the Thompsons had allowed Rob and his team access to the cabin so they could set up a display of the documents and research that had brought them to today. There would be tours of the hidden staircase running all afternoon.

Greta herself hadn't been back down there, not since finding the letters and nearly coming face to face with Fitz. She grimaced at the memory. She was still working through the loss of her friendship with a guy she trusted and respected.

A group of volunteers, including Dolores, Celeste, and Sadie, started shepherding those in attendance to their seats.

"They'll be coming up soon," Sadie said when she circled toward them, excitement clear in her rushed delivery.

The professional historic artifact team was below ground, excavating the site of the buried diamond. Or, as Greta kept reminding everyone, the alleged site. They wouldn't know for sure if Julian Vance had actually left secret treasure in Larkspur until they dug in. Literally.

Greta, Iris, and Anthony took their seats at the back of the crowd. Josie and Ed slid in next to them.

"Did we miss it?" Josie was breathless. "We had a crisis at the cabins."

Greta frowned. "What happened?"

"One kid dared another kid to shimmy through the stormwater pipe. The kid took the dare, got halfway through, and panicked. He wouldn't come back out. The guy who went in to drag him back through got stuck, so they were both wedged in there. It was a whole thing." Ed rubbed the back of his neck.

"Never a dull moment," Josie grinned at her fiancé before leaning over his lap and using a stage whisper to tell Greta and Iris, "Ed was the one who went in after the kid and got stuck."

Iris clamped a hand over her mouth, and Greta bit the inside of her cheek to keep from laughing out loud. Now that she looked at him, Ed was freshly showered. His face was also beet red.

Josie patted him on the arm. "My hero. Truly."

Ed rolled his eyes, but they twinkled when he looked down at Josie. "Yeah, yeah. But seriously," he said, turning to Greta and Iris. "What did we miss?"

"Nothing yet. They haven't reappeared." Iris craned her neck in an attempt to get a better view. "Oh, I hope they find something!"

Anthony smiled at her enthusiasm.

Greta sat back in her seat and blew out a breath. There had been a flurry of activity surrounding this project in the past month, as different teams were brought in and experts were consulted. It was incredible to watch history unfold before her eyes. But truthfully, she was ready to put the whole ordeal behind her. Summer in Larkspur was upon them. It was her favorite time of the year in the Northwoods. She and McHenry had made lots of plans to be out on the lake as often as possible.

Her eyes found him where he was positioned at the back of Bobber's Bar. As if sensing her stare, his gaze connected with hers. He nodded ever so slightly. She grinned back at him, before their attention was caught by movement near the cabin entrance.

The excavation team paraded out the door. Their faces were so stoic, Greta was sure they'd come up empty-handed. Her stomach plummeted. She had been expecting it, but it was still a disappointment.

One of them stepped over and conferred with Rob.

When he turned to the crowd with an enormous smile on his face, Greta sat up straighter. Iris grabbed for her hand. "Oh my gosh, this is it."

"Everyone, if I could have your attention." Rob spoke into the microphone they'd set up. "We have some good news."

A smattering of cheers and clapping reverberated through the crowd.

Rob grinned. "They found what appears to be an old Bobber's Bar cash box."

At this, it was as if a question mark hovered over the crowd.

"Why would they find something from Bobber's Bar buried underneath there?" Iris whispered, voicing the question on everyone's mind.

"Don't know."

"Shhh," Josie shushed.

Rob had a crooked smile on his face. "You may be wondering where Bobber's comes into all this. As it turns out, after Blythe Prescott approached my father about the potential for buried treasure on our family's property, he started doing some digging himself. As you know, Bobber's has been passed down in our family for years. We used to keep a book by the front entrance. And by 'used to', I mean many decades back. Before my time." The crowd chuckled. "Back then, the owners asked that anyone passing through make notes in the book. Who they were. Where they were going. What brought them to town. It's a neat snapshot of history."

"I'd love to get my hands on that. How fascinating," Greta whispered.

Both Josie and Iris nodded next to her.

"Anyway, Dad found a notation from April of 1934. The only name that was listed was 'JuJu,' but under the section primarily used for folks to explain why they were in town, he had written, 'To keep something special safe.'"

When Rob delivered this punch line, everyone tittered.

He was beaming from cheek to cheek at this.

"The kid knows how the hold the attention of the crowd, I'll give him that." Josie shook her head. "But let's get on with it!"

"Patience, dear," Ed teasingly said from her side.

Greta chuckled but zoned back in on Rob, who was saying, "When we discovered this, we thought for certain JuJu was referencing the diamond ring Blythe was searching for. My mom and dad have spent the past several weeks looking through old family boxes. They came across the diary of the wife of a previous Bobber's Bar owner. In it, they found a notation that shared an anecdote from that day in the bar. I thought I'd read it for you here."

Rob cleared his throat.

"A patron came in today and told us he was desperate to keep something safe. He was looking for a container that was water-resistant and sturdy. He wouldn't tell us why. I thought it was strange, but he didn't look like the kind of character you question, if you know what I mean. I could tell Lars wanted to press him, but I swooped in and offered him one of our

old cash boxes. We use them for events around town when we need to travel with our money. Anyway, the gentleman was thrilled. He gladly took it. I wish I knew who he was. I watched him go out the window, and he disappeared into the cabin out back. I'll have to ask the landlord his name once he leaves town."

Rob paused and then added. "This was the diary entry from my many times over great aunt Silvia on April 25, 1934. As you can see, the timing lines up if Julian Vance had fled from Manitowish Waters earlier in the week. He found himself here, and since he was on the lamb, he wanted to stow 'something special', in other words, the engagement ring he'd purchased. That's why, the discovery of a Bobber's Bar cash box is significant. So, without further ado, let's see what we have, shall we?"

The crowd cheered, and Rob stepped to the side. Ace and Suz joined him, along with Sadie.

Nico and Jake were close at hand for the big reveal, as well.

One of the historians donned protective gloves after they pried the box open, and everyone held their breath. He reached inside and plucked out a jewelry box with a hinged cover. When he cracked the lid, Suz clasped her hand over her mouth. Rob stood on his tip-toes for a better look, and Nico and Jake exchanged an excited glance.

"Can you see what it is?" Iris asked, rising to her feet as the group in front of them stood and tried to get eyes on the prize.

"Ladies and gentlemen," Rob spoke into the microphone. "We've recovered Julian Vance's long-lost engagement ring!"

Applause sounded. Rob hugged his parents. McHenry stepped forward along with Officer Clarkson, Chief Sorenson, and several other members of the Larkspur PD. They corralled the crowd into some semblance of order, and a single-file line formed as people walked forward to get a better look at history.

"I don't know," Josie said as they waited. "I'll take my ring any day."

"Well, that's a relief." Ed mimed, wiping his brow before grinning down at her.

Greta smiled at the couple, even as her eyes sought out McHenry. She gave him a small wave when he looked back at her, and he disentangled himself from the people he was talking to and joined them.

"Exciting day," he said with his no-nonsense delivery. "The ring looks beautiful," he added.

Something about McHenry referencing an engagement ring while he stared at her had Greta's heart beating in overdrive.

"I can't wait to see it," she told him.

He held her gaze and smiled.

Yep, she loved this man. Maybe someday, they'd do some ring shopping of their own.

Acknowledgements

All glory to God, now and forever.

Thank you to everyone at Level Best Books for giving Greta and the Larkspur crew such a cozy publishing home. To my editor, Shawn, thanks for all the time spent and work put into this one. I'm proud of what we created.

To Ana, thank you, once again, for sharing your amazing talent and designing the perfect cover. This is the yellow book of my dreams.

To the authors who took time out of their busy schedules to read an early copy of *A Killer Hold* and provide a blurb. Janna, Kara, and Sarah—I look up to all of you as writers and people! Thank you for your support and kind words.

To the Inky Fingers Critique Group. You saw this story from its early stages through to now, and you were integral in helping me to form it into what it is. I'm so grateful for your advice, encouragement, and perspective. I'm already looking forward to our next monthly meet-up. I'm glad to be walking this author journey with you!

To my local librarians and booksellers. The only thing better than being surrounded by books is being surrounded by book people, and you're some of the best book people I know! Thanks for your support and for all you do to make our community a bookish one.

To my Well Read Mom book club ladies. I love our book chats, and I admire each and every one of you. Thanks for the great conversation, fellowship, and support.

To you, dear reader, if you're here, reading this acknowledgements section—thank you! There are so many books in the world, and I'm honored you gave one of mine some of your time. I hope Greta and the gang made you smile, and I hope this mystery kept you turning pages.

To my family. You are the very best, and I love you. Thanks for everything!

To my kids. Keep reading. Keep writing. Keep asking questions. I love you the most.

To Nick. Thanks for believing in me. I love you madly.

About the Author

Leah Dobrinska is the author of the Fall In Love romcom series, the Larkspur Library Mysteries, an award-winning cozy mystery series set in the Wisconsin Northwoods, and the Mapleton novels, a series of standalone small town romances. She earned her degree in English Literature from UW-Madison where she was awarded the Dean's Prize and served as a Writing Fellow. She has since worked as a freelance writer, editor, and content marketer. As a kid, she hoped to grow up to be either Nancy Drew or Elizabeth Bennet. Now, she fulfills that dream by writing mysteries and love stories.

A sucker for a good sentence, a happy ending, and the smell of books—both old and new—Leah lives out her very own happily ever after in a small Wisconsin town with her husband and their gaggle of kids. When she's not writing, handing out snacks, or visiting the local library, Leah enjoys reading and running. Find out more about Leah, join her newsletter community, and connect with her through her website, leahdobrinska.com.

AUTHOR WEBSITE:
  https://leahdobrinska.com/

SOCIAL MEDIA HANDLES:
  https://www.instagram.com/whatleahwrote

https://www.facebook.com/whatleahwrote
https://www.bookbub.com/authors/leah-dobrinska

Also by Leah Dobrinska

THE LARKSPUR LIBRARY MYSTERIES
Mayhem In Circulation
Death Checked Out

THE FALL IN LOVE SERIES
Exes Don't
Enemies Don't
Friends Don't

THE MAPLETON NOVELS
Together With You
Good To Be Home
Love at On Deck Café

www.ingramcontent.com/pod-product-compliance
Lightning Source LLC
Chambersburg PA
CBHW050305110726
47899CB00007B/2115